Contents

One	1
Two	4
Three	8
Four	12
Five	16
Six	20
Seven	24
Eight	28
Nine	32
Ten	37
Eleven	41
Twelve	45
Thirteen	49
Fourteen	52
Fifteen	58
Sixteen	62
Seventeen	66
Eighteen	70
Nineteen	74
Twenty	78
Twenty-One	82
Twenty-Two	86
Twenty-Three	90
Twenty-Four	94
Twenty-Five	98
Twenty-Six	102
Twenty-Seven	106
Twenty-Eight	110
Twenty-Nine	114
Thirty	118
Thirty-One	122
Thirty-Two	125

Thirty-Three	129
Thirty-Four	134
Thirty-Five	138
Thirty-Six	142
Thirty-Seven	146
Thirty-Eight	151
Thirty-Nine	155
Forty	160
Forty-One	165
Forty-Two	169
Forty-Three	174
Forty-Four	178
Forty-Five	182
Forty-Six	186
Forty-Seven	191
Forty-Eight	194
Forty-Nine	198
Fifty	202
Fifty-One	206
Fifty-Two	211
Fifty-Three	215
Fifty-Four	219
Fifty-Five	223
Fifty-Six	227
Fifty-Seven	231
Fifty-Eight	235
Fifty-Nine	239
Sixty	244
Sixty-One	248
Sixty-Two	252
Sixty-Three	256
Sixty-Four	260
Sixty-Five	265

For Michael and Susan

One

Marjorie Blackburn grabbed the spoon from her husband's hand as it travelled uncertainly towards his mouth. 'Have you finished?' she snapped.

Drops of milk spattered onto the table as she slammed the spoon into the cereal bowl. This made her angrier and she stormed over to the sink and dropped the half-eaten breakfast into the murky water of the washing-up bowl.

'I have now,' her husband answered rather daringly.

Marjorie watched the soggy cornflakes rising to the surface of the bowl. 'Why d'you have to spoil everything?' she demanded.

'Me?' Ted Blackburn's eyebrows rose with genuine surprise. This was the closest his usually inscrutable face ever came to an expression. According to his wife's family he was a dark horse and never let his feelings show.

'You know how much this house means to me,' she said, turning to glare at him. 'It's me what's inherited it. Not my brother Sid – nor my twin sister. Because I was the one what looked after Nan all those years. No one else. I was the one what helped her onto the toilet and washed and changed her, year in and year out.'

Ted refrained from saying it was difficult for her sister Pam, seeing as she lived in Australia and had done for the past twenty-five years. Sighing, he rose from the table and reached for the sports bag containing his railway guard's uniform.

Marjorie squeezed the water out of a filthy dishcloth and furiously wiped the drops of milk from the table. Ted stood at the door and watched her.

'When we lived on the Ramslye estate,' he said, 'you didn't mind me being seen in my uniform then.'

'That was Ramslye. This is Molyneux Park Road, and I'm not having you coming and going in that uniform. It lowers the tone of the neighbourhood.'

'I hate going to work in civvies,' he moaned. 'It's awkward having to change at work.'

It was a token protest. He knew it was useless to argue.

'Civvies!' she shouted as he shuffled off down the hall. 'Anyone'd think you were in the Services – not a guard on the railway.'

He stood by the Victorian hallstand, listening in case she followed him to the front door. He was reassured by the clatter of crockery in the sink, quickly slid his hand behind the hallstand, withdrew a paperback book from its hiding place and transferred it to his sports bag.

'See you tonight,' he called as he zipped up his anorak.

It was cold outside, but at least it was dry and sunny, and he welcomed the brisk walk across the common to the station. And more than anything he looked forward to the few precious moments he could spend alone with his secret.

***

Mike Longridge brushed the hairs away from his client's neck and offered up the mirror.

'How's that?' he asked.

His client, the once-famous Dave Whitby, comedian and impressionist, nodded gloomily. Life was not so very funny these days.

'Thanks for dropping by at short notice,' he said, standing up and brushing the hairs off his lap onto the kitchen floor.

'You got some work on?' Mike asked.

'Not so's you'd notice. Masonic night in Folkestone. By the time I've paid the petrol...'

He shook his head gloomily and dug into his pocket for change. Mike packed his combs, scissors, mirror and hairdryer into his Gladstone bag and checked his watch.

'I've got to shoot over to Molyneux Park Road. I've got a client there who lives next door to a woman whose husband works on the railway. She won't let him leave the house or come home in his uniform in case the neighbours notice. What she doesn't realise is, her next door neighbour's had his ticket clipped by her husband on the train to Charing Cross.'

Dave Whitby managed a small chuckle. 'There's nowt so queer as folk,' he said, slipping easily into his native Yorkshire dialect. He handed Mike a crumpled five pound note and four pound coins. 'Sorry I can't make it any more.'

Mike pocketed the money without looking at it. 'No, that's fine. I hope it goes well in Folkestone.'

'Huh!' exclaimed the comedian bitterly. 'I'll see you to the door.'

'If only you could get back on the telly again,' Mike said.

Dave Whitby's face suddenly broke into a broad grin. 'You never know. I've got a great publicity stunt coming up. The tabloids'll be swarming all over High Brooms, and I'll be back in the public eye with a vengeance.'

Mike waited for him to elaborate but the comedian shook his head emphatically.

'Sorry: if I tell you, Mike, it'll be all round Tunbridge Wells. But I will tell you one thing: the bloke who lives opposite me'll be livid. And you know what they say. Revenge is sweet.'

Two

A ndrew stared defiantly at his mother. It was a look full of hostility and hatred, guaranteed to wind her up.

'Don't be so damn selfish,' snapped Claire Longridge, angrily straightening her son's duvet. 'You know I've got work to do on the computer.'

'Which happens to be in my room.'

'It won't take long. Just a few hundred words.'

Andrew sneered. 'The computer still happens to be in my room.'

Claire lost her temper and began yelling. 'Which you never ever tidy. Look at this room. It's a tip.'

Ignoring his mother's outburst, Andrew stared into a mirror plastered with stickers, and began squeezing a spot on his chin. This total disregard for his mother's presence made her feel worthless and she gestured dismissively at the computer games strewn untidily across his desk.

'Stupid moronic games, that's all you ever use the computer for.'

As soon as she said it, she regretted it. She saw his vulnerable, wounded expression in the mirror before he bent down to retrieve his hooded top from an untidy heap of clothes on the floor.

'Chloe's twice as untidy as I am. You never say anything to her.'

'How can I? She's gone back to university.'

He stopped at the door and gave her the sulky, contemptuous expression. 'God! You're pathetic.'

She fought back the tears and tried to think of a reply. But he had already gone. There was a tremor in her voice as she called after him: 'Where're you going?'

'Does it matter?' He stamped angrily downstairs. 'The only thing that seems to matter in this house is your brilliant daughter's education.'

She started to reply but stopped herself. What was the point? The times they had argued like this, going round in circles. And it always left her feeling drained.

The front door slammed and the house shook as if a gust of wind had attacked it. She crossed to the window and watched her son, his shapeless but fashionably baggy clothes billowing in the icy wind as he shuffled along the road, no doubt heading towards the town centre. She remembered him as he was aged six. The sweet smell of his hair when she cuddled him; the cheeky grin and sparkling eyes.

***

Like the Terminator throwing off an assailant, Dave Whitby hurled open his neighbour's gate, marched up to the front door and rang the bell. He saw the movement of the net curtain at the window and he knew it was deliberate. There was no way anyone could hem him in his car like that without meaning to.

'I know you're in there,' he yelled through the letterbox. 'I saw you peering through the curtains.'

He rang the bell and waited. No sound came from within the house.

'Right!' he shouted. 'You want to play games? Here's a good game. It's called keeping your finger on the bell until the battery runs down. And I bet you get tired of it before I do.'

After two minutes of continuous ringing, the door was flung open.

'You see,' gloated the comedian, 'I said you'd get fed up before I did.'

His neighbour towered over him and was shaking with anger. Dave began to have doubts about the car parking war. The neighbour was also well-built. If it came to the crunch, he didn't fancy his chances.

'What the hell d'you think you're doing?' yelled the neighbour.

Dave took his finger off the bell and jabbed it angrily towards the street. 'Your car is blocking me in. Move it!'

'Don't park outside my house then.'

'When you bought the deeds to your house, it didn't include parking space in the street. So move your car before I move it for you.'

'You touch that car and...'

Having ascertained that his neighbour must be at least seventy five, maybe even older, Dave became fearless. The finger that had been used for the doorbell was now turned on his neighbour.

'Shall I tell you what I'm going to do? he began. He was stopped by the sudden appearance of his neighbour's wife, small, wizened and grey, like a stage granny.

'Oh move it, Stan,' she pleaded. 'We don't want trouble.'

Her husband glared at her. 'Okay,' he said, as if it was all her fault. 'If that's what you want.'

Dave returned to his car. After a few minutes his neighbour appeared, determined to have the last word.

'I'm warning you,' he said. 'Don't park here again. Stick to your own side of the street.'

The comedian brought his finger into play again.

'And I'm warning you: next week you'll come crawling on bended knees, begging me for forgiveness. What I've got planned for you, mate, is nobody's business.'

As he drove away, he chuckled to himself, and did a mental action replay of the incident, but this time slightly altered by the witty ripostes he made to floor his opponent.

***

Marjorie knew Ted had a secret. He was a dark horse, that one. Furtive. And recently his behaviour had been more furtive than usual. Especially since they had moved from their Ramslye council house to their house in Molyneux Park Road.

Suddenly she made the connection. At Ramslye he had his workshop at the bottom of the garden, and was never bothered by her. But here in Molyneux Park Road, from the large kitchen window, she could see clearly into the garden shed which was close to the house. Whatever Ted was hiding, she felt, it must be here in the house. And she was determined to find it.

Starting upstairs, she searched every possible hiding place. And it didn't take her long to find one of his books, cleverly concealed in the bottom of the sponge bag he always took on holiday.

She opened the book, which had been disguised with a brown paper cover, and turned the pages slowly. As her eyes scanned the words, her anger bubbled and boiled, and she hated him as she had never hated him before. But at least now she had the evidence to destroy his pathetic little secret.

She would show him that she knew. She placed the book face up on the kitchen table and looked forward to watching him squirm.

Three

Nigel Pooley caught Mike looking pointedly at his watch and hastily ended his telephone conversation.

'Sorry about that,' he said. 'The phone just hasn't stopped all day. I'll put it on answer. No more interruptions.'

Mike moved a chair close to the computer workstation.

Nigel tutted. 'It's a bit close to the computer. I'm thinking of all those little hairs. I know you've got to plug in your hairdryer but....'

'Don't you have a cover for it?' asked Mike, running short on patience.

'I don't know what Betty's done with it. Betty's my new secretary. Two days a week. Nice lady. Very well spoken. Lives in Cranbrook, so I have to give her petrol money as well. But she's worth it. A very tidy person. I can't bear clutter...'

Mike sighed audibly. 'Look, I don't want to rush you....'

Nigel looked aggrieved, until he realised he'd kept Mike waiting throughout three telephone conversations.

'I'm sorry to keep you. It won't take a minute to change out of my suit and rinse my hair.'

As he was leaving the room, Nigel was distracted by a newspaper cutting on top of a filing cabinet.

'Have a look at that,' he said, handing Mike the cutting. 'And let me know what you think.'

Left alone in the office, Mike studied the cutting. Sales Executive, it said. Early fifties. Interests include travel and music. Would like to meet mature and attractive lady with similar interests, with a view to marriage. Must be a non-smoker and committed Christian.

Mike flung it with disgust onto the desktop. 'Sales executive,' he thought. 'Selling garden tools from his spare bedroom in Crowborough. Who's he trying to kid?'

8

Nigel returned, wearing a towelling bathrobe. He looked a bit sheepish. Mike wondered why he had been given the cutting to read.

After an awkward silence, while Mike prepared to cut his client's hair, Nigel asked him what he thought.

'About the newspaper ad? I suppose it's as good a way as any to meet someone.'

'Exactly! And it's a short cut to finding someone with the same Christian beliefs as yours truly.'

Mike remembered being given an ear-bashing the last time he'd cut Nigel's hair, and quickly changed the subject.

'You still selling unusual garden tools?'

'That was only ever a sideline. I'm concentrating all my energies on what I do best – selling telephone systems. And it's still a vertical market. I was speaking to a client only today....'

Mike thought it was time for another change of subject.

'What sort of music you interested in?'

'I don't really know,' replied the salesman with an apologetic tone. 'You see, I had to put something in the advert. I don't have any interests outside of work. I don't watch TV; I don't read – other than my Bible. So I had to put something interesting about myself. I suppose I quite like Country and Western music. Something with a nice tune. I know what I like when I hear it.'

Mike was becoming depressed. He couldn't wait to get to his bolthole, drive across Ashdown Forest to a pub in Rusthall, where he could sink a few beers and forget about customers like Nigel Pooley.

The salesman chuckled suddenly. 'I've already had some response to the ad. Very attractive she looks in the photo. I'm taking her out to dinner on Saturday night.'

You poor bitch, thought Mike. Little do you know what you're letting yourself in for.

***

As soon as he had finished his shift, Ted fancied a pint in the Bedford Arms, opposite the station, and was relieved to find it was quiet at the pub. He bought himself a pint of lager and sank into a comfortable seat. He took a couple of sips of beer, then opened the sports bag containing his uniform and took out the paperback book. He turned to the last page and began to read, his lips delicately miming the words: 'If we shadows have offended, Think but this, and all is mended – '

'Good book, is it?'

Ted was startled at the intrusion. He hadn't paid much attention to the man at the table next to his. He was a middle-aged man with thinning grey hair, wearing an expensive-looking brown leather jacket. He smiled pleasantly at Ted.

'Covering it in plain paper's a dead giveaway,' he said.

Ted felt himself blushing. 'No,' he protested. 'It's Shakespeare. A Midsummer Night's Dream.'

'And here was I thinking you had something to hide.'

'No ... I....'

'This is a coincidence, our meeting like this. I'm also extremely fond of Shakespeare. I suppose you'd call me a bit of a buff, really. And I just happen to have a couple of tickets for the Royal Shakespeare Company season at the Albery next Saturday. Would you like to come with me?'

Ted shook is head nervously. 'I start the next shift on Saturday. I'm a guard on South Eastern Trains, you see.'

'Well how about Friday then?'

Ted eyed him suspiciously. 'I thought the tickets were for Saturday.'

The man grinned. 'Would you like to come or not?'

'Yes,' said Ted, making the most spontaneous decision of his life. 'Yes, I would.'

Four

'This is what I call good timing,' said Mike as he entered the White Hart, making sure his mobile was switched on now that he'd finished work. 'Cheers, Brian!'

Brian raised his eyes towards the ceiling and said, 'We don't see him for weeks, then he walks in just as I'm paying.' He pointed towards the Harvey's pump, and called to the landlord: 'Give him a pint of the real stuff, Ken.'

'About the only thing in here that is real,' said Mike to wind Ken up. 'I bet that so-called Victorian mirror comes from Taiwan.'

'That mirror cost me an arm and a leg.'

'In other words it was cheap. Where's Marion?'

'She's on holiday. And if I'd known you were coming in, Mike, I'd have gone with her.'

Mike laughed, then spotted another customer further down the bar, who scowled as he caught Mike's eye.

'Hello, Trevor. Didn't see you lurking there. But then I never notice insurance salesmen.'

Trevor mumbled what he thought was a witty riposte, which was lost in the succession of comments following Mike's insult. Mike downed half of his pint as Ken strolled along the bar to where some regulars were watching a Premiere League football match. 'Come on!' he said. 'Don't let the football slow your drinking.'

Mike downed half of his pint before he realised his mobile was ringing. He fumbled in his pocket and clicked it on as he headed for the door.

'She'll know you're in the boozer,' called Brian after him. 'They can smell it down the phone.'

As it happened, Brian was right. Mike hadn't managed to make it outside before Claire caught the background noise. 'Where are you ringing from?' she demanded.

'Pub in Uckfield,' he lied. This would give him more drinking time in Rusthall before he went home. 'I've just stopped for a swift half before I do my last client.'

'But it's gone half-eight.'

A whine crept into her voice, which irritated him, making him feel less guilty about lying.

***

'You know some of my clients don't get home until late. What's the problem?'

'It's Andrew.'

A cold shiver ran through him.

'Where is he?'

'He's upstairs. In his room. Can't you hear the music blasting out?'

Relieved his son was safe, Mike relaxed and decided he could return to the bar and have a few more pints. Face the problem later.

'He's always playing his music too loud, sweetheart. Why is tonight any different?'

'Because tonight he seems really angry. He went out this morning in a really foul mood and came back this evening in the same foul mood. I can't stand it. And over the past few months I've noticed money missing from my purse. I didn't mention it because I wasn't sure. But this morning, after he stormed out, I checked my purse. I know I had two ten pound notes, and one of them was gone.'

'But Andy's always broke,' he protested. 'If he's nicking money...'

'Exactly,' she replied. 'Where's the money going?'

***

'You smell of beer,' said Marjorie, sniffing distinctly. 'Have you been to the pub?'

Ted wiped his feet diligently on the doormat.

'I might have called in for one on the way home.'

There was a triumphant gleam in Marjorie's eye. 'Oh, might you,' she said ominously. 'I expect you could still manage a cup of tea.'

She led the way, and Ted followed, to the kitchen. She switched on the kettle and turned to face him, dying to see him wriggling from the pain of discovery. But she was disappointed. He spotted the book, but his face was a mask. He put the sports bag containing his uniform down, eased the book to one side, and sat at the table.

'What's that book,' she demanded, 'which I found hidden in your wash bag?'

'Oh that.'

'Oh that,' she mimicked. 'Since when have you taken to reading Shakespeare?'

'I like Shakespeare,' he explained quietly. 'I always have done. Ever since I was at school.'

She snorted contemptuously. 'Just because you went to the grammar school. A pity you didn't do something better with your life then.'

It had always rankled that her husband had gone to a grammar school, whereas she had gone to Sandown Court. She picked up the copy of Richard III, sniffed disparagingly, and dropped it back on the table.

'Why you thought you had to hide it, God only knows.'

'Because I didn't think you'd understand.'

'What is there to understand? If you want to skulk about hiding your books from me ... but if that's the best thing you can find to hide then God help you. Shakespeare! It's pathetic. Thank goodness we've got something lively to look forward to on Friday night.'

His heart sank. Friday was the night he was invited to see Macbeth with that chap Donald he'd met in the pub. And, come hell or high water, nothing was going to stop him from going.

'Why? What's happening on Friday?' he asked.

'Alec and Freda are coming over. To see the house. They've not been before. Ted! What's wrong? You're not working Friday, are you?'

'No. But....'

'But what?'

'Nothing.'

'Why d'you always look so guilty?' she said, tutting loudly. 'As if you'd got something to hide.'

Five

As soon as Mike arrived home, Claire knew he'd had more than a 'swift half'.

'Had a good evening?' she asked pointedly.

He shrugged and tried to sound normal. 'Not too bad. I've done quite well. Financially.'

He hoped the reference to his earnings might allay criticism of his drinking. But he could see by the pursed lips and resentful look in her eyes that he was onto a loser.

'Don't try to kid me that you haven't spent some time in the pub.'

'One of my last two clients cancelled and I had an hour to kill.'

'That was convenient. So you've driven all the way from Uckfield in that state. You're going to lose your licence one of these days, then bang goes your livelihood.'

'I've only had a couple of pints,' he lied. He'd had five, but he'd only driven back from Rusthall, taking the scenic route down Teagarden Lane. The lie about Uckfield had been to give himself valuable drinking time.

'I don't want to nag you,' she said, her tone softening slightly, 'but it's just that I worry about you drinking and driving....'

'It slops all over the steering wheel,' he quipped.

'Seriously.'

'I'm sorry,' he said, looking suitably contrite. 'I'll be very careful. I promise.'

Relieved that the subject was closed, he watched her sinking into the armchair and pick up the remote control. From force of habit she always watched the ten o'clock news on BBC 1, although she invariably talked throughout it.

'What about Andy?' he asked. 'I don't hear pounding music.'

It stopped about ten minutes before you came in. I think he must have got bored with it.'

She switched the TV on, with the sound turned off, and they watched in awkward silence scenes of bloodshed in Syria. The camera zoomed in close on a wounded man on a stretcher, and this seemed to trigger an explosion in Claire.

'I keep asking myself why. Is it my fault Chloe's a high achiever? What were we supposed to do? Hold her back because Andrew felt threatened. What's he going to do with the rest of his life? He can't go on doing night work at Sainsbury's, stocking shelves. He's just so ... so negative about everything. That's what I can't take. You should have heard him this morning. He sounded as if he really hated me. I had my article to write for the wedding dress supplement but I couldn't concentrate. It was useless.'

Her voice petered out and Mike could see she was on the verge of tears. He placed an arm round her shoulders.

'D'you want me to have a word with him?'

'If you think it'll do any good.'

'I can but try. How certain are you he's nicking your cash?'

'I'm positive.'

He started towards the door. 'In that case, I'll talk to him.'

'Mike.'

He stopped, and he could see that she was crying now.

'Try not to lose your temper. It won't do any good.'

***

Dave Whitby turned to the classified section of the local paper, found the advertisement he was looking for, and dialled the number. While it rang he looked at his watch. It was a bit late to be phoning but what the hell! The bloke selling this heap of junk should consider himself lucky.

'Hallo?'

It was a gruff voice, more defensive than annoyed.

'I'm ringing about your advert for the MOT-failed Nova. If it's still available I'd like to come and see it.'

'What? Now? Me an the missus was just about to....'

Dave interrupted hurriedly, and grinned as he imagined what the rest of the bloke's statement was about to reveal. 'No, tomorrow's soon enough. Tell me, is there much rust on the car.'

A slight pause. The man cleared his throat before speaking in an overly defensive tone. 'It says in the advert I'm selling it for spares. You can't expect much for thirty notes, you know.'

'Excellent,' Dave stressed delightedly. 'If it's got heaps of lovely rust. It's just what I'm after.'

Another pause. He hurriedly assured the man it wasn't a wind-up, took down his address, then hung up. He could imagine the bloke telling his wife about this nutter who wanted to buy his car because of the rust. Well, pretty soon he'd know the reason. If all went according to plan, Dave would be the owner of the most famous clapped out bit of junk in Britain.

***

Andrew was hunched over the computer keyboard, fiercely concentrating on a futuristic war game.

'Can you switch it off? I want to talk to you.'

He ignored his father and carried on staring at the screen as if his life depended on it. Mike knelt down and switched off the computer at the socket.

'Hey! What d'you do that for?'

'Because I want a word with you.'

Mike sat on the edge of the bed and fixed his son with a steady look. 'What's the problem, Andy? Why don't you tell me and I'll see if I can help?'

Avoiding his father's stare, he shrugged. 'Nothing.'

'Something's wrong. You act as if you hate us.'

Andrew made a show of sighing deeply. 'I told you: nothing's wrong.'

'You do two all-nighters at the Sainsbury's; I know it's not much of a job but for someone of your age the money's not bad. And it's not as if you're asked to contribute to any household bills. Not that we want you to. It's just that you always seem to be so broke.'

Mike's mouth suddenly felt dry and there was a queasy feeling in the pit of his stomach. He swallowed noisily before continuing.

'And Mum's had money taken from her purse.'

Andrew looked his father straight in the eye. 'You're not blaming me for that, are you?'

Mike realised his son's answer was just a little too ready, almost as if he'd been expecting a scene about the money.

'No,' Mike said. 'I made a mistake. I'm sorry.'

He stood up and started to leave the room. He needed time to think. He could tell Andrew was lying, and hoped that by leaving it in the air like this his son might eventually feel troubled enough to come and talk about it. But, as he looked back, he saw that Andrew was kneeling by the socket, switching the computer back on.

Six

Having locked the fish and chip shop up for the night, and carrying two parcels of cod and chips, Craig Thomas slid into the back seat of the taxi.

'Working men's club?' the driver asked.

'Right,' said Craig. 'You're new, aren't you?'

'Started last night.'

Craig had a sinking feeling deep inside him that tonight was going to be one of those nights. The end of another lousy day.

'Did they tell you my method of payment?' he asked the driver when they were almost at the club.

The driver replied with more hostility than was necessary.

'Did who tell me what?'

'Your firm. I always pay in kind. A large cod 'n' chips for the fare.'

'No, they didn't tell me.'

The taxi stopped at the traffic lights. Rain began to drum heavily on the roof of the car and the driver switched the wipers on, which squeaked irritatingly as they waited for the lights to change.

'So how about it?' said Craig. 'D'you want the cod 'n' chips or not?'

'Nah. Stick your fish 'n' chips.' A sneer in the driver's voice. 'I work for cash. An' if you ain't got it, I'm round the corner to the cop shop an' you can sort it out with them.'

Craig felt like punching him in the back of the head, and would have done if the lights hadn't changed.

'Don't remember me, do yuh? The driver said as they pulled away – Craig saw him grinning as he adjusted his driving mirror – 'We were in the same cell block. I recognised you right away, even without the pony tail.'

'I'm sorry,' Craig began. 'I....'

'Name's Rice. Tony Rice.'

'Oh yeah,' said Craig, his tone indicating he had no intention of discussing his recent sentence with this fellow inmate he couldn't remember from Adam. He fiddled nervously with his earring and was relieved when they pulled up outside the Working Men's Club. The driver turned round.

'Haven't you got any dosh then?'

'I've got enough to pay the fare, if that's what you mean.'

The driver grinned and waved away the offer to pay. 'Nah, go on. It's on the house. I wouldn't like to deprive a man of his pint.'

'Cheers, mate!'

'An' if you can trade the greasy leftovers for an extra pint, you're laughing.'

'Nothing wrong with these fish and chips,' said Craig as he opened the cab door. The driver put a restraining hand on his arm.

'If you hear of anything that's going, I wouldn't mind a piece of the action.'

Craig shook his head firmly. 'I'm going straight.'

'That's what they all say. You can't be earning much at that fuckin' chippie.'

'I get by,' Craig replied. 'Thanks for the lift.'

As he hurried towards the club entrance, the taxi driver let the window down and called out: 'You know where to find me if you hear of anything. Just give the cab firm a ring.'

Craig had no intention of contacting him. Ever. It was a past he wanted to remain buried. He was determined to keep out of trouble this time. But when he got inside the club, there was a disappointment awaiting him: the regular bar steward was off sick, and the misery-guts replacing him wasn't interested in swapping a pint for a portion of fish and chips, and as no one else wanted the food, Craig ended up binning it.

He stood quietly at the bar, sipping the one pint he could afford, his mood growing darker by the minute as he thought bitterly about life's cruel blows and the pittance he was being paid to work in his brother-in-law's chippie. He knew he was being tested. He also knew he would eventually give in to the temptation of improving his financial status the easy way.

***

Gary Branston rubbed a liberal amount of Giorgio Armani into his neck and shoulders. In the bathroom mirror he could see his wife eyeing him suspiciously. He picked up a pair of cosmetic scissors and snipped a hair that had grown too long on his neatly-trimmed beard.

'You're going to a lot of trouble over your appearance,' said Maggie. 'Especially at half-ten at night.'

'I had my hair cut earlier,' he explained, somewhat testily. 'And you know I can't stand feeling itchy.'

'Where is it you said you were going?'

'To see this bloke at his club, to discuss the possibility of forming a partnership.'

'Doing what, exactly?'

'Oh – this and that.'

'And what time will you be back?'

He shook his head and avoided her eyes. 'I've no idea. The meeting'll be as long as it takes. Maybe you'd better not wait up for me.'

He went into the bedroom, removed his bathrobe and began dressing hurriedly. She followed him.

'You're hardly ever at the chip shops these days, and now you're starting to talk about starting another business.'

'I own the chip shops. Other people can work them for me.'

'Yeah. People like my brother.'

'Don't start that again. He's lucky to get a job so soon after he came out.'

'Oh yeah – very lucky,' she said, sarcastically.

He ignored it and continued dressing.

'Daryl and Hannah are all tucked up,' she said after a while. 'Why don't you go in and see them. They look really sweet.'

He knew it was a form of moral blackmail, trying to make him feel guilty, so he glanced at his watch. 'Not now,' he said.

She followed him downstairs to the front door. 'Gary,' she began, 'I get worried ... about the way you live ... the money you spend....'

'You didn't complain about that on St Valentine's Night. I spent a wad that evening, I can tell you.'

'That was different. It was special.'

'Look, don't worry about this business venture. It might not even come to anything.'

She knew then that he was lying. He had no intention of attending a potential business meeting.

'If I find out who she is,' she hissed, 'there'll be hell to pay, Gary. That I can promise you.'

'What are you talking about?' he said innocently. 'I've told you it's a business meeting.'

He'd learnt that much from his brother-in-law: if they've got no evidence, and you deny it, they can't prove a thing.

Seven

'Sorry to drag you all the way to Crowborough just to trim this bit,' said Nigel Pooley, tugging at a small tuft of hair at the end of his parting. 'But this will drive me doolally.'

'I know you like a regular trim,' grumbled Mike, 'but I only cut it four days ago.'

'Yes I know. I expect it's me being a fusspot,' continued the salesman. 'But I'm pitching to an important client this afternoon.' He lowered his voice to a conspiratorial whisper. 'And I have a meeting with a lady this evening.'

Mike didn't bother to disguise the lack of interest in his tone. 'This the one you were telling me about? The one who answered your ad in the lonely hearts column?'

Nigel sniggered like a mischievous child. 'This is another one. I've had a good response from the advert. Of course, there were one or two that were a bit – how shall I put it? – a bit suspect. But I've whittled it down to three possibles, including the one I'm having dinner with tomorrow night.'

Mike stared closely at the top of his client's hair and carefully snipped the tiniest bit.

'That should do it.'

He undid the protective mantle round Nigel's neck and gently shook it onto the carpet, taking care to do it away from the desk and computer.

'I know you missed that tuft of hair the other night,' said Nigel. 'But I'd be happy to pay you five pounds for your trouble.'

Mike shook his head. 'I was passing anyway.' He was annoyed because he'd had his hairdressing skills brought into question.

'I'd feel better if you took it,' offered Nigel, tentatively holding out a ten pound note. 'Only I haven't anything smaller.'

'That settles it then,' replied Mike. 'Neither have I.'

He noticed the tenner had disappeared back into Nigel's wallet pretty sharpish.

'Oh well,' said the salesman, 'you must allow me to buy you a drink one of these days.'

Chance would be a fine thing thought Mike. He nodded non-committally and moved towards the door. Nigel placed a hand on his shoulder.

'Something bothering you, Mike? You don't seem to be your usual self.'

'Oh, just the problems everyone has with teenagers. God knows what my son spends his money on. I wish I knew.'

'Could it be drugs?'

Mike thought about it. 'I don't think so. I hope not.'

'That's one of the biggest scourges in society today – lack of meaning; lack of direction. Perhaps your son needs some spiritual guidance. I'd be happy to come and have a word with him.'

For once Mike was lost for words. Nigel continued.

'I could explain to him the way to discover a deeper meaning to life.'

'Look, I don't want to be rude,' Mike almost snapped, 'but he'd see you coming a mile off.'

'What d'you mean?'

'I mean he'd be suspicious if you tried to sell him something. You're a salesman: you start peddling God to him and he'll back off straight away.'

Mike thought he might have gone too far, but Nigel was thick-skinned and saw all heathens as potential prospects.

'We're all salesmen,' he began smoothly. 'Everyone in the world is selling something. Some of us sell good things, while others sell bad things. Like drugs dealers, for instance....'

Mike edged nearer the door. 'I really must....'

'What's your son's name?

'Andrew.'

25

Nigel suddenly produced a paperback book with the eye-defying speed of a conjuror and thrust it at Mike. 'Please give Andrew this, with my compliments. He might read it; he might not. But I hope he does. It may save him.'

Mike accepted it and read the title. He wondered what his son's reaction would be to The Search for Truth.

'Thanks,' he said. 'One of Andy's favourite films is Monty Python's Life of Brian. He should enjoy this.'

Nigel looked blank. It was wasted on him.

Grinning, Mike added, 'I expect you've led a sheltered life.'

***

Exotic Savoury Dips caught Marjorie's eye. She picked up the packet, read the ingredients on the back, sniffed noisily, then put it back on the cold shelf. She walked on up the supermarket aisle slowly, with Ted following closely, pushing the trolley.

'I'm looking for something special,' she explained. 'Something what'll go down well with a few schooners of cream sherry.'

Ted was churning with agony inside. He glanced at his watch. Only another seven hours before he was due to meet Donald at the station. As he saw the exciting prospect of the trip to London to see the Royal Shakespeare Company slipping away, he was suddenly stirred into action.

'I don't think I can face Alec and Freda tonight.'

Marjorie turned slowly to face him, incomprehension spread across her face. 'What?'

'I said I don't think....'

'I heard what you said,' she snapped. 'You've been behaving peculiar all week. What's wrong with asking Alec and Freda over? Just because we live in Molyneux Park now, they'll think us stand-offish if we don't.'

'It's just...' he stammered, 'I ... I ... might have to go out tonight.'

Her eyes widened. 'Go out? Go out where?'

'Um...union meeting,' he said lamely.

She tutted and turned away from him. 'Don't be stupid. We've never been one for unions.'

He knew it was a stupid excuse. But how could he possibly tell her the truth? Tell her he was going out with a man he'd met in the pub. A total stranger. He could imagine what her reaction would be. But he was determined that he should go. This time she would not stand in his way.

'Marjorie,' he said. 'I'll just go outside and order our taxi. I'll get a better signal outside.'

'Use the supermarket phone. It's free.'

'The firm I use is cheaper,' he lied.

He knew she wouldn't argue with that. But she still had to have the last word.

'Tell them quarter past,' she commanded as he walked towards the exit. Outside in the Sainsbury's car park, before phoning the taxi firm, he telephoned Alec and Freda and apologised for having to cancel their arrangements that evening. He was now committed to his contingency plan. There was no turning back. Come hell or high water, Marjorie was not going to stand in his way. Even if she had to suffer the consequences.

Eight

While Marjorie unpacked the shopping, Ted took a packet of pork chipolatas out of the fridge and placed them next to the cooker. Marjorie eyed them suspiciously.

'What's that?' she demanded.

'Pork chipolatas,' he retorted boldly, feeling braver now that he had committed himself to scuppering his wife's plans for tonight.

'I can see that!' she snapped. 'When did you take them out of the freezer?'

'Last night, when you said we'd go to Sainsbury's first thing this morning. I thought you might like a cooked breakfast afterwards.'

'Oh did you? And who's going to cook it? I've got a pile of ironing to get through.'

'I don't mind cooking it,' Ted offered innocently, avoiding her gaze and unwrapping the sausages. He held his breath, hardly daring to cast a glance in her direction. He could feel her eyes boring into him. Was she suspicious? What if she said she wasn't hungry. And what if the chipolatas were to smell disgusting? There was so much of his plan that he had left to chance.

'As long as you don't get under my feet while I unpack the shopping,' said Marjorie.

'You'd like some breakfast then?'

She snorted disdainfully. 'I just said I did, didn't I?'

Ted tried to control the crafty smile that tugged at the corners of his mouth. As Marjorie turned away to unpack a plastic shopping bag, he secretly sniffed the sausages. They had a slightly sweet aroma and he wondered if this was normal. It would be just his luck if they turned out to be perfectly innocuous after all the trouble he'd taken. Surely they couldn't. He had taken them out of the freezer on Tuesday, sneaked them into his sports bag, taken them with him on the train all day, then put them back in the freezer in the evening. Wednesday night he'd left them to defrost overnight at the bottom of the airing cupboard, followed by another spell in the freezer until last night. No. They couldn't possibly be safe to eat.

'Mmm, that smells good,' said Marjorie once he'd got the bacon and sausages cooking under the grill. 'I feel quite peckish now.'

'How many eggs d'you want?'

'Just the one. I'll have four of them chipolatas, though. They smell really nice.'

While Marjorie took a fresh bottle of bleach and disinfectant upstairs, Ted laid the table carefully and dished out the breakfast. The hard part was yet to come. The part where he had to get rid of his own sausages.

'It's on the table!' he called, then impulsively snatched a chipolata off his own plate, broke another one in half, and hastily transferred the one and a half sausages into the plastic bag he kept in his jacket pocket for this purpose. Now he only had two and a half chipolatas to somehow sneak into his pocket while Marjorie was at the table with him. And this he planned to do while she got up to get the milk which he had deliberately forgotten to put on the table.

***

Craig had just finished frying the first batch of fish and chips when his sister dashed breathlessly into the shop. She threw his wage packet onto the counter.

'Sorry, love, I know we normally pay you on Thursday, but I've been up to my eyes.'

He started to tear open the envelope. 'What's wrong with Gary then? Is it too much like hard work to visit one of his chip shops from time to time?'

'I can't stop, Craig. I've left the car on a double-yellow.'

'Maggie!'

She stopped in the doorway. He could see her eyes were red and puffy, as if she'd been crying.

'You're the one who does all the running around, looking after your husband's business empire.'

She smiled weakly at his sarcasm. 'Well,' she shrugged, 'you know how it is.'

'Yeah, too right I do.'

He flicked quickly through the notes in his wage packet, a pitifully lean amount for the hours he'd worked. He felt angry suddenly.

'He's walking all over you, Maggie. And you just let him.'

'Not anymore, love. I've had enough. This time he's gone too far.'

'What's he done?'

'He never come home last night. Went out about half-ten – a business meeting he said.'

'And you believed him?'

'What do you think, Craig?' she snapped; then added in a more apologetic tone: 'But there was nothing I could do to prove otherwise.'

'So where is he now?'

'How should I know? I told you: he never come home.'

Craig slammed the metal lid shut on the fish fryer. But this wasn't enough to assuage his temper, so he kicked over the rubbish bin, which fortunately was empty.

He always lashed out at inanimate objects when he was angry.

'The bastard!' he yelled. 'I'll be round your place tonight and I shall have 'im.'

'No you won't, Craig. Because if he comes home between now and tonight, I'm gonna....'

Craig didn't find out what his sister had in mind, because at that moment the first customer of the day entered.

'I'll see you then, Craig,' said Maggie as she hurried away.

The customer, an elderly woman in a headscarf and massive overcoat, watched her leaving, then regarded Craig suspiciously. She knew she had interrupted a scene and would have loved to know more of what had gone on.

'Oh dear!' she said, nodding at the waste bin lying on its side. 'Had an accident, love?'

***

Ted glanced at his watch. It was four o'clock. Only another hour to go until he had to meet Donald. And still there was no indication that the chipolatas had worked. He stared across the kitchen table at Marjorie, who was reading Woman's Realm and noisily slurping tea. Suddenly she winced painfully and a low animal moan came from the depths of her stomach.

'Marjorie!' exclaimed Ted with exaggerated concern. 'What's wrong?'

Marjorie ran from the room and just about made it to the downstairs cloakroom before throwing up in the small hand basin.

As Ted listened to the revolting sound of her retching, a grin spread across his face. Eureka! he thought. It worked.

Nine

Having spent the last two days waiting for a reaction from his neighbour across the street, Dave Whitby was bitterly disappointed. He had left the clapped out Nova right outside the bloke's house on Wednesday afternoon; it was now Friday evening and still the proverbial hadn't hit the fan. Then, as he was about to leave for his Masonic do in Folkestone, the doorbell rang.

'Bingo!' he cried and, picking up his dinner jacket, he walked to the front door, singing loudly: 'It must be him, please make it him or I shall die.'

He flung open the door. The neighbour stood framed in the doorway, blocking out the fading light.

'Is that your heap of junk?'

Dave took his time replying, enjoying the situation.

'I'm sorry?'

'You know damn well what I'm talking about. That eyesore you've parked outside our house is yours presumably? Or does it belong to some other ignoramus?'

'If you are referring to Betty,' Dave began, 'you are talking about the vehicle I have fallen for. It was love at first sight, you see. She may not be the best looking car in the world, but Betty's got character – which is more than I can say for a lot of people not a million miles from here. Betty's poor old tired body may be blemished....'

'That vehicle,' interrupted the neighbour, jerking a thumb in the direction of the Nova, 'is committing an offence. And I'd like you to move it.'

Dave stared defiantly at the man. 'Oh, yes? What offence am I committing. Pray do tell.'

'Well, it's hardly roadworthy, is it? Consequently it means it's parked illegally.'

Dave shook his head. 'You're out of luck, sunshine. That car is taxed for another couple of months – which I intend renewing – and I've insured it. Admittedly she failed her MOT – poor old cow! – but I only bought her because I knew how attractive she'd look outside your gaff.'

There was a wounded, incredulous expression surfacing on the man's face. 'You mean you've gone to all this trouble and expense of buying an old banger just to upset us?'

Dave was lost for words suddenly. 'Well...'

'God! You're pathetic.'

The neighbour turned and began to walk away. Dave felt he was losing control of the situation. 'You're the one who's pathetic, getting territorial about parking. This is to teach you a lesson.'

The neighbour looked back and spoke calmly and confidently. 'Didn't you wonder why I didn't storm round here straight away when I discovered it was your car? It's because I wanted to speak to a solicitor friend of mine first. And I'm afraid you're the one who's out of luck. A car deliberately abandoned like that will be considered an obstruction. So you'll have to move it or pay a fine. Too bad. You've chucked your money down the drain.'

The man gave Dave a smile before walking away.

'We'll see about that,' Dave called after him. 'Wait till the press gets hold of this, we'll see who looks pathetic then.'

But as the comedian stood watching his neighbour returning to his own house, he suddenly felt very unsure of himself.

***

When Gary tried to unlock the front door his key wouldn't fit. At first he couldn't work out what the problem was, then he noticed how shiny and new the lock was. The penny dropped.

Cursing quietly, he strode across the front lawn, hoping Maggie hadn't done the back door as well.

'You needn't bother trying the back door. That lock's been changed as well.'

He hadn't heard the bedroom window opening. He craned his neck back, shielding his eyes from the last rays of sunlight, and stared up into Maggie's resentful face.

'What's going on, Maggs?'

'That's what I'd like to know.'

'Look, I'm sorry about last night. I didn't want to ring you. It was too late to disturb you.'

'Oh!' she yelled sarcastically. 'You're so thoughtful, Gary.'

He looked towards the street, hoping there were no neighbours passing on their way home from work.'

'What's wrong?' she shouted. 'Am I ruining your image?'

He had always been proud of his manipulation skills and his ability to smooth-talk his way out of any tricky situations; but this time he realised he had gone too far.

'Please, Maggs,' he pleaded, 'let's talk about this.'

'No way. You are not coming back into this house. You can go back to whoever you were with last night.'

'It's not like you think it is.'

'Don't treat me like an idiot.'

She was about to close the window.

'Maggie! At least give me a chance to explain.'

'I've heard it all before. What's the story this time? How you had one too many drinks and fell asleep on a mate's sofa?'

He gazed up at her, his mind a blank. She had word for word guessed what his excuse would be. And his silence proved she was right.

'Don't tell me you were really going to use that excuse.'

'Look, Maggie, I swear to you....'

'I've had enough, Gary. I'll get your things together tomorrow and you can pick them up. I'll leave them outside the back door. But you are not coming back in this house.'

'What about the kids?'

'They're at my mother's. So leave them out of it.'

Recovering slightly, he made one last ditch attempt to rescue the situation.

'Listen Maggie, if I can prove to you where I was last night ... if I can get my mate to ring you...'

But she had already slammed the window shut.

***

As Claire placed an enormous mountain of a dinner in front of her husband, the phone rang.

'Sod's law!' she said. 'If it's for you, shall I say you're out?'

'No, I'll take it.'

She went out into the hall and took the call, returning to the breakfast room moments later. 'It's for you,' she said. 'Someone called Gary Branston.'

Mike frowned. 'I only cut his hair yesterday.' He got up from the table. 'I wonder what he wants?'

'Try not to be long. You're dinner'll get cold.'

Claire tried to listen to the conversation but the washing machine, which was on its final spin, was making too much of a racket. When Mike returned he continued eating in silence before Claire asked:

'What did he want?'

'Wanted to know if I fancy a quick drink.'

'You're not going, are you?'

Mike stared at his food and muttered, 'I thought I might pop out for a couple.'

'I know you and your quick ones. You'll stagger back at half-eleven tonight, reeking of booze.'

Ten

Any sense of responsibility Ted might have felt towards Marjorie he put behind him as he sneaked out of the house. She would be left in the darkening silence, calling out for him to attend to her needs, and he couldn't have cared less.

Having arranged to meet Donald at ten-past-five, he arrived breathlessly at the station five minutes late. Donald was nowhere to be seen, and Ted felt nauseous waves of irrational panic. What if Donald had gone without him? But the train wasn't due until twenty-one minute past. Perhaps something had gone wrong. Maybe Donald had changed his mind. The thoughts of walking back across the common to face Marjorie filled him with dread. Not to mention loathing.

Suddenly a taxi pulled up and there was Donald, waving and smiling from the back seat. Ted glanced at his watch, feeling anxious about catching the train. As Donald walked towards him, Ted thought he looked older than he remembered. A man in his mid-sixties, at least. But then he was wearing a sober, dark suit, so perhaps that aged him.

'Sorry I'm late. I had to wait ages for a taxi,' he explained. 'I'd better get our tickets.'

'I've already got mine,' said Ted. 'I don't have to pay.'

Donald regarded him with amusement. 'Oh yes, I forgot – you work for the company. Well I still need a ticket.'

As they joined the small queue at the ticket office, Ted noticed the quality of Donald's suit and compared it to his own inferior sports jacket, with its bulging pockets. Suddenly he went hot and cold. One of the pockets contained the plastic bag with the virulent chipolatas. He had intended disposing of it on the way to the station but in all the excitement it had slipped his mind. Somehow he would have to get rid of it on the train.

As they neared the front of the queue, Donald said, 'I had to leave Bamber to lock up the shop. We have an antique shop in the Pantiles – jewellery and china's our speciality. And leaving Bamber in charge is dangerous. Talk about a bull in a china shop.'

Donald laughed uproariously at this. The person in front of him turned round to look.

'Who's Bamber?' Ted asked, speaking quietly, hoping that Donald might do the same. But Donald was a naturally loud person and continued in stentorian decibels.

'Bamber is the friend with whom I share my abode. I sometimes allow him to do some work for me; when he's not going through a clumsy time. Unusual name, isn't it?'

Donald stared at Ted, waiting for a response. Ted nodded passively and it was all the encouragement Donald needed to continue.

'His mother was a fan of University Challenge – poor sod! She lives in Brighton. She's quite well off but she's a dipsomaniac. There won't be much left for Bamber by the time she pops her clogs. Spends every waking moment doing The Times crossword. What a waste of an agile brain. Ah! Here we are. One return to London, please.'

They caught the train with only minutes to spare. As soon as they had settled into seats opposite one another, Donald asked: 'Whereabouts in Tunbridge Wells do you live, Ted?'

'Er – Molyneux Park Road.'

Donald looked surprised. Ted leaned forward and explained as quietly as possible, 'We used to live on Ramslye. Then Marjorie – my wife – inherited our house from her grandmother.'

'How absolutely splendid.'

Ted looked as if it was far from splendid. As the train moved off he leapt to his feet, excused himself and dashed to the toilet. Making certain the door was locked, he took the chipolatas out of his pocket and stuffed them into the waste bin, covering them with layers of scrunched-up paper towels. When he got back to his seat, Donald commented on how flustered he looked. Ted nodded and smiled thinly.

'What's your favourite Shakespeare play?' Donald asked.

Without thinking, Ted blurted out, 'Titus Andronicus!'

Donald frowned. 'That's a curious choice. Bit bloodthirsty. Bit morbid. Isn't it the one where the queen is fed her own sons in a meat pie and collapses over the dinner table?'

Ted looked confused. Somehow Shakespeare's rarely performed play of mayhem and murder had slipped out of his subconscious. Now thoughts of poison and police and prison rattled about inside his head. What if Marjorie died? That would make him a murderer.

He noticed Donald staring at him, frowning. 'I – I don't know why I thought of Titus Andronicus,' he explained. 'It's not my favourite. Not by a long chalk. I think I like A Midsummer Night's Dream best.'

Donald leaned forward and tapped him on the knee. 'You must allow me,' he said conspiratorially, 'to take you to the Open Air Theatre in London during the summer. It's a magical evening.'

'Could I see your tickets, please?'

Ted looked startled. He hadn't heard the guard approaching.

'Hello, Ted,' said the guard. 'Where are you off to then?'

'Mmm. London,' Ted mumbled.

'We're going to see Macbeth at the Albery Theatre,' said Donald, showing the guard his ticket.

'Oh well,' replied the guard, looking suspiciously from one to the other, 'each to his own.'

Donald smiled and looked across at Ted, whose hands were tightly clenched and he was blushing to the roots.

***

Maggie had been on the phone to her mother for an hour. She hadn't long hung up when it rang again. She thought it might be Gary and braced herself for another argument.

'Yes!' she snapped.

'Could I speak to Gary?'

'He's not here.'

She heard pub noises in the background. She was about to slam the phone down when the man's voice shouted urgently over the noise:

'It's Mike Longridge. I cut your husband's hair yesterday. Sorry about last night. I don't suppose he'll be allowed out to play for a while.'

'What d'you mean?'

'It's the longest poker session I've ever known. Gary did all right for the first couple of hours. But by the end of the game I think he was down about two hundred. Pity I bumped into him last night. I feel it's down to me he lost his shirt.'

'He's old enough to make his own decisions,' she said, her voice frosty.

'Well, anyway, sorry about that. You don't know what time he'll be back, do you?'

'No, I don't.'

She slammed the phone down.

At his local, Mike rejoined Gary at the bar. 'I think it might have worked,' he said.

Gary slapped him on the back. 'Cheers, mate! That's one I owe you.'

Eleven

Jackie Ingbarton stared at the pile of greasy crockery in the sink. She knew she had to confront the girls about it but she hated scenes.

'Oh, Vanessa....' she began, and gestured helplessly at the draining board.

'That wasn't me,' her daughter snapped, defensively.

Jackie sighed long-sufferingly. 'It never is you. Or Nicky. It's so depressing to come home to. You could at least make the effort.'

Vanessa ignored her mother and busied herself at the kitchen table, scrolling through the photographs on the back of her camera. Jackie switched the kettle on and started to clear a space at the sink, ready to tackle the washing-up herself.

'How did it go today?' she asked.

'I did my first project. It was a photo-journalism assignment.'

'How exciting!'

Vanessa shrugged indifferently. 'It was alright.'

'What did you choose to do?'

'I went down to the Animal Rights protests. I got a terrific one of Nicky with her banner. Come and have a look. You might need your glasses.'

Jackie peeled off her rubber gloves, fumbled in her handbag for her reading glasses, then peered over Vanessa's shoulder. She tutted disapprovingly.

'I didn't realise Nicky was so heavily involved. What about her job? If she spends all this time protesting....'

'She's due some annual leave.'

'All the same, I don't suppose the insurance company would be happy to see one of their employees protesting in public.'

'Oh, Mummy, you're so spineless.'

Hurt, Jackie turned away from the table and returned to the sink. Vanessa, realising she had been spiteful as usual, added:

'Well, you must admit, you don't exactly stick up for yourself. Look at the way Daddy walked all over you.'

'That's because he was a....' Jackie paused.

'He was a what? You can't even say it, can you?'

'He behaved very badly.'

'Oh, Mummy!'

Jackie felt she was being pitied, and this made her suddenly very decisive. She went and sat opposite her daughter and said, 'I was going to wait until Nicky was here. But as we seem to be ships that pass in the night, I may as well tell you my news now, while I've got the chance. You know I've been seeing Nigel?'

'You never told me where you met him. He just appeared suddenly and took you out to dinner.'

Jackie avoided eye contact with her daughter and fiddled thoughtfully with the edge of a tea towel she was clutching like a comfort blanket.

'I suppose,' continued Vanessa in a haughty, sarcastic tone, 'he's one of the leading lights in your amateur dramatic society.'

'No, I met him through a newspaper advertisement.'

Vanessa snorted. 'I don't believe this. Not a lonely hearts column?'

Jackie felt her heart sinking like a stone. In a small voice she said, 'He's asked me to marry him.'

'What?'

From the incredulous expression on her daughter's face, Jackie seemed to gain some strength. It was like being with her amateur acting society, now she felt the thrill of stepping from the wings to centre stage.

'He's an extremely nice chap. A real gentleman. And a regular churchgoer.'

'So what's the catch?'

'Pardon?'

'You've known him just over a week and already he's proposed to you. What's wrong with him?'

Jackie's voice became strident. 'Why do you have to spoil everything? You girls ... you always spoil ... everything I do.'

'Hey now just a minute! You're not actually thinking of marrying this creep, are you?'

'No, I'm not thinking about it. I've thought about it. I'm going to say 'yes'. And he's not a creep.'

***

The portable radio vibrated tinnily on the shelf next to the sauce bottles as Craig dipped a portion of haddock in the batter, then chucked it sizzling into the fryer. He hummed tunelessly along as Abba sang "Thank You for the Music" and didn't hear his first customer entering. He started slightly when he looked up..

'Remember me?'

Craig recognised him immediately. It was the taxi driver; the fellow inmate from the same cell block.

'Yeah, course I do. You gimme a lift the other night.'

'I didn't mean to make you jump. Sounds like you was miles away.'

'Yeah, thousands of miles; lying on a golden beach, underneath a coconut palm, with several dusky maidens plying me with an exotic and intoxicating beverage.'

The man shook his head seriously. 'I used to have that dream when I was banged up. It don't mean a thing. Cos you ain't ever gonna get further than dreaming it without any gelt.'

'Nope,' Craig agreed. 'I won't get far on what I earn here. About as far as Uckfield, I reckon. That's if I'm lucky.'

The man reached across the counter and held out a fleshy hand. 'You've probably forgotten. Tony Rice.'

Craig shook Rice's hand, a surprisingly limp handshake for such a big bloke.

'Craig Thomas. You hungry? I can fix you something to eat on the house.'

Rice declined monosyllabically, walked to the door to check that no customers were about to enter, and said, 'The cabbying's a dead loss. I just need something to tide me over ... just one quick job.'

'As a matter of fact,' Craig said, 'I've been starting to think along the same lines.' He glanced towards the door and began to speak hurriedly. 'You know the club where you dropped me off? I know it's on my own doorstep but ... it's so easy. Upstairs, outside the snooker room is the Gents toilet. And inside the toilet is a trapdoor leading to a loft. If we help each other up into the loft during eyes down in bingo....'

'We can wait there till after closing and help ourselves,' Rice finished with a grin.

'Exactly. The trouble is, with my form, the finger of suspicion's going to point my way. I'll have to get an alibi first.'

Rice shrugged nonchalantly. 'I'll get you an alibi. No worries.'

'As long as it's not a poker game. No one believes that old chestnut anymore.'

Twelve

Surrounded by piles of clean washing, Claire looked up from the ironing board as Mike walked into the kitchen.

'You're early,' she said.

'I've got an hour to kill, so I thought I'd pop back for some tea.'

'Was the pub closed then?'

Ignoring the barb, Mike opened a copy of the Kent & Sussex Courier he'd picked up earlier on and came and stood next to his wife at the ironing board.

'Feast your eyes on that then,' he said, shoving the paper in front of Claire. 'You know my client – that comedian I was telling you about? He said he'd be back in the news again. Well, that's him. I think he's upset the whole of High Brooms.'

Claire glanced at the story. There was a picture of Dave Whitby posing in front of the offending car, and the caption said 'Comedian's Car Caper Backfires'.

'I don't think he's come out of it as well as he hoped,' continued Mike brightly, oblivious to his wife's darkening mood. 'Mind you, he's managed to get some publicity, which can't be bad in his game, I s'pose. Shame he didn't manage to hit the national papers.'

Claire sniffed disapprovingly. 'How pathetic can you get? I hope they throw the book at him. Stupid wally.'

'It's not entirely his fault. If his neighbour hadn't been so territorial over his parking space....'

'You sound as if you approve.'

Mike hesitated. He could sense Claire wanted an argument. 'Well,' he began uncertainly, 'it's only a bit of a laugh.'

'Oh, very amusing.'

'What's up?'

There was a pause while she moved a pile of ironed clothes onto a chair, then struggled to take down the ironing board.

'Here, let me give you a hand,' offered Mike.

'I can manage!' she snapped, and shoved the ironing board into its cubby hole behind the fridge.

Mike sighed and busied himself with making a pot of tea.

'I'm sorry, Mike,' said Claire. 'I'm sorry I shouted. It's just that everything's ... Tom phoned to complain about the lack of advertising in the wedding supplement, as if it's my fault. I know I'm the general dog's-body there, but I am only a part-timer. Then I had two weeks' washing and ironing to catch up on. And Chloe phoned.'

She sat at the kitchen table, waiting for Mike to join her. He sensed there was more bad news on the way. He poured out two mugs of tea and sat opposite her.

'What was Chloe ringing about? Is she okay?'

'Andrew's been in touch with her recently. Trying to borrow money from her.'

Mike took a small sip of tea and slammed his mug down.

'What? She's not leant him any, has she?'

Claire shook her head. 'She refused. But she said she found it difficult. He wouldn't tell her what it was for but he pleaded with her. Offered to pay her back with interest.'

'What the hell is he spending his money on?' questioned Mike. 'Drugs? Gambling? Booze?'

'Whatever it is, the problem's going to get worse. He'll be eighteen in three months' time, and he'll get the inheritance Mum and dad left him.'

'Oh, hell!' moaned Mike. 'I'd forgotten about that.'

'I hadn't.'

'What the hell will he do with ten grand?'

***

Gary was on his best behaviour, pretending he was suffering guilt and remorse from losing so much on a poker game. All week Maggie had been watching his every move and he knew he didn't dare put a foot wrong. The atmosphere was strained but at least he was back in his house. Things would soon be back to normal. Unfortunately, he hadn't anticipated that Sharon would be so stupid as to call him at home. Why couldn't she text him on his mobile, then none of this would have happened?

He was out in the garden being a model father and playing with the children when the phone rang. He dashed into the house but Maggie got there first.

'Hello? Hello?'

Maggie listened for a moment, replaced the receiver, picked it up again and dialled 1-4-7-1. Then she wrote a number down on a notepad and started to redial.

'Who is it?' Gary asked, starting to fear the worst.

'I don't know yet.'

'What are you doing?'

'I'm finding out who just rang.'

'It was probably a wrong number,' he offered with little hope.

'Shut up, Gary!' she barked. 'I can't concentrate. Go and make me a cup of coffee.'

He slunk away into the kitchen, hovering at the door to listen to the conversation. He heard her say something about not being a double-glazing canvasser but someone doing market research about fast food. He missed the next part of the conversation while he put the kettle on. He quickly spooned instant coffee into a cup then moved swiftly back to the door. He panicked as he heard Maggie ending the conversation with:

'Thank you, Sharon. You've been a great help.'

He couldn't think straight. Sweat broke out under his arms and he braced himself for the confrontation, wishing now he'd never become involved with the stupid little tart.

'That was Sharon,' said Maggie with satisfaction as she entered the kitchen.

'Sharon?' He put on a puzzled expression.

She smiled, enjoying his discomfort. 'You must know Sharon. She works for us at the Maidstone shop. That little scrubber with the crooked teeth.'

He tried to make his voice sound light, disinterested. 'What did she want? Did she say?'

'Don't be stupid, Gary. She called here and hung up when I answered, and I traced the call. Now why would she call then hang up?'

Gary's throat felt dry. He tried to swallow. 'I don't know. Maybe she....'

'Maybe she what?'

She was staring at him, her eyes like cold steel.

He shrugged helplessly. 'Maybe she was going to hand in her notice then changed her mind.'

'Of course, she could have dialled 1-4-1 before the number then I would never have known who called. I wonder why she didn't?'

Gary pursed his lips, suggesting it was all beyond his comprehension. Maggie suddenly smiled sweetly.

'The children are waiting for you to finish the game.'

'Oh. Right,' he said, making a sideways move towards the back door.

She smiled again, though her eyes were cold. He found her behaviour unsettling. This was far worse than any argument.

Thirteen

Ted laid his guard's uniform out on the bed, folded it neatly, then squeezed it into his sports bag. Marjorie came into the bedroom, wearing rubber gloves and carrying a duster and an aerosol of furniture polish.

'My stomach's still not right,' she complained. 'I don't think I could face sausages ever again.'

'It can't have been the chipolatas,' repeated Ted for the umpteenth time. 'Or anything you'd eaten. I had exactly the same as you and I was alright. It must have been a virus.'

Marjorie squirted a jet of lavender polish onto the dressing table. 'It's funny,' she mused, 'you used to moan about having to change into your uniform at work. All the time. But recently you've stopped complaining.'

She stopped polishing, her head turned slowly like a tank turret and her eyes fixed him in her sights. Ted concentrated on zipping his bag.

'I expect I'm getting used to it,' he said, his voice light and inconsequential.

He could feel the twin lasers of her eyes boring into him. He glanced at his watch and cleared his throat delicately. 'I shall be back later than usual tonight. There's been a change in the rota.'

He had arranged to meet Donald for a quick drink after work. Marjorie noticed the crafty little smile that was teasing the corners of his mouth as he picked up his bag and shuffled towards the door. She knew something was up but had no idea what it was.

'Oh, before you go,' she said. 'There's something that's been bothering me.'

He stopped in the doorway. All traces of a smile had vanished.

'When I phoned Freda and Alec and said I'd come down with a stomach bug, Freda said you'd phoned up on Friday morning to cancel. I said you couldn't have done. I wasn't taken ill until the afternoon.'

Forcing himself to look her straight in the eye, Ted said, 'Well, there must be some explanation. I wouldn't have known you were going to be ill in advance, would I?' He gave a small nervous chuckle and glanced at his watch again. 'Bloomin' heck! Is that the time?'

'Never mind,' she said, as he made his getaway. 'We'll talk about it later.'

***

Maggie let herself into the Maidstone chip shop, which had just closed for the afternoon, glad to find Sharon on her own. Sharon's mouth fell open as Maggie handed her a brown envelope.

'What's this?'

'It's your wages made up to the end of the week. And you can count yourself lucky you're getting paid.'

'What have I done wrong?'

'Oh come off it, Sharon: Gary's told me everything.'

Sharon dropped the envelope unopened into her handbag and started to leave. She stopped in the doorway and told Maggie, 'It weren't my fault, Mrs Branston. It was Gary. He come on really strong. Wouldn't take no for an answer.'

Maggie smiled humourlessly. 'Oh well, Sharon. Thank you, anyway.'

Sharon frowned. 'What for?'

'For confirming my suspicions.'

***

'Sorry I'm late,' said Nigel as Mary Fernhill slid into the passenger seat. 'Only I had a tender to get out this morning and I was running a bit behind.'

He sniggered naughtily, as if caught out by a daring double entendre.

Humouring him, Mary returned his smile and said, 'I haven't been waiting that long.'

As he drove off, Nigel glanced at his passenger and frowned. The dress she was wearing was just a trifle loud. Perhaps that teashop in Eastbourne was not such a good idea.

'Something the matter, Nigel?'

'I thought we might have some tea in Eastbourne. Only....'

'Oh, I like Eastbourne.'

Suddenly Nigel's mobile rang insistently. He braked sharply and swung the car to the side of the kerb, oblivious to the obstruction he was causing. He assumed an important expression as he answered his mobile. 'Excuse me. It might be a client.' But his expression changed to one of slight panic. He had forgotten that he had given Jackie his mobile number.

'No – er – sorry. I can't talk now. I'm in a meeting.'

He clicked off the phone and shoved it into the glove compartment.

'I don't want to mix business with pleasure,' he said smoothly. 'Now then, let's head for that nice teashop in Eastbourne, where we can have that serious talk.'

Fourteen

Having sold most of his CD collection in a second hand record shop in Camden Road, Andrew stepped into the nearest pub. He bought himself a pint of lemonade and a packet of prawn cocktail flavoured crisps and sat staring at the fruit machine. It was late afternoon, and some of the regulars were already knocking back pints of Guinness. They were roofers mainly, and at this time of the year they knocked off work reasonably early.

Andrew watched while one of them – a large, bull-necked bloke with a shaven head – fed the fruit machine. Andrew had already been in the pub the previous night, counting the money being fed into the machine. He thought he had a system now and was certain it would work. He was convinced the machine was due to pay out any minute now. As soon as the bloke had lost ten pounds, he returned to the bar. Andrew shot to his feet and crossed quickly to the fruit machine. He had about twenty pounds in coins and fed the entire amount into the slot. Lights flashed furiously as he hit the first button. He was so engrossed, he didn't notice the man who loomed up beside him.

'So this is what you spend all your money on.'

Andrew froze. 'Dad! What are you doing here?'

'Watching you chuck your money away.'

Andrew ignored his father and continued playing the machine, frenetically hitting buttons, his eyes wild with concentration. Suddenly the wheels clicked smoothly into jackpot, the machine coughed and spluttered, and seventy-five coins fell into the tray. Feverishly, Andrew hit buttons. Lights flashed and more money spluttered into the tray. Again and again, until the machine won him well over a hundred pounds. The roofer at the bar glared at him. His father glared at him. But Andrew couldn't care less. He had been proved right. He had known the machine was due for a big win.

'Okay,' sighed his father. 'You might have won this time, but ultimately you can't beat the machines. It's not possible.'

'That's where you're wrong, Dad. I've cracked it.' He scooped the coins from the winning tray into his pocket. He was going to show his father he could leave the machine alone now that he'd won.

'Cracked it! Listen, Andrew, when other people start paying for your habit....'

'Like who for instance?'

'Like Chloe. She needs all the money she's got now that she's at university. She rang Mum and told her you tried to tap her for some.'

'The bitch! She promised she wouldn't say anything.'

'Now listen!' Mike's voice rose. 'Don't involve other people in your habit. Is that understood?'

'Keep your voice down.'

'And keep your thieving mitts out of Mum's purse.'

Andrew stuffed the last of the coins into the bulging pockets of his anorak and gave his father a confrontational stare. 'Are you accusing me of stealing?'

'That's what it sounds like.'

'Great! Mum's always losing things. Stupid cow!'

Mike waved a finger angrily at his son. 'I'm warning you, Andrew. There's only so much we can take.'

'Oh, get stuffed!'

Andrew barged past his father and marched out of the pub.

'Andrew!' Mike called out, but didn't attempt to follow him.

The man who had been playing the fruit machine prior to Andrew had been watching the scene with interest. He raised his eyebrows sympathetically and said to Mike, 'Kids, eh. Who'd have them?'

***

The tearoom was crowded. Nigel and Mary hovered awkwardly near the door, getting in the way of a plump waitress.

'I had no idea it would be so crowded this time of the year,' Nigel said.

Mary felt irritated and said flatly, 'And it was a long drive just for tea.'

The drive had been strained with awkward silences. And when Mary asked Nigel how he had been since they last met, he had prattled on about telephone systems he had sold to prestigious clients and boasted about the competitors he had beaten. And they both knew he was just talking to fill the silence.

'Ah!' exclaimed Nigel brightly. 'There's a table about to become free.'

He hurried over to the table and stood poised over four elderly ladies about to depart. One of the old ladies tried to free her ample bottom from where it had become lodged between the corners of two tables, as the plump waitress tried to clear the table, adding to the congestion. Eventually, after some complicated manoeuvring in spaces ill-suited to the more fulsome figure, the old ladies departed maladroitly and Nigel and Mary sat down.

Grabbing the menu, Nigel asked Mary if she was hungry. When he saw her hesitate, he waved a hand carelessly and said, 'Don't worry. It's on me. I know I paid for dinner the other night but you've got two young mouths to feed. I bet they're a handful, aren't they?'

'You must come and meet them soon.'

Nigel frowned and studied the menu. 'Buck rarebit, pot of tea and a selection of pastries do you?'

Mary nodded. 'Yes, that's fine, thank you.'

The waitress finished clearing their table, took their order and went off to fetch a pot of tea. Nigel caught Mary's eye, smiled tentatively, then looked down at the tablecloth and began fidgeting nervously with the cruet set. Mary wondered if she had upset him in some way. He was certainly behaving most strangely. The silence between them grew longer. Nigel cleared his throat noisily, and it looked as if he was about to speak when the waitress returned with the tea things.

'Shall I be mother?' Nigel said as he reached for the milk jug.

The waitress laid the table and went off again, leaving Nigel to pour the tea. He looked more comfortable now that he had something with which to busy himself, and he set about the task meticulously, his actions bordering on effeminacy. Mary watched him carefully. She knew this elaborate performance was a delaying tactic. But from what, she had no idea.

'You do want to meet them, don't you?' she said.

'Who?'

'My two little boys – Simon and Thomas.'

'Who's looking after them today?'

'They're at school. Then going round a friend's house for tea. Why?'

'Oh, just wondered. Is that alright for you?'

Mary took the cup from him. 'Yes. And you didn't answer my question. Don't you like children? Is that what it is?'

'Of course not. I've got a son of my own. A real chip off the old block, that one. Very good at selling....'

Mary found it difficult to contain her irritation. 'Yes, you've already told me all there is to know about him.'

'Oh!' he exclaimed, slightly taken aback by her impatient tone. 'Have I?'

There followed another long and uncomfortable pause, during which Nigel slurped his tea noisily. The waitress brought them their meal and Nigel immediately set about his with gusto. A large dollop of egg yolk missed his mouth and attached itself to his cheek. He noticed Mary staring at him.

'Is something wrong? You're not eating.'

'I'm not hungry. I want to know what's happening. About us.'

Sighing, Nigel put down his knife and fork. 'I'm sorry,' he began, 'I've – er – I've been trying to find the right words ... it's not easy but ... I ... um ... I want to get married.'

Mary's eyes widened and became moist. 'Oh, Nigel ... I didn't think ... well, I suppose I was hoping....'

Nigel panicked. 'No, no! Not to you. To someone else.'

'What?'

'I'm sorry. I really am. But you weren't the only one to answer my advertisement. I'm afraid I've made my decision and you weren't successful on this occasion.'

She rose angrily, fighting back the tears. Crockery rattled. Heads turned to look at her.

'Then why did you bring me here?'

'I thought it would be nice to let you down gently.'

'Call yourself a Christian!' she hissed. 'You pompous hypocrite.'

'I ... I'm sorry,' he stammered, 'if I gave you the impression our relationship was ongoing.'

You did more than give me that impression. You consummated it – our second night together.' She shuddered. 'To think I let you touch me....'

'I've suffered the most awful pangs of guilt about that,' he said, half rising. 'If you want me to give you a lift home now....'

'Don't bother,' she snapped. 'It's an awkward journey from here, but I'd sooner catch the train.'

She stormed out. There was a brief silence in the tea room before tongues began wagging again. Nigel sank back into his chair, relieved that it was over. He was embarrassed but he was also hungry. So he finished his meal then devoured two pastries. He over-tipped the waitress when he settled his bill, and she followed him to the door as he was leaving.

'Excuse me, sir,' she said. 'I hope you don't mind my mentioning it – I don't like to think of you going around unawares, like – but you've got egg on your face.'

Fifteen

When Andrew arrived home he acted as if nothing had happened between him and his father. 'Hi!' he said going to the fridge and helping himself to a tub of yoghurt.

Claire looked at Mike expectantly. Andrew pretended not to notice. He took a teaspoon from the draining board and tucked into the yoghurt, carefully avoiding eye-contact with his parents.

'Have you eaten?' Mike asked him.

'Not really.'

'What have you been doing all this time? It's gone seven.'

Andrew shrugged. 'Oh ... things. I saw this accident at the roundabout ... bottom of Frant Road. A taxi hit a BMW. The taxi driver was a nutter ... started beating up the BMW driver. Going berserk he was. He nearly....'

Claire interrupted him. 'Dad told me you were in the pub playing the fruit machine.'

'So?'

Mike tried to conceal his temper. 'So what Mum is saying is that we know about your problem, Andy.'

'Problem? What are you on about? Problem!'

'Gambling's a sickness, you know. Like drug addiction. Or....'

'Alcohol?' Andrew suggested, looking pointedly at his father before disposing of his yoghurt tub beneath the sink.

'I don't make any secret of my drinking habits. If I fancy a few beers now and then....'

'A few!' Andrew scoffed. 'Don't make me laugh.'

'At least my drinking's under control; paid for with the money I earn.'

'What's that supposed to mean?'

'Do you want me to spell it out for you?'

'I think you're gonna have to. My spelling's pretty lousy.'

'Don't try to be clever, Andy. You know bloody well what I'm talking about.'

'Oh,' Andrew sneered. 'Hard words, Dad.'

Mike slammed his hand onto the kitchen table. 'Now look! I've had enough of your behaviour – moping around, feeling sorry for yourself. Making all our lives a misery. And if I catch you stealing to pay for your habit....'

'Stealing!' Andrew shouted indignantly. 'I don't need to steal to....'

'Nobody's accusing you of stealing,' Claire interjected, but Andrew had already pulled a building society payments book out of his back pocket.

'I told you I'd cracked it,' he said, opening the book to the relevant page. 'Take a look at that, then.'

Mike glanced at the book. 'You paid in sixty quid. So what?'

'That's my earnings from the fruit machines.'

'Earnings!'

'Winnings then.'

'You've had a lucky run, that's all. All gamblers do from time to time. Tomorrow it'll be gone again. And the rest.'

Andrew snatched the book and stuffed it back into his pocket.

'No, this is it. I know how to play them now. I can make fifty or sixty a day. Easily.'

Claire moved closer to him and spoke gently. 'Andrew, you can't live like this. It won't lead anywhere. You need some help, sweetheart.'

She tried to cuddle him but he brushed her off as if he found her repugnant.

'Yeah, well it's only a problem to you two. I don't have a problem with it. I've found a way to earn that beats working in a supermarket. If it doesn't work out, no big deal. But I've got to give it a go.'

He turned to leave.

'Where're you going?' asked Claire.

'To get a burger.'

'There's plenty of food in the house.'

The door slammed. Mike sighed deeply and shook his head.

'Mike,' said Claire. 'Come and hold me. I think I need a cuddle.'

He got up from the table and went to her. She held him close and buried her face in his neck. After a moment she looked up and said:

'Did you notice the way he pushed me away when I tried to touch him. Just as if he'd been burnt. He couldn't bear to be touched.'

'It's just some teenage phase he's going through.'

'This is more than a phase. He seems to be locked in his own world.'

'Good job you've got me then,' Mike whispered, pulling her closer and running his hands down her back. He began kissing her, parting her lips with his own. She drew back.

'Not now, Mike.'

'Why not?'

'I would have thought it was obvious.'

'Well, would you like to let me know when, so I can make an appointment in my diary.'

'Oh, men!' she complained. 'Not that there's any such thing. It's just boys growing up into bigger boys.'

***

Dave had just finished sending a text on his mobile when his landline rang. He went out into the hall to answer it, wondering if it was another neighbour ringing up to complain about the car.

'Hello?' he said warily.

'Is that Dave Whitby?'

'Who wants him?'

'Hello, Dave. Don't suppose you remember me. You did a little gig for me in ninety-two. Police do down in Torquay.'

'You're right,' said Dave. 'I don't remember you. A name would help.'

The man had a throaty laugh. 'It's Harvey Boyle. I saw your splash in the local rag today. Naughty, naughty. Opened a can of worms, you did. Still, there's no such thing as bad publicity.'

'I remember you, Harvey. You still an agent?'

'Yeah, and a club owner. You fixed up with a summer season yet?'

'Not really. No.'

'Might be able to put something your way.'

Dave sighed. 'I knew there had to be a catch.'

Boyle chuckled loudly, a rasping sound as if he was clearing his throat. 'I know you was never one for stag nights, but I need someone double quick. And there's two hundred of the folding stuff goes straight in your back pocket. No questions.'

It flashed through Dave's mind that if it was something Harvey Boyle was involved in, then it would be a night to remember, like the sinking of the Titanic. But right now two hundred quid was worth having.

Reluctantly, he said, 'Ah well, I'll just have to dirty up my act. When is it?'

Sixteen

'Ugh! What's this?' complained Daryl.

Maggie gritted her teeth. 'Shepherd's pie. You've had it before and you liked it.'

'I'm not eating it.'

'If you don't eat it, there'll be no ice-cream, no sweets and no mountain bike for your birthday. And I mean it this time. So you'd better bloody well eat it.'

He had never seen his mother scream with such uncontrolled vehemence before and he hurriedly began eating, while glowering at his goody-goody little sister who was dutifully tucking into her meal.

Gary, carrying a billiard cue, came rushing into the kitchen. 'What's all that shouting and swearing?'

'I hate shepherd's pie,' whined Daryl. 'And Mum's swearing at me because I don't like it.'

'I like shepherd's pie, Daddy,' said Hannah cutely, and her brother stared at her with loathing.

'You eat it, there's a good boy,' Gary said, patting his son on the shoulder. He looked accusingly at Maggie. 'Shouting and swearing's not going to help.'

'Don't interfere, Gary. And where are you going with that?'

'I'm gonna play snooker. Why?'

'No you're not.'

'Now what's the problem? It's the semi-finals tonight. It's been on the cards for some time. You know it has.'

'That's tough, Gary. You should have thought of that before – '

'Before what?'

She turned away from him, opened one of the cupboards and reached for a bottle of Cinzano. He watched as she poured herself a liberal measure.

'You can't play snooker tonight because we're short staffed at Maidstone.'

'Oh blimey! Millie's not ill again, is she?'

Maggie fetched ice from the fridge and threw Gary a sidelong look of triumph. 'Who said anything about Millie?'

'Oh. It's not ... er....' He couldn't bring himself to say her name.

'Sharon,' Maggie finished for him. 'Yes, I'm afraid Sharon's no longer with us. I fired her this afternoon.'

'What the hell did you do that for?'

'Do you want me to spell it out for you, Gary? In front of the children. Do you really want me to say why I got rid of her?'

'You can't sack people without good reason.'

'Oh, I've got a good reason alright.'

'But what am I gonna do about the snooker?'

Maggie dropped her ice cubes into her drink and stared incredulously at her husband. How thick-skinned could he be?

Daryl, who had been listening carefully to this exchange, found the slight pause he had been waiting for.

'Dad's been shagging Sharon,' he told his sister.

There was a deathly silence in the room. He hadn't truly understood the significance of his statement, but he could feel the ripples of discomfort it had caused, and it gave him a wonderful feeling of power.

***

Craig finished wrapping two portions of pie and chips then snatched up the phone. It was Tony Rice.

'It's not a good time to ring,' Craig told him. 'I'm on my own and I've got a shop full of customers.'

'Bugger 'em,' said Rice. 'We on for this little caper on Friday night? Because I've fixed you up with a watertight alibi.'

'There's no such thing.'

'You interested or not?'

'Yeah. Why not? Let's go for it.'

'Can you meet me tonight in Hastings? We're meeting a guy called Harvey Boyle. I'll explain later. Here's the address'

Craig glanced along the queue of customers as he hastily scribbled the address on a chip wrapper. Those at the back of the queue looked more irritated than those at the front.

'I'll see you later then. I should be there about half-eleven. Who's this Harvey Boyle?'

'Owns a club in Hastings,' explained Rice. 'He's the owner of the club. And he's got your alibi lined up. Quite tasty she is, an' all."

***

Donald was already into his second large gin and tonic by the time Ted arrived at the pub.

'Sorry I'm late,' Ted said, sheepishly. 'Points failure at Hither Green. Can I get you a drink?'

Donald smiled congenially. 'You mean there really is such a thing as points failure? I always thought it was an excuse for staff shortages. I'll have a single gin to add to this one, please.'

Ted placed his sports bag on the floor near Donald and went to get the drinks. When he returned with a gin, and a pint of bitter for himself, he noticed his new friend had an amused expression on his face.

'Tell me, Ted, what do you cart about in this bag of yours? You had it with you the first time we met.'

'It's my uniform.'

Donald grinned knowingly. 'I see. And it's not really Molyneux Park Road, is it?'

Ted felt the start of a blush. Donald patted him reassuringly on the knee.

'Take no notice; I'm only teasing. But for some time I've had this kinky fantasy about a man in uniform.'

Ted didn't know where to look. His blush deepened as he stared into his beer.

'Tell me,' continued Donald, 'why did you get married?'

'Oh, I suppose we ... er....' Ted began falteringly. 'We must have loved each other.'

'And now?'

'Now I can't stand her. I hate her.'

'So what are you going to do about it?'

Ted shrugged. 'I wish I knew. She's waiting to talk to me tonight... about the chipolatas again.'

'Chipolatas?'

Ted felt the need to unburden himself. Slowly he began to explain about his plan to poison Marjorie. But he realised Donald wasn't listening. Looming over their table was an overweight young man in denims and a white T-shirt under a black leather, studded jacket. He was in his early thirties and sported a Freddie Mercury moustache which didn't suit his large round face.

'Who's she?' he hissed, glaring at Ted.

'Bamber,' Donald said, cheerfully, 'I'd like you to meet Ted.'

Seventeen

Feeling threatened by the young man's towering and hostile presence, Ted gave him a weak smile and said, 'I'm, er, pleased to meet you.'

'Wish I could say the same for you,' Bamber replied.

Donald laughed softly. 'You must excuse my friend. He thinks everyone is...' He stopped and fixed Bamber with a stern, fatherly look. Now please don't take it out on everyone because you've had a bad day. Ted is interested in Shakespeare, that's all. End of story.'

'And what does she do when she's not watching Shakespeare?'

'You'd better ask him, hadn't you,' said Donald, emphasising the pronoun. 'Now what would you like to drink?'

'I'll have a pint of lager.'

While Donald went to the bar, Bamber sat opposite Ted, who felt uncomfortable and gripped his glass tightly.

'Whereabouts d'you live?' Bamber asked him.

'Molyneux Park Road.'

'What number?'

Without thinking, Ted told him, then immediately regretted it. Bamber repeated the number several times, committing it to memory for some reason.

'You in the antiques game?'

Ted flushed. 'No, I work for South Eastern Trains.'

Bamber's eyes lit up. 'Really? I've always wanted to be a train driver. Ever since I was so high.'

'I'm not a driver. I'm a guard.'

'Oh,' Bamber said with a sneer in his voice. 'Didn't quite make driver, eh? So what's a British Rail guard doing living in Molyneux Park Road?'

'My wife inherited the house.'

'Your wife!' Bamber stressed with mock surprise. Ted had the distinct impression the young man was toying with him, waiting for an opportunity to humiliate him. He was relieved when Donald returned.

'Why you have to drink pints at this time of night,' Donald complained as he placed the beer in front of Bamber. He sat next to Ted and said conspiratorially: 'If he has too many beers, he snores. Either that or he'll be up half the night.'

'Chance would be a fine thing,' Bamber said.

Embarrassed by this glimpse into their personal life, Ted cast his eyes down.

'Oh pleeeease!' Donald said with pretend shock. 'Save us from these inane Carry On style double entendres.'

Bamber leaned across the table. 'Well how's this for a single entendre? Up yours!'

Deliberately ignoring him, Donald spoke to Ted. 'Our interests have always differed. I like opera and he likes noise.'

'Heavy metal,' Bamber explained.

Donald brushed it aside and continued. 'I adore Shakespeare and Bamber lives exclusively on a diet of violent films featuring muscle men, morons and robots.'

'You're a cultural snob,' Bamber said flatly.

'He just can't understand how two people can enjoy a non-physical relationship.'

'Don't give me that old cobblers. Non-physical, platonic and oh-so-intellectual, darling! I think your new friend is gay. He just doesn't know it himself yet.'

Ted blushed again, opened his mouth to protest but was unable to speak. Bamber stood up, downed what was left of his pint, then leant over them threateningly.

'I think it's time Ted was outed.'

Donald laughed. 'You can only 'out' someone who's a celebrity, dear boy. Ted's sexual preferences would not make the back page of the Nether Wallop Gazette. It's just not news.'

'It might be to his wife.'

This was Bamber's exit line. Without looking at either of them he walked out into the street, leaving Ted frozen with terror.

'Take no notice,' said Donald. 'He's only bluffing.'

'But it's not true,' mumbled Ted.

'I know it's not. You know it's not. But Bamber....'

Ted felt angry suddenly. 'How can you sound so bloody cheerful? As if it's all a game.'

'Don't get upset.'

'I don't think we'd better meet each other again. Not if it's going to be....'

Donald took a small envelope out of his pocket. 'And what am I going to do with these? I'd bought us tickets to see The Barber of Seville at the Coliseum. I thought you might like it.'

Ted sighed and sipped his beer. 'Look, I appreciate the ... er....'

'It was more than a gesture, Ted. I bought them because I like you. I couldn't take Bamber. He'd only fidget throughout. Whereas you ... you share the same interests as me.'

Ted looked lost. Confused. 'But what am I going to do about...'

'Your wife? You were telling me how much you hate her. Sooner or later you're going to have to decide what you want to do.'

'I know,' Ted agreed mournfully. 'But just for tonight I wish I could disappear and not have to go back and face her. Especially now. Bamber might be with her at any moment, telling her about us.'

***

Millie carried in a bowl of batter from the back room and chuckled. 'It's good to see the boss in working clothes. A treat. A rare treat.'

'If I had a pound for every time you've said that tonight,' Gary said, scooping a batch of fresh chips from the fryer.

Millie laughed irritatingly. 'Well, you must admit, Gary, we rarely see you this side of the counter.'

'Is it usually this quiet?'

'Not usually, no. But Man-U's playing an important match tonight.'

'You might as well shoot off home then,' offered Gary.

She looked suspicious, so he gave her his most disarming smile.

'I'll still pay you the full rate, have no fears. I just thought you might fancy an early night.'

She didn't wait to be asked twice. As soon as she had gone, Gary shut the shop and called Sharon on his mobile.

'Hi, sweetheart,' he said. 'It's me. All alone in the Maidstone chippie. Fancy a drive out in my passion wagon to a secluded spot?'

Eighteen

Instead of kissing him on the lips, Jackie offered her cheek to Nigel. The gesture irritated him and he tried to suppress the anger that was welling up inside him. With tightly puckered lips he pecked the coldly offered cheek and said, 'Sorry, but I think I may have to cancel our arrangements for the weekend.'

Jackie felt like screaming, he was so childish. She managed to contain herself and stepped outside the front door, pulling it almost closed behind her, so that Vanessa and Nicky wouldn't hear.

'Why are you behaving like this?' she whispered.

'Like what?'

'You know jolly well what I mean.'

'Do I?'

'Yes, you do. You've been sulking all evening. And it was our first family get-together. The girls were dying to get to know you.'

'I bet they were.'

'Yes, they were, actually. And you start behaving all moody and horrible, sighing all through dinner.'

'If you must know, I can't stand the way they treat you. Like a servant. I couldn't believe it. Nicky came downstairs after washing her hair and just dumped her towel on the living room floor, leaving it for you to pick up. Which you duly did. And neither of them lifted a finger to clear away the dinner things.'

Jackie began to raise her voice. 'I don't see why you're getting so upset about it.'

'Oh don't you! Well, has it occurred to you that after we're married we'll all be living under the same roof?'

'If this is how you feel about it, perhaps we'd better call it off.'

'Oh there's no need to....' Nigel began, but he didn't get any further because she had gone inside and slammed the door. He stood for a moment staring foolishly at the closed door.

'If that's how you feel,' he grumbled, 'it would serve you right if I did call it off.'

He drove home rather fast and recklessly, and was immediately ashamed of himself for having done so. He went into his office, turned on the lights and sat at his desk. He took out his Bible and opened it to the beginning of Isaiah, making occasional notes on a jotter pad. But after a while he became distracted about random thoughts of Mary. He felt guilty about the way he'd treated her. Perhaps he could make it up to her in some way. That's if she would speak to him following the embarrassing scene in the Eastbourne teashop earlier that day.

Sighing, he snapped the Bible shut, picked up the phone and dialled her number. He glanced at his watch, saw that it was past eleven and decided to hang up. But the phone was answered after only two rings.

Nigel spoke in a hushed tone. 'Is that you, Mary?'

'This is her mother.'

'Oh. Er, sorry to ring so late. Could I possibly speak with Mary?'

'She's not here. She had to go out for the evening. Who's calling?'

'It's, er, it's a f-friend of hers,' Nigel stammered. 'I'll give her a call tomorrow.'

He hung up quickly, then sat staring into space, wondering if Mary was out with another man. Someone else she had met through the dating service. Although he had no right to be jealous, if she was already out with another 'prospect', he felt miffed, as if she had already wiped him clean out of her life.

He grabbed the phone again and dialled Jackie's number. She answered his call in a subdued tone, as if she had been expecting him to ring.

'I couldn't let the sun set on our quarrel,' he said. 'Sorry if I was like a bear with a sore head. Only today's been fraught with problems.'

She put on a girlish voice. 'I'm sorry, my poppet. Bunnykins should have realised you'd been overdoing it.'

'Let's forget it, shall we?' He sniggered. 'We'll celebrate at the weekend.'

'Celebrate?'

'Yes, our very first quarrel.'

***

In a Hastings side street Craig eventually came across the seedy drinking club belonging to Harvey Boyle – theatrical agent, ex-wrestler, sports promoter, charity fund-raiser and fingers-in-pies man. He found Rice waiting for him at the bar.

'Pint of Export?' Rice offered.

'Cheers.'

'You found it alright then?'

Craig looked around at the fading establishment and dropped his voice. 'Bit of a dump. How we getting home? In your cab?'

Rice shook his head. 'I picked a funny way to resign from the firm this morning. I hit this silly bastard in a BMW. First I hit the car. Then I hit him.'

'Oh great!' Craig complained. 'There's no more London trains till the morning. How we supposed to get back?'

'No problemo. I borrowed some wheels for the night.'

Craig looked doubtful. Laughing, Rice patted him reassuringly on the arm, then led him towards a corner table and chairs. He sat close to Craig, and spoke out the side of his mouth, as if he was still back inside. 'No worries, mate. These wheels won't be missed till the morning, by which time we'll be back in Tunbridge Wells.'

'And what if we're stopped and they ask for your documents?'

Rice's grin widened. 'My driving licence is in the name of Colin Stonegate.'

'Who?'

'You may well ask. But I reckon Colin popped his clogs a while back. Don't worry, my son, it's all taken care of. And we'll be giving your alibi a lift home.'

Rice gave Craig a lascivious grin. 'Harvey's fixed you up with a tasty alibi. And I mean tasty. You might be alright if you play your cards right.'

'You mean he's fixed me up with some bird who's going to say she was with me....'

That was as far as Craig got. Rice nudged him and nodded at the door marked 'Private'.

'Hang about. Here's the man himself. With your alibi.'

Craig looked up as Harvey Boyle, a fair-haired, thickset, middle-aged man came over, accompanied by an attractive, nervous-looking, woman.

'Don't get up,' Boyle told them.

Neither of them had been going to.

'You must be Craig,' Boyle continued. 'This is your young lady you'll be spending Saturday night with. If you know what I mean.'

He grinned and winked at Craig.

'You'll have to get to know one another. Craig, let me introduce you to Mary Fernhill.

Nineteen

Nearing the house, Ted saw the living room light was on. And Marjorie had decreed that the front room was to be used for special occasions only. In other words, when they had visitors, so perhaps Bamber was with her this very minute, telling malicious lies.

His hand shook as he turned the key in the lock. 'I'm back!' he called out, trying to sound normal. There was no reply. He dropped his bag next to the hallstand and listened for a moment. It was very quiet. He pictured them both, she and Bamber, eyes glued to the door, waiting for him to enter. Waiting to make him squirm.

Fearing the worst, he eased the door open. But he was surprised to discover the room was empty, bathed in the over-bright glare from Marjorie's teak and gilt chandelier. He noticed there were three sherry schooners and an empty sherry bottle on the coffee table.

Puzzled, Ted switched the light off and went stealthily upstairs, hoping Marjorie might be asleep by now. He spent ages in the bathroom, scrupulously cleaning his teeth, and closely examining his face in the mirror, as if searching for his ambivalent feelings in his relationship with Donald.

Unable to delay a minute longer, he tiptoed to the bedroom door, took a deep breath and entered. Marjorie was sitting up in bed, reading one of her Mills and Boon books. She peered over her reading glasses at him.

'You're later than I expected. I suppose you've been to the pub.'

'Mmm,' he muttered. 'Has, um, has anyone... have you had any visitors tonight?'

'Alec and Freda turned up. Didn't even phone to say they were coming. Just turned up.'

'Anyone else?'

'What d'you mean, anyone else?'

'I just wondered if there'd been any other visitors, that's all.'

She snapped the book shut crossly. 'Of course not. Were you expecting someone.'

He breathed a sigh of relief.

'No, no. I just wondered if....'

He sat on the edge of the bed and started to take off his shoes. Marjorie folded her arms, and her voice cut into the night like an oracle of doom.

'We've got to get to the bottom of that phone call you made to Alec and Freda. They still swear blind you called them in the morning, as if you knew I was going to be ill. So why did you phone and cancel when you did?'

Ted avoided her stare. He caught sight of the title of the book she was reading. The Prophet of Love. Prophet! It brought him the inspiration he so desperately needed.

'I've a confession to make, Marj. I kept it to myself because I didn't think you'd believe me. I knew you were going to be ill that day. I had a premonition. A glimpse into the future. It's hard to explain. I think I might be clairvoyant. That's why I rang Alec and Freda. To save them a wasted journey.'

Marjorie was frowning hard, trying to take in what he was telling her.

'But why didn't you tell me?'

Ted smiled, suddenly very sure of himself. 'Be honest. You'd never have believed me. Not in a million years. But I think it's possible I might have secret powers.'

She looked him up and down and shuddered. 'I've always known you were a weirdo, Ted, but this sort of thing gives me the heebie-jeebies. I don't like it.'

He shrugged. 'I'm sorry, but....'

'I think you'd better sleep in the spare room for a while. In case you get any more of these....'

'Premonitions,' Ted prompted.

'Yes. I'd never feel safe in my own bed. Not with you next to me. It'd give me the creeps.'

Ted took his pyjamas from under the pillow. 'Well, as long as you're sure.'

'Oh, I'm sure alright,' she said, and picked up her book again.

He went to the door. 'I'll, er, see you in the morning then, Marj. Night.'

'Night,' she muttered without looking up.

As soon as he was outside the door, he did something uncharacteristic. He punched the air triumphantly with a clenched fist.

***

Maggie sat and watched an episode of Desperate Housewives and drank three quarters of a bottle of Chardonnay. She glanced at her watch. Gary should have been home long ago. The chip shop would have closed well over an hour ago and it didn't take that long to drive back from Maidstone.

She switched the television off and topped up her glass. She tried ringing the chip shop but, as she suspected, there was no reply. She began to smell a rat. She slammed the phone down and knocked back her drink, spilling some down her sweatshirt. She swore loudly. She was on her way to the breakfast room to get a piece of kitchen roll when the doorbell rang. Through the mottled glass of the front door she could just about make out the dark, distorted shape of a uniform.

Suddenly her world began to seem unreal.

She opened the door to a young WPC.

'Mrs. Branston? Can I come in and have a word with you?'

'It's Gary, isn't it? What's happened to him?'

'I'm really sorry, Mrs. Branston. Your husband was involved in a road accident.'

'Oh God! When? I mean, where? Where was this?'

'On the Ashdown Forest. I'm sorry to have to tell you, Mrs. Branston, but – when they got to him – I'm sorry – there was nothing anyone could do.'

Maggie fought back the tears. She laughed suddenly.

'No, you're wrong. It can't have been Gary. He was in Maidstone tonight. Why would he have gone to....'

The realisation stopped her.

'Was there anyone else in the car with him?'

The WPC nodded gravely. 'We haven't identified her yet. We wondered if you could....'

'Go to hell!'

Maggie slammed the door and collapsed in tears.

Twenty

It was well past time as Mike peered through the window of the White Hart. The police car was still parked by the green near the crossroads. Mike cursed quietly and asked Marion to order him a taxi. This would mean another argument with Claire. He had promised to run her to the station first thing in the morning. While the landlady ordered him a taxi, he chatted to Howard, one of the pub regulars,

'I don't see your mate in here anymore,' he said. 'You two were inseparable.'

'He moved to Cranbrook,' Howard told him. 'He had to buy a bungalow for his wife's knees.'

***

The following morning Mike sat opposite his son at the breakfast, sipping strong black coffee. 'D'you have to crunch those Frosties so loudly?' he complained.

Andrew, who was studying notes on a scrap of paper, replied, 'Does Mum know you've got a hangover?'

'Yes, I know,' Claire said in a resigned tone as she came into the kitchen. 'Which is why I've got to get a cab to the station.'

They had already exhausted the argument over his drinking. Claire checked her handbag contents to see if she'd got everything she needed. 'Shall I give Chloe your love?' she asked Andrew.

'If you like.'

'Not if I like.'

He looked up at her. 'Yeah, alright, give her my love. What are you going all the way up there for, anyway?'

'I told you – I knew you weren't listening – Chloe wrote to me. She sounds desperately unhappy.'

'It's probably just boyfriend trouble, as usual.'

'I hope that's all it is.'

'Why can't she tell you on the phone? Newcastle's a long way to go in one day.'

Claire snapped her handbag shut. 'What do you care, Andrew?

Mike tapped his watch. 'If that taxi, doesn't come soon, you're going to miss it. They're so unreliable.'

Claire's mouth tightened. 'Like someone else I could mention not a million miles from here.'

'We've been through all that,' Mike snapped.

Claire was about to respond, but Mike was spared by the front doorbell as her taxi arrived. She dashed out to the hall. 'I don't suppose I'll be back until quite late,' she called.

The front door slammed. Silence. Apart from Andrew's intermittent crunching noise.

After a brief interval, Mike asked, 'What's that you're reading?'

'Oh – just some notes I made.'

'In other words, mind your own business.'

Andrew gave his father a defiant stare. 'If you must know,' he said, 'this is list of pubs... pubs where the fruit machines are due a big win. And those that have just paid out.'

'You can't make a career out of feeding coins into a slot. What sort of life is that?'

'Well, it's a hell of a sight more interesting than cutting hair. Snip, snip, snip, all day long. Boring.'

Mike sighed deeply. 'As it happens you're right. What's it all about, I wish I knew? What is the point of it all?'

Andrew wasn't in the mood to cope with his father's navel gazing, as so often happened following a night on the booze. He got up from the table and left his cereal bowl on the surface above the dishwasher.

Mike's eyes narrowed suspiciously. 'I've just realised, this is the crack of dawn as far as you're concerned. What are you doing up at this time of the morning?'

Andrew laughed. 'I've only just got in. That's why I'm off to bed.'

***

'I'm sorry, Maggs,' Craig mumbled as she opened the front door. Although she wasn't crying, he could see her eyes were puffed and smeared. As he entered, he could smell alcohol on her breath.

She led him into the living room, then stood there helplessly shaking her head. 'It's so unreal, Craig. I think I'll wake up in a minute from a bad dream.'

Craig cleared his throat before speaking. 'Where's Mum and Dad?'

'In the kitchen with the children.'

'Do they know yet?'

She nodded and her eyes filled with tears. 'But I'm not sure if they've really taken it in.'

'Maggs, I'm sorry.'

He held her close and she sobbed quietly on his shoulder. He stroked her hair soothingly, and after a while she composed herself, picked up a glass of brandy from the coffee table and finished it.

'I keep asking myself, why am I crying over that bastard? Because of the kids, I suppose. They'll never know what a 22 carat shit he was. Their innocent minds will stay innocent, and they'll wonder why I'm such a hard, unfeeling bitch.'

'You're not unfeeling, Maggs. It's understandable – in the circumstances.'

'You don't know the half of it, Craig. I expect it's the biggest laugh they've ever had at Pembury Hospital.'

'What d'you mean?'

'They weren't wearing seat belts. They would have got in the way of what she was doing to him.'

Craig tried to look shocked, but his impression was one of prurient interest. 'Not while they were driving?'

He tried to imagine it. He also tried to wipe the slight smile that was tugging the corners of his mouth.

But Maggie wouldn't have noticed. She laughed bitterly and said, 'At least he went out the way he would have wanted.'

Their mother put her head round the door and spoke softly. 'Hello, Craig.'

'Hi, Mum.'

'I've just made a pot of tea. Would you like some?'

He nodded. 'How are the kids?'

'Coping.'

She shuffled quietly back to the kitchen. Craig looked at his sister for a while before speaking.

'Do Mum and dad know about Gary and....'

'They know he was with another woman. Course, they don't know the sordid details. Funeral will be a farce, won't it? What will anyone find to say about Gary?'

Craig looked embarrassed.

Still, it's an ill wind,' Maggie continued with false brightness. 'Your brother-in-law's about to give you a bonus. On his behalf – cos he can't have been all rotten – I am giving you one of the shops. Well, you could look pleased about it.'

But Craig had remembered that on Saturday night he and Tony Rice planned to burgle the Working Men's Club. And if there was a change of plan, how would Rice and Harvey Boyle take it?

Twenty-One

A ndrew hit the buttons of the machine. His system wasn't working. He was now down more than fifty pounds. He decided to wait until other customers had fed maybe another thirty of forty into the slot, so he returned to the bar and ordered another Coke, which he drank from the bottle.

Sitting on a bar stool, doing The Times crossword, a man with a florid complexion peered at him over half-moon glasses and said, 'I expect you're into computer games, as well.'

Andrew shrugged and grunted. He didn't like the man's patronising tone. Computer games polarised youth and oldies more than music these days.

'So what sort of computer games d'you play?' the man persisted.

Andrew rattled off a lot of titles he thought would be meaningless to the man.

The man smiled. 'Sounds like a lot of war games. Ever thought about the end result of a direct missile hit?'

The guy's a nutter, thought Andrew. Humour him.

'Yeah,' he replied. 'Every time I bring down an enemy fighter, I always imagine the pilot splattered into a million pieces.'

'He'd be one of the lucky ones. The victims are the civilians unlucky enough to live within a certain radius of a military target. Tomahawk cruise missiles, for instance, have a circular error probability: they don't have to be bang on target to be effective.'

The man spoke in a slight monotone, as if this was a speech he'd made many time before.

'These computer games,' he continued, 'force feed us with the illusion that war is now fought without blood being spilled. You'd be too young to remember the Gulf War. At least eighteen years ago.'

Andrew nodded. 'I'd have just been born.'

'Well the television coverage of the Gulf War was a wonderful video game. From the comfort of our armchairs we didn't see the retreating Iraqi soldiers being cluster bombed, napalmed and burnt to a crisp.'

Andrew glanced at his watch. 'I've...er...'

'I'm driving you away. I'm sorry. I didn't mean to be rude. It's just I've lived with this for the past six years. I suppose I've become obsessed. I think I need another gin. Can I get you another drink? Go on, it's the least I can do.'

Andrew hesitated. In spite of his suspicion that this man might be the pub bore, his curiosity was aroused. 'OK,' he said. 'I'll have another Coke.'

The man grinned. 'Of course, if you were a baby during the Gulf War, you'd be breaking the law if you drank something stronger.'

'Cheers!' said Andrew after they'd been served. 'When you said you'd lived with it for six years....'

'I'm a writer. I'm writing a book about an arms dealer. Well, I've finished it, actually. My publishers paid me a handsome advance, then backed off. And no one else will touch it. But at least the advance means I can self-publish now.'

'How come your publisher backed off?'

'I opened a giant can of worms. Not far from here, in deepest East Sussex, tucked away and impossible to find, is a large rambling house surrounded by high walls. The home of one of the richest and most powerful men in the country. He made a personal fortune of twenty million selling weapons to Saddam Hussein in the early Eighties.'

Andrew frowned. 'But surely arms dealing is... well, I thought it was just one of those things that goes on.'

'If you went to a posh school, thinking your father was just a rich businessman, would you like your friends to know your father made money peddling death and destruction? And if you were his wife, cosseted from the truth, would you want it brought home to you that your husband deals in cluster bombs that explode into thousands of needle-sharp fragments, literally shredding people to death, women and children included? How would they feel knowing their father makes his riches out of other people's tragedies. He even has a company to outsource army interrogation of Iraqi and Afghan prisoners. And it's not just the money that motivates him. It's the power. Otherwise he could have retired years ago. And this man is so powerful he can guarantee his anonymity.'

'So he can put the frighteners on your publisher?'

The man smiled at Andrew's choice of words. 'What do you think?'

Andrew, who'd been distracted from the fruit machine, suddenly found all this intriguing. 'I'd like to buy a copy of your book,' he said impulsively.

'Thanks. That's kind of you but....' The man hesitated, then took a dog-eared business card out of his wallet and handed it to Andrew. 'Contact me next week. Proofs should be ready by then. I'll let you have a copy.'

'I don't mind paying.'

The man waved it aside. 'Please. It's on the house. The least I can do for boring you.'

Andrew blushed. 'No, of course not....'

'Just promise me one thing,' the man cut in. 'Next time you play your computer games, spare a thought for the death you could be dealing out. I know it's only a game but everyone seems to be losing their sense of reality.'

Frowning, Andrew suddenly wondered if this bloke was on the level. Perhaps he was just some pub nutter who drank too much. The local nuisance.

As if he guessed what Andrew was thinking, he added, 'Everything I've told you is true. When you read the book, you'll see.'

'No,' Andrew said hastily. 'I believe you. It's just... I was wondering what life would be like without my computer games.'

'They're not all war games, are they?'

Andrew laughed. 'The best ones are.'

***

Mary had just returned from taking the children to school when the phone rang. It was Harvey Boyle. 'I've just had a phone call from Craig – chap you met last night. He won't be needing your help now, Mary. I'm sorry, but it's all off.'

'Oh, no! I needed that two-hundred. I still owe the balance for the school trip.'

There was a slight pause. Harvey cleared his throat before speaking. 'I tell you what I'll do....'

As soon as he used that phrase, she knew there had to be a catch. 'You're still very attractive, sweetheart. Nice figure and that.'

'No, Harvey. No strip-tease.' She shuddered at the memory. 'I hate it.'

'You're a talented dancer, Mary. And this is a good venue. A private do for professional men.'

'I don't care if it's at the Oscars ceremony. I won't do it.'

'I can make it two-fifty.' She sighed, already feeling dirty at the thought of it. 'Okay. Just this once. For the sake of the kids.'

Twenty-Two

Claire arrived home late to find Mike and Andrew sprawled out in front of the television. The house smelt of beer and vinegar. Crumpled fish and chip wrappers littered the coffee table. She felt like screaming.

'Couldn't you even be bothered to eat off plates?' she said, trying to control her anger. But the television was too loud, setting her nerves on edge. 'Can you switch that bloody thing off?'

'Oh, Mum!' Andrew protested. 'We're in the middle of watching it.'

Claire stared with hostility at the screen. A thug in a Hawaiian shirt fired a few rounds from a machine pistol, then lobbed a grenade at a motor launch, which exploded vividly.

'Please, Andrew! Go and watch the rest of it in your room.'

'What about Dad?'

Mike's voice sounded slurred. 'I've seen as much as I want to see. Load of old... any film starring Chuck Norris....'

Impatiently, Claire switched the television off. Andrew got up, went to the door, and reluctantly stopped to ask, 'How was Newcastle?'

'Newcastle's fine. Thank you for asking.'

Andrew frowned, shrugged, then left the room, muttering, 'I'll go an watch the rest of the film then.'

Claire sat on the sofa next to Mike, poised on the edge, tension showing in her neck and shoulders.

'What's wrong?' Mike asked.

'I'm glad he's out of the room. I couldn't face telling him. Not right now.'

'Telling him? Telling him what?'

'About Chloe.'

'Well, are you going to tell me or not? I was hoping you'd phone from Newcastle....'

'I did, and you were out. I couldn't leave a message on the answering machine. Hello, I'm just ringing to tell you that you that your daughter's pregnant.'

Claire stared at Mike, watching his reaction. They heard the distant crackle of gunfire as Andrew switched the TV on in his room. Mike rubbed and pressed his forehead and sighed tremulously.

'All day I've been thinking about her, wondering what the problem was, and I didn't think that....' He felt angry suddenly. 'Why the hell couldn't they take precautions?'

'It gets worse, I'm afraid. It wasn't her boyfriend Mark. She'd had an argument with him. She went to a party, got drunk, and slept with another bloke just to spite him.'

'Oh, the stupid little... I can't believe this. If it was Andrew who'd come home and told me he'd got some girl in the family way, I could understand it. But not Chloe.'

'Not your little girl, you mean. She's nearly twenty-one, Mike.'

'Yes, I know but – what the hell is she going to do? What about her degree?'

'She says she doesn't know what she wants to do. She's going to come home this weekend to talk about it.'

'Well, she's got one of two choices. She can either have it or have an abortion. And what about the father? What was he studying? Anatomy?'

Claire shook her head. 'He wasn't a student. He worked in the Union Bar. He was Australian.'

'Was?'

'The night he slept with Chloe was his last night in this country. He went back to Australia the next day. And she can't even remember his name.'

***

Craig waited for Tony Rice in a pub near Tonbridge Station. The place smelled musty and stale and he wondered why Rice frequented such a down-at-heel dump.

As if in answer to his thoughts, Rice suddenly materialised at his side and whispered, 'Not exactly your old English pub – more of a karzy in Cairo – but at least I don't 'ave far to stagger home. If you can call it that.'

'You live near here then?'

'You catch on quick. I'll have a pint of Guinness, seeing as you're paying.'

As soon as they'd been served, Craig nervously started to explain about how he would inherit the chip shop. Rice interrupted him.

'Harvey's already told me you want out.'

'Does that bother you?'

'It might have done, if I didn't have nothing else.'

'I was a bit worried – you might be a bit upset, like.'

'Nah. Doing that club was too risky for my liking. But I was desperate.'

'So what you up to now? Or shouldn't I ask?'

A slow smile grew on Rice. 'I've got myself a nice little number punishing people.' He looked at his watch. 'I start tonight.'

'When you say punishing people....'

'I mean a bit of bone-breaking. I've got a keyboard musician's fingers to snap tonight – poor bastard. Still, at twenty a finger, mustn't grumble.'

Craig shivered. Rice leant close to him and added, 'Harvey took exception to this musician screwing around with his daughter. I got nothing against the bloke, so I'll probably put him out first. He won't feel a thing. Job done. Cheers!'

Craig raised his glass. 'Yeah. Cheers!'

***

Awake for most of the night, Claire eventually fell into a deep, trance-like sleep, but was immediately woken by a noise which made her start. She listened carefully. Mike was snoring, as he usually did after too much beer. Then she heard the noise again. A cry of pain, coming from Andrew's room.

She climbed out of bed, put her dressing gown on and crept quietly to her son's room. He was half sitting up in bed, sobbing.

'Andrew,' she whispered. 'What's wrong?'

She sat on the bed and put an arm round him. He let his head fall onto her shoulder.

'It... it was a nightmare,' he sobbed. 'It was so real. It was terrible.'

She stroked his hair. 'Hush. Shh. It's alright. Mum's here now. Everything's alright.'

'I was on the computer. Firing missiles at children. Small children. Crying and screaming. Blood everywhere. It was so real. I could see their faces.'

'It's alright, darling. It was just a nasty dream.'

She held him close, enjoying the cuddle.

Make the most of it, she thought. Make the most of it.

Twenty-Three

As Dave drove out of the pub car park, two drunks tapped on the nearside window and made obscene suggestions to Mary, who shrank into the passenger seat, staring straight ahead.

'Get lost, you ignorant pillocks,' Dave muttered, and swung the car dangerously close to one of them.

'Thanks,' whispered Mary as they pulled out onto the main road.

'What for?'

'Your moral support. Just because I did a striptease....'

'I don't know why you're thanking me. I didn't do owt. Unless you want me to go back and run over that wally's foot.'

'Why stop at just his foot?'

Dave chuckled. 'You really hated them, didn't you?'

'Did it show that much?'

'Well, they were a bunch of prats. Professional types skiving off for the afternoon; letting their hair down. Under pressure at work, they think they've earned the right to behave badly.'

Mary fumbled in her handbag for a tissue.

'Bloke running that pub must've made a packet. Thirty-five notes a head. Mind you, the food didn't look bad.'

He glanced at Mary and noticed she was crying. 'You alright?'

'Yes,' she sniffed. 'I'm just relieved it's all over.'

'You've not... not done any stripping before, have you?'

'Once. And I swore I'd never do it again.' She wiped her eyes, blew her nose, and stuffed the tissue back in her bag.

'Well, I know one thing: I don't think we'll be asked back. The feeling was mutual. I think they hated us, an' all.'

'Your act... your act was very good. I thought it was funny.'

'You were the only one who did.'

'No... really.' I mean it.'

'Apart from the four letter words.'

Well, I suppose they weren't really....'

'Necessary? No, that's 'cause I'm a family comedian. Like Jimmy Cricket. So when Harvey asked me to do this stag afternoon, I just did the same material with swear words. Idiot!'

Dave swerved to avoid a motor cyclist.

'So where d'you know the slimy Harvey Boyle from?'

'I used to go out with Harvey.'

'I'm sorry,' said Dave, backtracking. 'I didn't mean....'

Mary laughed. 'No, you're right. He's a slimeball. I was young and naïve when I went out with him. I was a dancer and he got me my first job in a professional pantomime.'

'What made you quit dancing?'

'I got married, had a couple of kids, then my marriage broke up, and I haven't danced professionally for eleven years.'

'Couldn't you take it up again?'

'Nobody loves a fairy over forty.'

Dave snatched a look at her. 'You're not forty, are you?'

'I'm thirty-six. It was a joke.'

'Oh, but, joking apart, from what I saw this afternoon, your figure's very... um... and your movement....' He could feel himself blushing. 'What I mean is....'

She smiled, secretly pleased. 'Thanks for the compliment. But this isn't the way back to Tunbridge Wells, is it?'

'I thought we'd cut across – go back a different way. Across Ashdown Forest. Be very pleasant at this time of day.'

She chewed her lip thoughtfully. She had only met him this morning. He seemed sincere, but....

As if he could sense what she was thinking, Dave said, 'I just thought it would erase memories of leering slobs. Don't worry: I won't run out of petrol.'

'Oh, I didn't think....' she began, feeling guilty for not trusting him. She didn't know what else to say, so she opened her window.

The smell of fresh cut grass drifted into the car, for an instant blotting out the still overpowering stench of stale cigarette smoke on their clothes, as the smoking ban at the venue had been ignored.

After driving in silence for a while, Dave cleared his throat delicately before asking, 'I don't suppose you'd like to come back to my place for a bite to eat, would you?'

Then he added hastily, 'No strings attached.'

She turned to him and smiled. 'Thanks for the offer. Maybe another time. If it's all the same to you, Dave, I'd like to get back and have a nice long soak in the bath. I feel dirty. Then a cuddle from my two boys should help.'

'Oh.' He sounded disappointed.

'When you drop me off, I'll give you my phone number. We'll make it another time. I promise.'

***

It was Nigel's birthday. He arrived at Jackie's like a small boy, full of eager anticipation. He was taken into the sunny living room where a walnut cake (his favourite) awaited him, with a bottle of chilled white Lambrusco.

His face lit up with surprise and pleasure, although he was secretly expecting it. Jackie handed Nicky a box of matches.

'Would you light the candles for me?'

Nigel chortled. 'I'm glad you've only put six on the cake.

'It's all we had,' said Vanessa.

She and Nicky had reluctantly agreed to attend their future stepfather's birthday celebration after much badgering from their mother.

Nicky lit the candles and Nigel blew them out, spraying the cake with a fine shower of spit. After singing a limp Happy Birthday,

Jackie and the girls gave Nigel his presents. They all watched as he pulled a BHS bathrobe out of its wrapping. He grinned impishly.

'Thank you, darling,' he gushed. 'Just the thing for our honeymoon.'

Nicky left the room, saying, 'I'll get a knife to cut the cake.'

'None for me,' said Vanessa. 'I'm on a diet.'

Jackie handed Nigel a small parcel. 'This is from the girls. Nothing very exciting, I'm afraid.'

'Ooh!' Nigel squealed, trying to sound enthusiastic. 'Socks! Thank you. Perhaps now might be an opportune moment to explain about my unique sock system.'

He raised his right trouser leg.

'Notice a piece of red cotton sown into the top of the sock? I have different colours for different days. It's because I only wear dark, plain socks, you see. That way I never get them muddled up. I call it my sock stock rotation. So when we're married, this little gimmick of mine will help you when you're sorting out the washing.'

Jackie stared at him, open-mouthed.

'Excuse me,' said Vanessa, 'while I throw up!'

Twenty-Four

After dropping Mary off, Dave arrived home to find three messages on his answering machine. The first was from an anonymous caller. A man's voice, young and aggressive.

'Your jokes are pathetic, Whitby. Like you. An' that car's an eyesore. Like you an' all. Think you can litter the street like that? How would you like it if we dropped litter through your letter box? Loads of dogs round here to provide the necessary. So get rid of the banger, Whitby. Now! Before we turn your gaff into a dog bog.'

The caller hung up and the machine bleeped. Waves of depression washed over Dave. His mouth felt dry, and for the first time in years, since giving up alcohol, he felt like a drink.

But the next message was from a theatre producer, offering him a summer season at the Pier Pavilion, Cromer. His depression vanished instantly. He scribbled the details on a notepad and waited for his final message. It was Harvey Boyle.

'Dave, I've just had a call from George, owner of the pub. He tells me you and Mary didn't exactly do a stormer.'

'That's an understatement, Harvey,' Dave replied to the machine.

'By all accounts it was a tasty venue. Professional types. Rugby supporters. None of your football riff-raff. So what went wrong?'

'I told you,' Dave yelled, 'I don't do stags. I needed the money.'

'I wish you'd told me you only do good clean kiddie-winkie stuff. Soon as you come in, give us a bell, will you?'

The machine gave its final bleep. Dave immediately picked up the phone and dialled Harvey's number. The agent answered right away, as if he'd been waiting for the call.

'H. B. Enterprises.'

'It's Dave Whitby here.'

'You got my message?'

'It's why I'm ringing.'

'I tried your mobile but....'

'I forgot to switch it back on after my act.'

'That's what I wanted to talk to you about. Your act. George was not too pleased with the standard of entertainment.'

'Now look – let's just get one thing clear – you asked me to do this as a favour, because your usual comic was not available. You know very well I don't normally do stags.'

Harvey sniffed loudly. 'Well, not to worry. I've managed to patch things up. I've offered him a return visit of my German stripper. Really dirty she is. He was quite happy in the end. So no worries. I'm still going to pay you.'

'Oh, thanks very much!'

'Well, you must admit, the act was a bit iffy.'

'They were a load of drunken pigs. You about tomorrow?'

'Yes. Why?'

Boyle exaggerated the suspicion in his tone, and Dave imagined the agent's eyes narrowing.

'Is it okay if I pop down to Hastings tomorrow to pick up some cash?'

'Cash!' Boyle sounded horrified. 'Did I say anything about cash? Sorry, Dave, there'll be a cheque in the post.'

The second broken promise, Dave thought.

As if the agent guessed what he was thinking, he chuckled and said, 'You'll get your money. No problem.'

Dave sighed. 'It's just that I start rehearsals in a couple of weeks. For a summer season. I'll be away for some time.'

'That was short notice. Someone drop out?'

'Probably.'

'And will you be closing the first or the second half of the show?'

Dave became almost inaudible through embarrassment. 'Um... I think they said something about opening the second half.'

Harvey laughed cruelly. 'How the mighty have fallen, eh? Still, it's work. And don't worry about the cheque. It won't be one of your broken promises. Good luck wherever it is you're going.'

'Cromer in Norfolk.'

'Yeah, well, you'll need it. Be seeing you.'

The line went dead. Dave replaced the receiver and thought about his situation. First of all someone in the street was out to get him, unless he got the car shifted. Secondly, he was stony broke; borrowing on his credit cards was up to the hilt.

The phone rang, making him jump. He snatched at it angrily, expecting another threatening call. It was a female voice.

'That was quick. Were you waiting for it to ring?'

Dave laughed. 'Story of my life. I know we exchanged phone numbers, and you promised to call soon, but that was only fifteen minutes ago, Mary.'

'How did you know it was me?'

'I recognized your voice. So what did you leave in the car?'

'Nothing. I just... I just felt like talking to someone. And you were really kind to me at that awful....'

'Is something wrong?'

There was a long pause. She sounded on the brink of tears.

'Mary. What's wrong?'

'It never rains but it pours. When I got home there was a letter from the landlord. I've had notice to quit. I've got a month to find somewhere else.'

'Can they do that? I thought occupation was nine tenths of the law.'

'That's what I thought. But the property's being sold, and the lease clearly states....' She started sobbing. 'I'm sorry. I didn't mean to burden you with my problems. It's just – I'm such an idiot. I'm so disorganised. I just hoped something would turn up.'

Dave took a deep breath, hoping he wouldn't regret what he was going to say.

'Well something has turned up. I've been offered a summer season in Norfolk. You can stay at my place until you find somewhere else. It'll be empty all summer.'

'Oh, Dave,' she said, controlling her flood of tears. 'How can I ever show you how grateful I am?'

She didn't see the smile that lit up his face.

'I'll think of something,' he joked.

Twenty-Five

Ted sensed trouble as soon as he arrived home. He could hear conspiratorial voices coming from the kitchen, which stopped as he shut the front door.

'We're in here,' Marjorie called out.

He dropped his bag next to the hallstand. He could smell fresh coffee and he wondered who merited such treatment.

'Come and join us.'

Marjorie's voice bubbled and boiled excitedly. Ted braced himself for whatever she had in store for him and, his expression bland, walked slowly down the hall towards the kitchen.

'I believe you two have already met,' Marjorie said with overpowering relish.

Ted stopped in the doorway. His eyes met Bamber's.

'Hello, Ted. I said I'd pop in and meet the wife, and here I am.'

Marjorie watched her husband closely, her eyes cold and hard. 'Why didn't you tell me?' she demanded.

'Tell you? Tell you what?'

'You know very well what I'm talking about, so don't try and deny it.'

'There's nothing to deny.'

'Oh isn't there! And what about this bloke's friend?' She pointed at Bamber. 'How long have you known him?'

Bamber stood up. 'I... er... think I'll be off now.'

'Now that you've come round to stir up trouble,' Ted snapped.

Ignoring him, Bamber addressed Marjorie with exaggerated politeness. 'Thanks ever so much for the coffee. Sorry I knocked the first one over. Must be going through a clumsy time. I'll leave you to it then.'

Marjorie pushed her chair back from the table.

'Don't bother to get up. I can see myself out.'

Bamber grinned at Ted, who avoided his look and stared at the floor.

'Ouch!' Bamber complained as he collided with the doorframe. 'I don't know what's wrong with me lately.'

'Thank you for calling round,' said Marjorie. 'It's been most interesting.' She glanced at Ted. 'Most interesting.'

'My pleasure,' came Bamber's reply from down the hall, followed by the slam of the front door. Then a long, uncomfortable silence. Marjorie stared at her husband with undisguised loathing.

'Well?' she demanded eventually.

Ted shoved his hands into his trouser pockets and returned her look with one of defiance. 'Well what?'

'How long have you been one of them?'

Ted laughed, which took Marjorie by surprise.

'I'm not one of "them" as you call it. Donald and I happen to like Shakespeare, that's all.'

'Huh! Expect me to believe that.'

She tried to imagine what this man and her husband got up to. Obscene pictures clouded her brain and she chased them away.

'My family always said you was a dark horse..'

'What's that got to do with anything?'

'They've always said you was a bit... funny.'

Ted snorted dismissively. 'Your family's as thick as two....'

'Ted!'

'Well, you're not going to pay any attention to what that fat slob said, are you? He could hardly stand up straight. He was drunk.'

'I couldn't smell nothing on his breath.'

'Anything.'

Marjorie looked confused. 'What?'

'It's... I couldn't smell anything on his breath. You said "nothing", which is bad grammar.'

Marjorie was stunned. Ted had never spoken to her like this before. His eyes blazed with defiance and she suspected his new friend and lifestyle had something to do with it.

'You're disgusting,' she sneered, her eyes narrowing. 'You and this other man. Ugh! Just the thought of it makes me....' She shuddered theatrically.

This made Ted angrier, but he kept himself in check, his fists tightly clenched in his pockets.

'Donald is my friend. I like him. But only as a friend.'

She got up from the table and started to clear away the coffee cups.

'I don't want to talk about it anymore. It's disgusting.'

Ted brought his hands out of his pockets. She had turned away to put the cups in the sink. He tried to imagine what it would be like to put them around her neck and squeeze. If he did it from behind, it wouldn't be so bad. But supposing, in the struggle, she managed to turn and face him. No. He knew he'd never be able to do it. Then he remembered how successful the food poisoning had been and a barely visible smile tugged at the corners of his mouth.

'Marjorie,' he began fawningly. 'You're right. I don't think I'd better see Donald again. Not that there's anything... you know... between us. But if it upsets you, well....'

She turned to face him, smiling the smile of the victor, mistakenly thinking she had won this round and Ted was now back in her power.

'Let's forget it, shall we? I know, as it's your day off tomorrow, why don't we pop down to Hastings and play bingo? Bloody Shakespeare, indeed!'

***

Dinner at the Longridge's that night was a strain. Chloe had come home for the weekend, and the family sat around the table making small talk in between the awkward silences. As soon as dinner was over, Claire suggested to Mike that he take Andrew out for a drink. Mike didn't need to be asked twice.

'Does Andrew know?' Chloe asked, as soon as they had gone.

Claire nodded. 'I'm sorry. I had to tell him.'

'Oh thanks, blabbermouth!'

'He'd have known something was up. Anyway, Andrew's a lot more sensitive than you give him credit for.'

'Oh yeah, and David Cameron's a socialist.'

'That's unfair, Chloe. Andrew can be very sympathetic when he wants to be.

Chloe sighed. 'So what happens now, Mum?'

'I suppose we have to look at the options.'

'Like the one I thought of on the journey home. I could always pretend to Mark that it's his baby.'

Claire was shocked at how calculating her daughter could be.

'And suppose he finds out the truth?'

'It would be a lot worse if he found out I'd had an abortion. He belongs to the New Life Church. He's a Born Again Christian.'

Twenty-Six

Tense and numb with grief, Maggie, Craig, their mother and father, and the two children squeezed into the first car.

'I don't want them to burn Dad,' Daryl moaned. 'Why can't they bury him?'

His grandmother stroked his hair and said softly but firmly, 'Your mum's already explained, Daryl. Now be a good boy. It's what Daddy would have wanted.'

Maggie glanced at the car behind, containing her in-laws and Gary's younger brother Brad. She thought she saw Brad looking at his watch, and wondered if he regretted his brother's funeral because of the inconvenience of missing a day when the money markets promised potentially good pickings.

'Gary always wanted to be like Brad,' she told Craig, incongruously.

'Brad'll burn himself out before long,' Craig replied, immediately regretting the choice of words.

'Still,' Maggie sniffed, 'I'm glad he didn't insist on bringing his Porsche.'

'I wanted to come in Uncle Brad's's Porsche,' said Daryl.

Hannah glared at her brother.

At the crematorium the mourners were ushered into a cramped waiting room, as airless as a hothouse. Time seemed to be suspended. Maggie found the situation as unreal as her sleepless nights. She went through the motions of playing the part of the grieving widow. She thought of it as a performance. A scene from a film. Especially when they were inside the chapel. The slow march down the aisle. Craig and Brad as two of the pallbearers. And the ancient chaplain, coughing, wheezing, and mopping his brow with a grubby handkerchief, struggling to his feet to begin the service.

'We are gathered here today to celebrate the life of....'

It was as far as he got. Suddenly his eyes rolled heavenwards, and his hands shot up, as if he was having a gospel experience. Then he fell to the floor.

The horrified mourners stood frozen for a moment. Then two of the undertaker's men dashed from the back of the chapel. One of them whispered urgently: 'It must be his heart.'

Brad, man of action, whipped out his mobile and said, 'Where can I get another vicar? Now!'

'Call for an ambulance first,' snapped the undertaker's man.

Following this hitch in Gary's last moments before being consumed, his mourners were ushered back to the waiting room, although most of them waited outside. An ambulance arrived and took the first chaplain away. Fifteen lifelong minutes ticked away before another chaplain could be found. By now the funeral was running almost thirty minutes late, so Gary was dispatched with one quick prayer, and it was all over.

As they left the crematorium, they stopped at the gates to let another hearse in. Maggie stared at one of the chief mourners in the car following it and burst into tears.

As soon as they were back at the house Craig took Maggie gently to one side and asked if she was okay.

'I'll be alright,' she responded. 'It was the other funeral that arrived as we were leaving. It was Sharon's. I recognised her mother. She used to come in the chip shop at Maidstone.'

Craig frowned. 'But why the funeral in this neck of the woods? If they live Maidstone way....'

'Craig, I never told you this: Sharon's mother phoned me up after they were killed. She said Sharon loved Gary. I put the phone down on her. But not before I told her when Gary's funeral was going to be. She must have had some sort of warped idea that they should be cremated in the same place and same day. Stupid bitch!'

Craig was at a loss. 'Can I get you something to eat?' he asked, after an awkward silence.

Maggie shook her head. 'I couldn't.'

Gary looked round at the other mourners. 'Gary's dad doesn't seem to have lost his appetite. Look at him tucking in like there was no tomorrow.'

Maggie looked disgusted. 'Let's go into the garden. Will you get me a glass of wine, Craig?'

'Sure.'

On the patio, Brad was wheeling and dealing on his mobile. He caught the look in Maggie's eye and said, 'Sorry, Jason: gonna have to go. Call you later, mate.'

Maggie stared at him with loathing. 'Your own brother's funeral.'

'Life must go on.'

'Not just yet!'

She snatched his mobile, and before he could stop her, she threw it into the children's paddling pool.

'What the hell did you do that for?' he yelled. 'Just as a strong Dow Jones had kicked the market into action.'

***

Days after Chloe had returned to university, Claire was sitting at the kitchen table, gazing into space. A smell of burnt toast hung in the air. Mike was about to leave for his first appointment.

'God! What a mess she's made of her life,' he said. 'If it was you – if it was your decision – what would you do?'

Claire shrugged. 'I'd feel exactly as she feels at her age. I wouldn't want to get rid of my baby, but I'd feel it was too soon to have one. It would get in the way of what I wanted to do.'

'I suppose you mean her career. I really don't think Chloe's that ambitious.'

'Don't be stupid, Mike, of course she is.'

'I think she tries to live up to your expectations of her.'

'Are you going to start blaming me for what's happened?'

'Did I say anything about blaming you?'

'You didn't have to.'

Mike filled a glass with water from the tap and gulped it noisily.

'I know you think I pushed her too hard. I just thought there was at least one member of this family who was going places.'

Andrew suddenly appeared in the doorway. The expression on his face made her regret her words.

'Andrew,' she began awkwardly. 'What I said about Chloe....'

Andrew shrugged, acting deliberately laid-back. 'You don't have to explain, Mum. You've always thought more of Chloe than me. It's no big deal.'

She could tell he was hurt.

'I love you just as much as I love Chloe,' she said.

'No problem then.'

He opened the back door.

'You off out?' Mike asked.

'Yeah. I'm going to see a writer friend of mine.'

As soon as he had gone, Claire looked at Mike guiltily and muttered, 'Oh, damn!'

Twenty-Seven

As Andrew neared the writer's flat in Queen's Road he saw an ambulance, light flashing but no siren, pulling away from the kerb, followed closely by a police car.

At first he thought nothing of it, but the closer he got to the house number, the more anxious he became. When he found the address he was looking for, he realised the ambulance had been parked at the same spot.

The writer's flat was in a large house, and was accessible via concrete steps at the side. Andrew rang the bell and waited. here was no reply. He rang again. After a moment he heard heavy footsteps clumping down the hall towards the door. The door was flung open by a tall, bulbous-nosed man with a mop of curly ginger hair.

'I think we're ready to....' he began, then stopped when he saw Andrew. 'Yes?'

'I'm... um... looking for Alan Hartswood.'

The man stared, his face expressionless.

'I'm sure this is the right address' Andrew said. He fumbled in the back pocket of his denims for the writer's business card.

Calmly, the man lit a cigarette. 'You a relative?'

'No, I only met him the other day, but....'

'Well, I'm sorry, you're too late.'

'Too late?'

'Yes. He's dead. That was him in the ambulance.'

'Dead! But I spoke to him last night – on the phone.'

'It was very sudden.'

The man started to close the door. Andrew stopped it with his hand.

'Hang on. What happened to him? Was it an accident or what?'

The man shrugged. 'We don't know yet. He was found dead. That's all we know at the moment.'

'Who's we?'

The man inhaled deeply on his cigarette and let out a thin stream of smoke. 'Sorry about your friend, but....' This was followed by a careless shrug.

'Last night, when I spoke to him,' Andrew persisted, 'he said he'd got a copy of his latest book for me. That's why I've come round.'

'I wouldn't know anything about that.'

'If there's a copy in his flat, can I have it?'

'You know as well as I do, nothing can be touched.'

'Isn't that when someone's been murdered?'

The man regarded the tip of his cigarette closely, then said, 'Forget it. Just be a good boy and clear off.'

'You got any identification?'

'You're trying my patience, son.'

Andrew started to back off, saying, 'Yeah, well, it's a funny way to behave when a bloke's been carted off to the morgue.'

'Morgue!' The man laughed. 'You've been watching too many movies, kid. Now push off.'

The door slammed. Andrew stared at it for a moment, feeling confused more than angry. He had spoken to the writer little more than twelve hours ago, and now....

Determined he was going to do something to unravel what was fast becoming a mystery, as he saw it, but having no idea what to do next, he ambled slowly towards St. John's Road. He thought he'd buy himself a beer, perhaps in the same Camden Road pub where he had met the writer. Perhaps drink a toast to his passing.

He caught himself grinning at his foolishness. Maybe that bloke had been right about seeing too many movies. He had only met the writer once, and already he saw himself as some Mel Gibson character in a film, toasting a dead buddy.

***

Jackie was looking at holiday brochures when Vanessa came downstairs.

'Someone's had a nice lie in,' she said, with abundant cheerfulness.

Vanessa gritted her teeth. She started to fill the kettle. Her mother hummed tunelessly and turned the brochure pages noisily.

'Do you have to?'

Her mother looked up with wide-eyed innocence. 'I'm sorry, darling?'

'That humming noise. It's irritating.'

'Someone's got out of the wrong side of the bed.'

'You don't know you're doing it half the time. It drives me and Nicky mad. We got any proper coffee?'

'Only decaffeinated. It's much better for you.'

Vanessa slammed the coffee jar onto the work surface. Jackie began humming again.

'For God's sake!' shouted Vanessa. 'You're doing it again.'

'There's no need to shout. My goodness me, you walk in here when it's nearly lunchtime and... I thought you were supposed to be finishing your project.'

'It's too sunny today. I couldn't be arsed.'

Jackie tutted. 'The devil makes work for idle hands.'

'You don't look exactly busy yourself.'

'I like that!' Jackie said indignantly. 'I've only this minute sat down. It may have escaped your notice – that pile of ironing....'

'Oh, not that again.'

'Somebody has to do it.

'Yeah, yeah, yeah!'

'What on earth's got into you today?'

Angrily, Vanessa spooned coffee into a mug. Her movements sharp and jerky, she felt she was about to explode in the atmosphere which was of her own making.

'Have you had a row with that boy you were going out with? What's his name? Terry?'

'Tony. And, no, we haven't had a row. We were never really serious about each other anyway.'

Jackie shook her head disapprovingly. 'I don't know,' she sighed. 'Young people these days.'

'And you oldies behave as if you're in your second childhood. Look at you and Nigel, can't wait to get off to some little love nest on the Mediterranean.'

'Oh, so that's what this is all about. You're jealous.'

Vanessa laughed sarcastically. 'Jealous! Of you and Nigel? Don't make me laugh.'

'You can't bear to think of me going off on holiday and enjoying myself for a change.'

A cruel thought struck Vanessa. 'No, it'll be a change to have the house to ourselves,' she said with a glint in her eye. 'Nicky and I can have a really wild party. I can invite half the students at West Kent College. It'll be great.'

Twenty-Eight

There were two messages on Dave's answering machine. The first was from Mary, asking when it would be convenient to come and look at the house. The other message was like a hand gripping his throat.

'Hello, Dave,' purred the voice, menacing in its familiarity. 'See you got rid of that eyesore. Bit naughty getting an AA tow. You've 'ad a good laugh at our expense. So now it's our turn. You're gonna have to pay for what you done.'

The caller hung up. Dave felt like crying. If only he'd known how sour this prank would turn. He wondered if he ought to call the police. But what was the point? The man was probably ringing from a public call box. Dave could have sworn he heard traffic noises in the background.

But there was Mary to consider. She would be moving in soon with her children. Should he warn her? On the other hand, he didn't want to frighten her unnecessarily. He would be going away soon. Perhaps the caller might see that his car was gone and stop calling.

He decided not to mention it.

He picked up the phone and dialled Mary's number.

***

Ted bundled his rail uniform into the sports bag, pleased that Marjorie had insisted on him changing at work. Now he could dump his bag in the shed and go off to the theatre with Donald.

'What are you smiling at?' said Marjorie, straightening a corner of the duvet.

Ted frowned. 'How d'you mean?'

'You were grinning to yourself. Care to share the joke?'

'Oh, it's nothing, Marj. I was miles away.'

'You don't want to tell me, do you?'

'Maybe my subconscious was having a bit of a laugh.'

'You what?'

'Nothing.'

He gave his hair a cursory brushing, not wanting to be seen to be taking to much care over his appearance.

'You really are a dark horse, Ted.'

He noticed she said it with a trace of affection in her voice. As he turned towards her, preparing to leave, she took his hand and sat on the edge of the bed.

'If you want, Ted, I don't mind if we go and see some of them plays you like. I know it means a lot to you.'

He looked down at her in amazement. She took this to be an expression of pleasant surprise and said, 'Since we've been sleeping in separate rooms, I've been starting to feel... well... different about you. Like when we was first going out together.'

'I... I'll be late for work.' His voice was a nervous croak. This was so unexpected, he was thrown off balance.

She tugged his hand gently, indicating that he should sit next to her. Reluctantly he allowed himself to sink down beside her. She lay back on the bed.

'It's so hot,' she whispered. 'I feel so.'..'

'Marjorie. I'm late.'

'All the better.' She smiled seductively. 'Remember how it was when we was first going out together? It was always last minute, before you left for work. Come on, Ted – let's do the London to Brighton in five minutes again.'

***

Mary sipped her wine. Dave toasted her with his cup of tea.

'Cheers!'

'I wouldn't have brought the wine if I'd known.' She sounded put out. 'Have you always been teetotal?'

Dave shook his head. 'I used to do two bottles of vodka a day. That was in the Eighties. When I was earning.'

She looked around at his cramped, rather squalid, living room. It seemed impersonal, like furnished, rented accommodation.

'Sorry,' he said. 'It's not much of a place.'

'Beggars can't be choosers.' She realised it sounded rude, and added, 'It's... it's OK, actually.'

He grinned at her. 'Don't tell fibs.'

She returned his smile. 'Well, I must admit, it could do with a female touch.'

'It could do with a lick of paint. Somehow I've never had the inclination. Nor the money.'

'I hope you won't think me rude if I ask what the kitchen's like. Only I've been used to... well, the flat where I am now has been thoroughly modernised.'

'You'll find this a bit different then.'

He stared into his tea cup, slightly annoyed by her attitude. He was doing her an enormous favour and she didn't sound at all grateful. He began to wonder if he was doing the right thing, offering his home rent free to someone he'd only just met.

'Oh well,' she sighed, 'not to worry. I can probably tart it up a bit for you. That's if you'd like me to.'

'I'm not bothered. I mean, you can if you want.'

'Have you ever been married?'

A distant, hundred-yard look closed the expression in his eyes.

'I'm sorry,' said Mary. 'Tell me to mind my own business.'

'Mind your own business,' he joked.

'Seriously. Have you ever been married?'

'I'll tell you about it sometime.' He stood up. 'Would you like to see the kitchen?'

But her curiosity was aroused. 'Don't you want to talk about it?'

'Not right now.'

She smiled reassuringly. 'OK. Why don't you show me the rest of the house? What are the bedrooms like?'

He started to speak and stopped, wondering if there was any hidden meaning in her question.

'What's wrong? Why are you looking at me like that?'

Thinking quickly, he said, 'I've, er, go to be away all summer, and this house'll not be much fun for your kids when they break up. You could always spend it in Cromer with me.'

She moved close to him and kissed him gently on the lips. 'That's really sweet of you, Dave. I'll give it some thought.'

He went to fold his arms about her waist but she pushed him away. 'Come on now. Don't rush things.'

'I've known loads of chorus girls like you. Like to tease and lead a bloke on.'

He had said it jokingly, but she caught the underlying seriousness of his tone.

Twenty-Nine

As soon as she got back from lunch, Nicky thought she had better clear her backlog of correspondence. The desk phone rang, seeming more shrill than usual, and telepathically something seemed to indicate that this was a bell of warning. She was right. As soon as she picked it up, just four words spat down the line:

'Nicky! My office! Now!'

The boss from hell. The sticky Malcolm. Late-thirties, but already a head of grey hair, jowls and a scowl to match. Reluctantly, she left the open-plan, walked along the corridor, the blazing sun streaming uncomfortably through the glass, and pushed open his door.

Without looking up, Malcolm said, 'A word, Nicky. Sit down.'

Demurely, she eased herself into the chair of doom, trying to guess what she could have done to upset him. She was a bit behind on her correspondence, but there had been meetings to attend, and then IIP report to type up. She hadn't exactly been idle.

'What about your e-mails?' Malcolm demanded. 'You stopped reading them?'

Nicky's throat felt dry. She coughed lightly before answering. 'I checked all my e-mails mid-morning.'

He stared at her, his eyes full of hate. Why did he hate her so much? she wondered. So much negativity. Perhaps it had something to do with last December, when he had come on a bit strong during the firm's Christmas party, and she had made it clear that she wasn't going to come across with the goodies, and certainly not with a married man almost twenty years her senior; but she thought he had got over that rejection. He had been drunk at the time, and she didn't think he would remember much about the incident the day after. And for a long time he behaved as if nothing had happened, for which she was glad. But just recently, he had become unbearable.

'I sent you an e-mail at eleven-forty-five,' he said crisply. 'I wanted you in here before your lunch break, and now it's two-fifteen.'

'Sorry,' she muttered weakly. 'What... um... what was it you wanted?'

He jerked a thumb at the wall behind him. 'See my clock. What time does it say?'

'Um... one-fifteen.'

'More than a month ago, someone should have moved it forward an hour. And as you're a lowly admin assistant, that someone should have been you. Now take it off the wall, go back to your office, re-set the clock to the correct time, then bring it back here. At the exact time. Not a minute fast or slow. Understood?'

She nodded dumbly, her mouth slightly open. She couldn't believe she was hearing this. She went behind the desk, lifted the clock from its hook and was halfway across Malcolm's office, when he added:

'You know our M.D. saw you in the precinct with those Animal Rights protesters. Perhaps what you don't know is our M.D will be out on the glorious bank holiday Monday hunt. It would be a fine thing if one of his admin assistants turns out to be a hunt saboteur.'

'Actually, I'm in London on the bank holiday,' she said weakly.

'But you don't deny parading yourself in the precinct with those nutters. Our illustrious M.D. mentioned seeing you handing out leaflets, in your sensible shoes – your Doc Martens – and he wondered if you're a lesbian. Are you, Nicky?'

She felt tears welling up and fought against them. 'No,' she managed. 'I've never....' She struggled to say something. Anything.

Impatiently, Malcolm snapped, 'There is so much legislation to protect staff these days. But I think you will want to leave this company soon, Nicky. And it goes without saying, I shall deny ever having had this conversation with you. Now go and correct that clock.'

***

Mike dashed in through the front door, having forgotten to pack his hairdressing mirror. He saw Claire putting the phone down and could tell by her serious expression there was something wrong.

'Who was that?'

'Chloe.'

'What's the latest news?'

'Why don't we discuss it later, Mike. I know you've got a load of appointments for tonight.'

'If it's something serious, I'd like to know about it now.'

Claire sighed deeply before she spoke. 'Chloe's decided to have an abortion. She's booked herself into a clinic at the end of the week.'

Even though he was half expecting it, it was still a shock. He stared expressionlessly at Claire.

'Well, you might say something.'

'I'm trying to think. Is this her decision?'

She stared back at her husband, her eyes piercingly defensive. 'I know what you're thinking, and the answer's no. It's her decision. And hers alone.'

'I'm sorry,' Mike muttered. 'It's just that....'

She saw him glance at his watch. 'I know: you've got to go. We'll talk about it when you get home.'

'It's a bit tricky tonight. I'm taking Andrew to the pub.'

'Charming!' Chloe's voice rose a notch. 'Chloe's having an abortion. So off you go to the pub. Can't you take Andrew another night?'

'It wouldn't be the same. Like me, you've obviously forgotten what tomorrow's date is.'

Claire looked as if she'd been hit in the stomach. 'Oh, Mike! What with all this trouble with Chloe, I've forgotten his birthday.'

Thirty

'My God!' Donald exclaimed. 'You look like a lobster. Have you been out in the sun?'

Ted had left the house early, pretending he was going to his usual afternoon and evening shift, and to pass the time he had gone into the Beau Nash for a pint, then lay down on the common and fell asleep for an hour.

'I thought I could feel my face burning up,' he replied.

As they walked towards the station, he asked Donald what excuse he had given Bamber about tonight.

'You're not worried he'll show up at your house again, are you?'

'Well, yes, of course I am.'

'And whatever would wifie say? Would she get the whip out? Chance would be a fine thing. Eh, Ted?'

Ted was silent. Brooding. Thinking about the way Marjorie had suddenly become amorous just as he was about to leave the house, almost as if she could sense a need to cement a marriage that was fast sinking into a morass.

'Your marriage,' said Donald. 'Bit of a farce, isn't it? On second thoughts, strike out the "bit of".'

'What about you and Bamber?'

'Ditto. So where does that leave us?'

'Us?'

'Yes, and don't pretend you don't know what I'm talking about. We like each other, don't we?'

'Well, yes... but....' Ted hesitated. 'Not in the way you mean. I mean....'

Donald stopped walking and turned towards Ted. Irritated. 'I suppose you're quite happy for things to continue the way they are. Sneaking off to share in our passion for the Bard. Can't you realise,

Ted, it makes Bamber and your wife more jealous than if we were lovers.'

An embarrassed laugh caught in the back of Ted's throat. 'But that's ridiculous.'

Donald shrugged. 'Yes, I know. But that's how it is.'

He walked on again and Ted followed.

'I think I know what you mean,' Ted said. 'This morning, Marjorie said she'd like to come and see some plays with me.'

Donald chuckled knowingly.'There you are, you see.'

'But I know she'd be bored.'

'So what's the answer?'

'I could always murder her. I've actually thought about it. Planned it in my imagination.'

Donald laughed. 'Nothing too gruesome, I hope.'

'Poison. I can't stand the sight of blood.'

'Ted, you're not serious, are you?'

Ted shook his head emphatically. 'I feel guilty even thinking about it. And the time I gave her food poisoning... well, I could have killed her then.'

Donald sniggered mischievously. 'Well, if it's any consolation, we won't be rocking the boat tonight. I told Bamber I was going to London to see a friend who's dying.' He saw Ted frowning. 'Bit sick, I know. But no worse than poisoning your wife.'

Ted beamed at Donald, and they arrived at the station giggling like schoolboy conspirators. Donald stopped Ted at the entrance, suddenly serious.

'Let's not worry about anything, just for tonight. It'll be a fun evening. Whatever happens with our respective partners, we'll at least have a wonderful night to remember.'

'I think I prefer things like this,' Ted said.

'How d'you mean?'

'Secretive. You know, forbidden fruit and all that.'

'You dark horse, you.'

'That's what Marjorie's always telling me.'

'If I tell you something, Ted, you must promise you won't let it ruin our evening.'

'All right. I promise.'

'Well, you obviously didn't get that tan working on British Rail. You're going to have to think up a bloody good explanation for that pillar box complexion.'

***

Nigel held his breath as Mike trimmed round his ears with the cut-throat razor. As soon as it was done, he relaxed and said, 'You're very quiet this evening, Mike.'

Mike's reply was brusque. 'Got a lot on my mind.'

'Trouble with your son?'

'Something like that.'

'Still causing you problems, is he?'

Staying silent, Mike brushed his client's hair with rather more force than was necessary. Feeling Nigel squirm under the pressure, he realized he was behaving unprofessionally and stopped brushing.

'Where is it you're off to?' he asked politely.

'Crete.'

'Very nice too. Ever been before?'

'No, but Jackie has. My fiancée's a very cultured lady. Knows a lot about history and opera and such like.'

Mike had stopped listening. He began untying the mantle around Nigel's neck.

'If you need a sympathetic ear,' hinted the salesman, dying to know what was troubling his hairdresser.

Mike ignored it and rummaged in his black bag for his mirror.

'I mean it, you know. It helps to unburden oneself. One shouldn't keep things bottled up. I can assure you, I wouldn't tell a soul. There'd be no point. You have my word.'

Mike held the mirror at all angles, catching Nigel's eye, who seemed less interested in his haircut than in Mike's problems.

'This time it's my daughter,' said Mike, suddenly relieved to get things off his chest. 'She's got herself pregnant. And she's having it aborted at the end of the week.'

There was a moment's stunned silence before Nigel said, 'But that's terrible. Can't she... I mean, won't she consider an alternative?'

'Have it, you mean?'

'Well, yes, anything's better than killing an unborn child.'

Mike shoved the mirror back in his bag, angry with himself for having told Nigel.

'Couldn't you persuade her....' Nigel began.

'It's not up to me,' Mike snapped. 'Sorry. I don't want to talk about it anymore. I shouldn't have told you in the first place.'

'I quite understand. But if there's anything I can do....'

'Yes there is. Just the nine pounds for the haircut, please.'

Nigel handed him a ten pound note, saying, 'Don't worry about the change.'

'Thanks.'

Mike packed up his gear and left hurriedly. As soon as he was behind the wheel of his car, he said through a tightly clenched jaw. 'You idiot! What did you have to tell him for? You idiot! You fuckin' great idiot!'

He thumped the steering wheel angrily.

Thirty-One

Mike stood at the bar with Andrew. 'Have whatever you like,' he offered. 'A few hours won't make any difference.'

'Cheers, Dad! I'll have a snakebite.' His father frowned. 'It's cider and lager.'

'I know what it is, Andy. Since when have you been on the serious drinker's potion?'

'Since this afternoon. I met some old school mates down at the Sussex.'

'Snakebite'll do your head in.'

'You just said I could have what I like.'

'Within reason.' Seeing his son's sullen expression, he added, 'Oh go on then: snakebite it is.'

He ordered the drinks. Next to him, a man on a bar stool was talking loudly.

'...I mean, why do these young girls wear such scanty clothing if they don't like us to look?'

'They feel pressured,' said Mike, an unholy glint coming into his eye. 'They've got to wear scanty clothes because all the other girls are wearing them.'

The man pounced on it. 'Exactly. No individuality. Follow-the-herd instinct. That's what it's all about.'

Mike had hooked his quarry. Time to reel him in. Staring at the man's tie, he said, 'It's a bit like blokes wearing a tie. They wear them cos they feel they've got to. But a tie's nothing more than an adornment. It serves no useful purpose.' He let his eyes drop pointedly at the man's bulging stomach. 'Unless it's to cover a beer gut.'

The man laughed nervously. 'You can talk. You're not exactly sylph-like.'

'No, but then I don't feel a pathetic need to wear a tie like the rest of the herd.'

The man looked at his near-empty glass, pretending he was ready for another drink, and rummaged in his pockets for some change.

'Dad, mind if we sit down?' asked Andrew.

They got their drinks and went and sat in a far corner of the bar.

Andrew stared at his father, frowning. 'Why d'you always pick on people?'

'I don't. Well, only on the prats who deserve it.'

'You'll get your head kicked in one of these days.'

Mike shrugged. 'I like living dangerously.'

'I thought you might be taking it out on that bloke because of what's happened to Chloe.'

Mike chuckled. 'My pub behaviour's always been the same. Nothing more I like than a good wind up; a bit of banter. By the way, has Mum told you the latest developments with Chloe?'

Andrew nodded, toying with his glass, staring at the murky concoction.

'It's because of what's happened,' continued Mike, 'that your mum and me... well, it's about tomorrow.'

'You've forgotten, haven't you?'

'It's been a difficult time for us.'

'Yeah, well, it's just one of those things. No big deal.'

'We'll make it up to you.'

'It doesn't matter, Dad. It really doesn't. I'm going to inherit the ten grand Nan and Grandpa left me. Why should you and Mum forgetting my birthday bother me?'

***

Thinking it was Chloe ringing, Claire hurried into the hall and grabbed the phone. There was a slight pause before the person spoke.

'Hello. My name's Jackie Ingbarton. Your husband cuts my fiancé's hair.'

'Oh?'

'Yes, I'm sorry to ring so late. t's a bit difficult to explain. It's just that....'

'Did Mike ask you to ring?'

'Mike?'

'My husband.'

'No, it was my idea. I'm sorry, I don't know your name.'

'Claire.'

There was a long pause, followed by a quick intake of breath before Jackie spoke again.

'The thing is, Claire, your husband confided in Nigel – that's my fiancé – that your daughter's about to terminate her pregnancy.'

'What's that got to do with you?'

'Well, as a Missionary for the Pre-Born, I would like to have a word with your daughter about saving the life of her child, instead of....'

Claire snapped, 'It's got fuck all to do with you. Mind your own damn business!'

She slammed the phone down and burst into tears.

'Oh, Mike,' she sobbed. 'How could you? How could you?'

Thirty-Two

The train was already at Platform 1, waiting. Claire stopped by the entrance and looked searchingly at Mike.

'I hope Chloe will be OK,' he said. Then, realising how feeble it sounded, he added, 'Tell her I'll be thinking of her.'

Claire's lips tightened, showing the first sign of wrinkles along the top edge.

'Physically there shouldn't be any problems. Emotionally I'm not so certain. That may take longer to heal. She'll suffer from feelings of guilt.'

'I'm sorry about the other night – that religious nut phoning up.'

Claire glanced impatiently towards the platform. 'I'd better go.'

'Look, I've said I was sorry....'

'I know you have. What d'you want me to say, Mike?'

'It's just that you still seem so angry about it.'

'How d'you expect me to feel?'

'None of this is my fault, you know.'

'I've got to go, or I'll miss the train. I'll give Chloe your love.'

She turned abruptly away, flashed her ticket at the collector, and hurried onto the platform. Mike felt hurt, the way she had gone off without the usual parting kiss, however perfunctory that might have been.

'Sod you then,' he muttered, starting to choke back tears of self pity.

A strapping tourist, rushing for the train, barged into Mike with his rucksack.

'Why don't you look where you're bloody going!'

***

125

It wasn't yet lunchtime when Ted met Donald in the Duke of York. He noticed his friend's face looked drawn, haggard.

'I'll get the drinks,' he offered. 'You look as if you could do with a large one.'

In spite of his downcast appearance, Donald couldn't resist saying, 'Depends what you're referring to, dear boy.'

But it was said on automatic pilot. Donald had lost his usual sparkle. Ted laughed dutifully, and bought a large gin and tonic for Donald and a pint of bitter for himself. They sat near the window, and Ted glanced surreptitiously at his watch.

'Eleven forty-five,' he said. 'Bit early for drinking.'

Donald nodded, then stared miserably into his glass.

'Is something wrong, Donald?'

As if he hadn't heard Ted, Donald continued staring into his glass. After an uncomfortable silence, he cleared his throat, and looked up and smiled at Ted, shaking off whatever was troubling him.

'What excuse did you give wifie for our little assignation today?'

'It was just luck. Marjorie had one of her migraine attacks. She'll be in bed for at least three or four hours.'

'And how did you explain the sun burn the other night?'

Ted looked pleased with himself. 'Simple. I said the sun's rays were shining through the guard's van window...'

'And she believed it?'

'Why wouldn't she? In fact she went on and on about the railway. She said they ought to have window blinds to protect the staff. If we have a hot summer, she said, she'd seriously think about making me a set of curtains to take.'

Donald laughed. 'How very camp. The only British Rail guard with swags and tails in his little cab.'

Donald's laughter ended abruptly. He seemed to feel guilty for enjoying himself. He took a large swig of gin and tonic.

Ted watched him carefully. 'That went down without touching the sides.'

'I could do with a whole bottle. To deaden the pain.'

'D'you want to talk about it, Donald?'

'As you've probably guessed: it's Bamber.'

'Well, yes, I thought as much.'

Donald shook his head with frustration. 'Bamber and I have such little in common. Zilch in fact. He's into all that ghastly Heavy Metal cacophony. Ghastly stuff. But in spite of all that, I do love him. I can't think why, but I do.'

'Well... I... I suppose,' Ted waffled, unable to think of anything to say.

'Our trip to the theatre the other night, Ted. I did enjoy it. And I swore I wouldn't feel guilty. In fact, I didn't at the time. But now....'

'Has... has something happened between you and Bamber?'

'I think Bamber's....' Donald pressed hard on his eyelids with a thumb and index finger. 'I'm not sure if he's going to get any better, you see.'

A cold shiver passed through Ted, followed by waves of nausea. He opened his mouth to speak but his mind was blocked. Sensing what he was thinking, Donald took his hand away from his face and smiled grimly.

'It's not what you're thinking, Ted. Bamber has a brain tumour. Did you notice how clumsy he was? I expect you thought he'd been drinking.'

'Of course not,' Ted said, although it was exactly what he had thought when he saw Donald's friend barging into the furniture.

'I banned him from the antique shop. Called him a clumsy oaf. God! I feel terrible.'

'But you weren't to know. You mustn't blame yourself.'

Donald laughed bitterly. 'No. I guess I'm not such a sensitive person after all.'

***

Mike rang the doorbell and waited, whistling tunelessly. Through the glass of the front door he saw someone approaching. His heart beat a little faster when he saw it was her, and he hoped she was wearing her mini skirt and black stockings.

'Hello, Maggie,' he said as she pulled open the door. She was dressed in just a T-shirt and her legs were beautifully tanned.

'Mike!'

She seemed surprised to see him. No, more than surprised. Shocked.

'I have got the right date, haven't I? It's in my appointments book.

'Oh God! Didn't you know. Didn't you read about Gary in the local rag?'

'No, I....'

'Gary died last week. The funeral was on Monday.'

Thirty-Three

'Maggie... I... I'm sorry,' Mike burbled. 'I had no idea. Gary always had a fixed appointment. I just don't know what to say.'

'My fault. I should have let you know. As you can imagine, it's not an easy time.'

'How did it happen?'

'It was a car crash. On Ashdown Forest.'

'Was anyone else involved?'

'No other cars, if that's what you mean. But the girl he was with was killed as well.'

Although her face was expressionless, her eyes said it all. Mike nodded slightly, to show her he understood. Then he glanced at his watch.

'I may as well shoot back home. I don't have another appointment now for....'

'Your welcome to come in for a coffee.'

Mike hesitated, his mind shifting into another gear as myriad thoughts of comforting the grieving widow bombarded his brain.

'Or perhaps you'd like something stronger?'

'I could fancy a beer. If you've got some.'

'I think I can manage to find you a beer.'

'Well, if you're sure.'

'Why not? Let's give the neighbours something to talk about. Anyway, there's something I'd like to ask you.'

Mike frowned as he followed her through the house and into the kitchen. What could she possibly want to ask him?

He watched as she turned her back on him and got a beer from the fridge. He found himself admiring her legs, staring at her shapely figure and wondering what she was wearing beneath the floppy T-shirt.

'Kids at school?' he asked, his voice softer than normal.

'Yes, they've gone back today for the first time since Gary died. But they won't be back for tea. My parents have taken them to Hastings to take their mind off it.'

She handed Mike a bottle of Becks and a bottle opener. 'There you go. D'you need a glass?'

He shook his head. 'Bottle's fine. What did you want to ask me?'

'That time you phoned about the poker game. Was it true?'

Mike twisted the top off the bottle, giving himself thinking time. After taking a sip of beer, he said, 'I'm sorry. I didn't want to lie to you. But Gary insisted.'

'He made you do it, did he?'

'Not exactly, but....'

'But you allowed him to get the better of you. As we all did.'

She poured herself a glass of white wine from a box in the fridge and raised her glass to Mike. 'Cheers!'

He lifted his bottle sheepishly. 'Yeah, cheers. I'm sorry if I....'

'Forget it. You didn't upset me. Gary did. I knew he was lying. But then, when you phoned....'

'If it's any consolation, I couldn't understand why the hell he'd want to go with anyone else. He was lucky to have such an attractive wife.'

'You're not trying to chat me up, are you?'

'No, I mean it. Whenever I came round to cut Gary's hair, I sometimes didn't dare look at you, in case it showed.'

'In case what showed?'

'What do you think?'

She put down her glass and smiled at him. 'I think I'm behaving stupidly, but I don't really care.'

His beer bottle clunked loudly as he abandoned it on top of the fridge. He put his arms around her waist and pulled her close to him. He swallowed noisily and his voice sounded hoarse when he spoke.

'Just tell me if I'm out of order.'

She giggled softly. 'You're out of order. But I tell you something, Mike: now it definitely shows.'

***

'Mum, I'm bored.'

Mary sighed deeply. 'Your tea's nearly ready.'

'I'm not hungry.'

Mary could feel herself about to explode. 'Go outside and play with Thomas. I'll call you when I've dished up.'

'It's a dump out there. It's not a proper garden. You said we'd have a proper garden in this house.'

'Well it's not as bad as our flat. We didn't have any garden there.'

'We did. We had the garden opposite.'

'That was the park, Simon.'

'You were the one who called it our garden.'

'That was because....' She searched desperately for a pair of oven gloves and just managed to rescue the pan of peas from boiling over.

'Because of what?' Simon demanded, stressing every syllable.

'Go outside and tell Thomas I'm dishing up.'

She folded a grubby tea towel in two and lifted a tray of fish fingers out of the oven.

'Can we go swimming after tea?'

'No we can't.'

'Why not?'

'It's too late in the day.'

'I don't mind.'

'Well I do.'

Thomas appeared at the back door. 'Are we going swimming?'

'No, Mum won't take us,' Simon moaned.

His mother's voice became shrill as she tried to dish up. 'I've already told you....'

The telephone rang. Thomas prepared to dash off.

'Blast! I'll get it. Simon, put the oven chips on the plate – and mind you don't burn yourself.'

She dashed into the hall and answered the phone. There was a confused type of pause before a man said, 'You 'is bit of stuff, are you?'

'Who is this? Who's speaking?'

'You're Dave Whitby's tart, are you? I see 'is car's not around. I'll be round later tonight. I might give you a good seeing to, darling. What sort of knickers d'you wear?'

She slammed the phone down and returned to the kitchen. Thomas looked up as she entered.

'Mum, what's wrong?'

Mary stood in the doorway, trying to catch her breath. 'That settles it,' she said, more to herself than her children. 'I don't like it here either.'

Through a mouthful of chips, Simon said, 'Let's go somewhere else then.'

'Fine. We'll do that for half term.'

Simon, who hadn't expected that response to his flippant suggestion, stared open-mouthed at his mother, revealing a mouthful of half-chewed chips and tomato ketchup.

'Where are we going?' asked Thomas. 'We haven't finished unpacking here yet.'

'We're going to a place called Cromer. It's by the sea.'

'Has it got a sandy beach?' Simon wanted to know.

'Yes. At least, I think so.'

'How are we getting there?'

'The man whose house this is will come and pick us up.'

Thomas looked at his mother closely. 'Have you asked him yet?'
'No. Not yet.'
'Then how d'you know he'll pick us up?'
Mary smiled knowingly. 'I just do.'

Thirty-Four

A ndrew walked up to the bar with barely a glance at the fruit machine. 'Bottle of Bud, please.'

While the barman turned to get the beer from the cold cabinet, Andrew sat on the bar stool. His bar stool. The one where the writer had sat less than two weeks ago.

The barman turned back with the Budweiser. 'D'you wanna glass?'

Andrew shook his head, handed the barman a twenty pound note, and said, 'Bottle's fine.'

As he was handed his change, he asked, 'Has anyone left anything behind the counter for me? My name's Andrew Longridge. I just wondered – on the off-chance – I met this bloke in here, couple of weeks ago. He was a writer, and he promised me a copy of his latest book. I wondered if he might have left me a copy behind the bar.'

The barman gave the shelf a cursory glance, then made the token gesture of rifling through some postcards and papers. 'There's nothing I can see. But I'll ask the landlord if you like. He's not here at the moment.'

'No, don't bother. It doesn't matter.'

The barman shrugged. 'Well, it's up to you.'

'No, it doesn't matter, thanks.'

Andrew took a long swig of his beer and the barman went to the far end of the bar to continue a heated discussion about a penalty goal in an important match.

Andrew stared at the shelf behind the bar and could almost see the brown paper package waiting for him. It was what was supposed to happen. If this had been a film, the writer would have known someone was out to silence him; and he'd have known Andrew would return to this bar and ask for the book after he was

134

dead. But this wasn't a film. This was the hard disappointment of reality. Things like that just didn't happen in real life.

***

As Mike dressed, Maggie said, 'You're not as good looking as Gary, and he wasn't overweight, but you're much more attractive, Mike.'

'Is that what they call a bank-handed compliment?'

'Gary's problem was that he loved himself so much.' She sat up in bed suddenly, remembering. 'I'll never forget one night, I heard him panting and breathing heavily. I wondered what he was up to.'

'And?'

'He was doing sit-ups on the floor there.' She giggled at the memory. 'He was trying to work off the beer he'd drunk. I've never known anyone as vain as Gary.'

Mike sat on the edge of the bed and took her hand. 'Does it help to talk about him?'

'I suppose it must do. Does it bother you?'

'No. It's just that this situation feels unreal. Bit strange, that's all.'

She ran her fingers softly along his arm, saying, 'It seemed real enough to me.'

'You know what I mean.'

'I refuse to feel guilty,' she said with sudden defiance. 'It's not my fault he's dead. I know you're not supposed to leap into bed with someone so soon after the funeral, but at least I didn't go behind his back when he was alive.'

'This is revenge,' laughed Mike, 'without the guilt.'

As soon as he'd said it, he knew it was wrong. She snatched her hand away, looking hurt.

'Is that what you think? That I jumped into bed with you just to get back at Gary?'

'Well, I haven't had much time to think about it. I'm sorry, I didn't mean to....'

'The reason I jumped into bed with you, Mike, is because I feel so free suddenly. Free to have a bit of fun for a change.' She brushed a hand through his thinning hair. 'Why do hairdressers go bald, I wonder?'

'I've got loads of hair left.'

'Whoops! Touched a nerve, have I? Found a weak spot?'

'OK. So you've got your own back. We're quits.'

'Well, it was a horrid thing to say. Morbid. You can't get back at the dead.'

'Depends on how religious you are. And if you believe in life after death.'

'You mean Gary could have been watching?' She suddenly went into peals of laughter and looked up at the ceiling. 'You see how silly you looked, Gary, from that angle. Oh, God! I think this is hysteria setting in. It's not that funny.'

She stopped laughing as suddenly as she had begun. Mike leant forward and kissed her gently on the lips.

'Thanks,' she whispered seriously, 'for giving me the fun and pleasure I never had with Gary.'

Mike smiled. 'So your husband wasn't exactly Master of the Universe between the sheets.'

'Put it this way: he was more of your hundred metre dash than a marathon man. Whenever I tried to talk to him about it, he just brushed it aside and said, "I've never had complaints in that department before." God! He could be arrogant.'

'What attracted you to him? I mean, why did you marry?'

'I was an immature young girl. I fell for him for all the wrong reasons. Looks, flash car, nice clothes. So I got what I deserved.'

Mike kissed her again. 'You're fantastic. Out of this world. I mean it.'

She laughed, then frowned. 'When you suggested I slept with you to get back at Gary – no, I'm not having a go at you – I just want to know: is that what you're doing? Taking revenge on your wife?'

'I hadn't really thought about it.'

'In other words, yes!'

Maggie swung her legs out of bed, grabbed her T-shirt from where it had been discarded on the floor, and pulled it on over her head. She came round to Mike's side of the bed.

'Will you promise me something, Mike?'

'If I can.'

'If you want to carry on seeing me occasionally, will you patch things up with your wife? Take her out to dinner. Buy her a big bunch of flowers.'

Mike looked bemused. 'Well, yes. But....'

'Because I don't want to be like Gary. I don't want to break up a family. I just don't want any problems. Is that understood?'

Mike nodded solemnly. 'OK. I promise.'

Thirty-Five

Nicky was talking to Savita by the water cooler when Malcolm marched across the open plan office, making a beeline for them.

'Just relaxing, passing the time of day, I see,' he sneered. 'No work to do?'

Nicky began to stammer. 'Um, ac ...actually we were discussing the team report....'

Malcolm cut her short with a sarcastic laugh. 'Pull the other one. Oh, by the way, Nicky, I didn't tell you, did I? I've been having riding lessons. They're coming on a treat. Bank holiday Monday I'll be out hunting with our M.D. Of course, it's not quite the same as it was. They can't use a whole pack to tear the vermin apart anymore. Still, as long as the weather stays fine, it should be an excellent day.'

He winked at Savita, then strode across the office, whistling tunelessly, and walked through to the reception area. Nicky watched him go, then turned to Savita.

'I hate that man,' she said. 'I hope he falls off his horse.'

Savita grinned at her. 'Perhaps with a little help he might.'

Interest flickered in Nicky's eyes. 'How d'you mean?'

'I hate him as well. And I owe him. He's always making nasty remarks about my race, and curries and arranged marriages. I'm sick of it. Then the other day, he called me into his office for an appraisal. Know what he said? He accused me of having communication difficulties.'

'That's rubbish,' Nicky protested.

'I know. And he went on to imply that I have a chip on my shoulder. "That's fairly typical of..." he said. I think he was about to say..."typical of someone like me. You know, an ethnic minority person." I'm sure that's what he was going to say, then stopped himself in time. He probably knows he could get into serious trouble for it.'

Nicky frowned thoughtfully. 'So when you said that he might fall off his horse with a little help...'

Savita's grin widened. 'I've been telling my boyfriend about Malcolm. And he's furious. He's got something planned for the bank holiday.'

'What?'

'I promised I wouldn't tell anyone. But... what are you doing after work tonight?'

'Nothing. Why?'

'I'm meeting Damian for a drink. Why don't you join us? If he knows how much you hate Malcolm, he might let you in on what he's got up his sleeve.'

'Yes, I'd like that,' she replied.

Nicky suddenly felt more cheerful. Not only was this a burden shared, the prospect of revenge was exhilarating. And she was keen to know how Savita's boyfriend could unseat the odious Malcolm on the bank holiday hunt.

***

'Car's all loaded up,' said Dave as he came into the kitchen. 'Where are the kids?'

'Out in the garden,' Mary replied. 'I'll get them.'

'No rush. Let's have a quick cuppa before we go.'

Dave switched the kettle on, then came and sat opposite Mary at the hideously-patterned Formica table. He patted her hand reassuringly. 'As we'll both be away for a while, maybe the phone calls'll stop.'

'I hope so. But we're only away for half term.'

'And an extra week,' Dave added.

Mary nodded. 'Yes, the school secretary was a bit snotty about taking them out for an extra week at half term – but what the hell!'

Dave frowned and stared down at the edge of the chipped table. 'I hope the arrangements will be okay. Four of us squashed into a caravan for two weeks. Could be a bit cramped.'

'At least it'll be good to get away for a while.'

Dave caught her staring thoughtfully at the kitchen walls. He took her hand in his and squeezed. 'I don't mind doing this house up,' he said. 'Now that... well, I've got a purpose, if you see what I mean.'

She offered him a sympathetic smile, the sort you offer the recently bereaved. 'I think you're a lovely bloke, Dave, I really do. And I'd like it to work out between us. The kids really respond well to you.'

'I like them, an' all.'

'It's just that....'

'I knew there had to be a but.'

'You're not over her yet, are you? I've seen you staring at her photograph.'

'It's not what you think.'

Frowning, Mary asked, 'What d'you mean?'

'I'll tell you one day.'

'Why not now?'

Shaking his head, he rose from the table to make the tea. 'Time's not right. But I will tell you soon. I promise.'

'Oh well, I guess I'll just have to be a bit patient. Listen, Dave, when we get back in two weeks' time, d'you think we could talk about the other bedroom?'

Dave spoke hurriedly, panic in his voice. 'We'll be OK as we are. You can manage with two bedrooms, can't you?'

'I just thought it would be nice if Simon and Thomas had separate bedrooms.'

'No, I keep all my costumes in the third bedroom.'

'Why d'you keep it locked?'

'I've got lots of props and costumes in there. I don't want them to get spoilt. I wouldn't want Simon and Thomas to get into any trouble. You know what kids are like. Natural curiosity. They start mucking about and... well, I like to keep all my stage gear in tip-top condition.'

She realised he was protesting too much. And the way he avoided looking at her as he spoke, busying himself with making the tea.

She wondered what on earth he kept in the third bedroom under lock and key. And she began to have doubts about where their relationship might lead. Especially as she knew very little about the private life of Dave Whitby.

Thirty-Six

As they were leaving the house, Mary stopped and glanced back at the cabinet in the hallway. It was in one of the drawers that Dave kept the key to the third bedroom, and this time he forgot to take it with him. So, as soon as she, Simon and Thomas returned from Cromer in a fortnight's time, she intended to find out what the comedian was hiding in that room.

'Come on, Mum; it's a long way,' Thomas urged from the doorway, which caused Dave to look round. And, as if he could read Mary's mind, he clicked his fingers as if he had forgotten something.

'Whoops!' he exclaimed. 'Nearly forgot.'

He walked back down the hall, retrieved the key from the cabinet, and stuck it in his pocket. He smiled nonchalantly at Mary as they left the house.

They drove in silence, until they were the other side of Southborough. Then Mary found she couldn't contain her curiosity any longer.

'That key you took from the hall cabinet: is that the key to bedroom number three?'

There was a slight pause before Dave answered. 'Yes. Why?'

'I just wondered. So why do you always take it with you when you go away?'

'In case the house is burgled. I don't want to make it easier for them. My stage props and costumes are irreplaceable.'

She knew he was lying. But why? And what was in that room?

***

After work, Savita took Nicky with her to TN4, a pub that used to be known by the more traditional name of The George. Nicky wasn't sure what she was expecting in Savita's boyfriend, but he turned out to be thin and intense looking, dressed in black, and sporting much silver jewellery. The impression he gave was of a mid-thirties man trying to hang on to his youth, dressed slightly Gothic, but somehow not quite succeeding. It was probably the lack of any piercings or tattoos that showed his lack of commitment to the image he was trying to create.

After she had been introduced to Damian, Nicky could see him giving Savita sidelong, questioning glances, probably wondering why his girlfriend had brought along a work colleague. Sensing Damian's disquiet, Savita got straight to the point.

'Nicky's having terrible trouble with the boss at work.'

'Fat pig!' he exclaimed.

Savita giggled and said, 'Yeah, or words to the effect.'

'So what's he done to you?' Damian asked Nicky.

'During the Christmas party, he really came on strong. Started groping me and saying corny things like: "You and I could make beautiful music together".'

Damian made a throwing-up gesture with his finger in his mouth.

Savita said, 'Then Nicky laughed at him and turned him down. Since then he's been unbearable. Hasn't he, Nicky?'

'It got even worse after our Managing Director saw me in the precinct, handing out Animal Rights leaflets. He told Malcolm about it, and since then he's made my life unbearable.'

Damian frowned intensely. 'So why d'you stick with the job? Why not get something else?'

Nicky shrugged. 'I don't know. I suppose it's because I don't want to end up commuting to London every day. There aren't many large insurance companies in Tunbridge Wells.'

As if to prompt her boyfriend into revealing his intentions to get back at Malcolm, Savita said, 'Nicky hates Malcolm so much she'd like to see him dead.'

Nicky nodded gravely. 'Right now wouldn't be soon enough.'

'Why don't you tell her, Damian? I know she won't tell anyone.'

After a long silence, Damian coughed lightly before he spoke. 'I'm going to hide out in someone's garden along the main road between Bexhill and Battle – that's the road the hunt will have to set out along – then let Malcolm have it with a paintball. That should bring him down to earth with a crash.'

'Paintball?' Nicky said, frowning, wondering what he was talking about.

Savita explained. 'Damian goes paintballing regularly. You know, it's like war games, where one team stalk another, armed with paintball guns. Well, Damian's going to get one of the paintball guns and some ammunition, and shoot the back of Malcolm's horse.'

'I'm going to have to get the equipment off the internet,' said Damian. 'Because when you go paintballing, everything is checked. In the wrong hands, those guns could be lethal weapons. Fire one at someone's face who's not wearing a mask and....'

He left the unfinished sentence hanging dramatically in the air.

'But Malcolm won't be wearing a mask,' said Nicky, starting to worry about this plan, and worry about what she was getting into.

'That's why I'm aiming for the horse's rump.'

'Oh, but that's cruel,' Nicky protested. 'I've got nothing against the poor horse.'

Damian shrugged. 'Neither have I. But don't worry. Horses are strong creatures. A little bruising won't hurt it.'

'No, you can't do this. Because if you do, Malcolm will think it's anti-hunt saboteurs. He won't have a clue that it's anything to do with his behaviour in the office. It'll be a waste of time.'

'But, Nicky,' began Savita, 'when we were at work, you said you'd love to see Malcolm knocked off his horse. What's made you change your mind? Is it because you feel sorry for the horse?'

'Partly. But it's just occurred to me that unless he knows it's us taking revenge for how he behaves in the office, he'll just carry on in the same way.'

'But whatever we do to Malcolm, we can't let him know it was us two.'

Nicky nodded fervently. 'Yes we can. We need to find a way of getting back at him so that he knows it was us, but can't prove it.'

'She's right,' Damian said to Savita. 'What's the point of revenge if he thinks it's something to do with anti-hunt protesters? That'll only make him more set in his attitudes.'

A sulky expression clouded Savita's face. 'But what about our plan?'

'It was your plan, babe,' said Damian. 'And I told you the equipment would be costly. And if I get caught, I could be looking at a prison sentence. Nicky's right. Let's put out heads together and see what else we can come up with.'

Thirty-Seven

Claire slammed a dish of roast potatoes onto the table. Chloe didn't look up from the magazine section of the Sunday paper she was reading. Andrew continued to toy irritatingly with the pepper mill, a sullen expression on his face..

'Oh, joy!' exclaimed Claire. 'A family Sunday dinner. Just like old times.'

She turned to Mike. 'Haven't you finished carving yet?'

'Give us a chance. It's as tough as old boots.'

Claire's voice rose an octave. 'What!' Then, noticing the mischievous glint in his eyes, added, 'Oh, ha-bloody-ha! Why don't you do the shopping for a change?'

Chloe dropped her magazine onto the floor and helped herself to potatoes. 'Why are you so stressed out?' she said, sounding so reasonable it annoyed her mother even more.

'Because you and Andrew have done nothing but bicker all day. It's not like you're children anymore.'

'It's not my fault,' said Chloe, pouting.

'No, it never is. You go back to Newcastle tomorrow. I was looking forward to at least one last civilized meal together.'

'I'm sorry. All I said was....'

'I know what you said. As usual, you were trying to wind Andrew up.'

Chloe looked across at her brother and sniggered. 'By the look on his face, I think I succeeded.'

'Oh yeah!' Andrew began, aggressively.

'Now don't start again!' Claire yelled.

Mike put the platter of roast beef in the centre of the table, saying, 'OK. Let's cool it now. There you go. Tuck in.'

Claire felt she was over-heating. She flopped into the chair next to Chloe, blowing out her cheeks noisily. Mike sat opposite her. A strained silence descended.

'Well!' said Claire, after the scraping of cutlery began to grate. 'This is fun!'

Chloe dropped her knife and fork with a clatter. 'All I said to Andrew was that his behaviour is obsessive. You know it's true. He knows it's true. He just won't admit it. One minute he's hooked on computers, then it's fruit machines. Now it's some dead writer he met in the pub.'

'Someone has to do something about it,' said Andrew. 'The police know nothing about it. Or they say they don't.'

Chloe laughed. 'So it's ace detective Andrew Longridge to the rescue. Anyone notice the striking resemblance to Matt Damon?'

'Shut your gob!' Andrew yelled.

'That's it! I've had enough!' shouted Claire.

'"Shut your gob!"' Chloe mimicked. 'He's regressed. Surely this can't be the same bloke who unearthed the Tunbridge Wells conspiracy, a secret that'll rock the world. Bring down the government.'

'You think you're so clever, don't you?' Andrew raged, his eyes blazing.

'At least I'm not obsessional. You're a real Trekie, you are. A sad anorak.'

Deeply hurt, Andrew pushed his chair away from the table and stood up. There were tears in his eyes.

'Are you happy now? Claire yelled at Chloe, who hadn't expected quite that reaction from her brother and looked shamefaced.

'Don't be silly, Andy,' Mike said. 'Sit down and finish your meal.'

But Andrew had already grabbed his coat from the hall. 'I'm not hungry.'

'I hope you're satisfied,' Claire said through gritted teeth. 'Another meal ruined. I thought as you two got older, you might....'

The front door slammed. Claire looked pleadingly at Mike, who sighed loudly, shoved half a roast potato into his mouth and got up from the table.

'I'll try to catch him up,' he mumbled through burning hot potato.

'Have a talk to him, Mike. God knows – his behaviour is obsessional.'

'Tell me something I don't know,' Mike replied as he left.

The front door slammed again. Claire looked at the remains of the wasted dinner then stared accusingly at her daughter. Chloe had tears pouring down her cheeks.

'I'm sorry, Mum,' she blubbered. 'I know it's all my fault but – I just can't help it. I feel so... so depressed. I still can't get over what I've done. I feel empty. Like nothing else matters.'

Claire softened, putting an arm around her daughter's shoulders. 'I know it hurts now, Chloe. But you will get over it in time. I promise.'

Chloe let her head fall onto her mother's shoulders. 'And now I've ruined everyone's Sunday.'

Claire didn't say anything. Sympathetic though she was, she couldn't resist letting silence work some guilt into her daughter.

***

As the taxi from Gatwick neared Tunbridge Wells, Jackie gripped Nigel's hand tightly.

'What's wrong?' he whispered, casting a self-conscious glance at the taxi driver.

'I've got a confession to make. I told the girls a lie. I told them I was coming home tomorrow.'

'What on earth for?'

'Because of what Vanessa said about having a wild party.'

'Now that wasn't very sensible, was it?' said Nigel, in his patronising tone. 'If, as I suspect, it was an idle threat, your daughters will wonder why you lied to them. But if they do have a wild party, you returning earlier than expected isn't going to change anything. When my son was in his mid-teens, my wife and I were away one weekend. And when we returned on the Sunday evening – rather like we are now – we knew Martin had held a party the night before. We found a dustbin filled with empties. But I had to hand it to Martin, there was no other evidence. He'd done a thorough job of clearing up. It's the way Martin was brought up.'

'Yes, I know,' said Jackie in a monotone. 'You've told me.'

Warming to his subject, and forgetting the taxi driver's fly-on-the-wall presence, Nigel began to pontificate loudly.

'I like to think I ran a tight ship. If Martin cooked himself something, there'd be no television until he'd washed up after him. Favourite programmes or not.'

Jackie tutted without meaning to. 'That seems a bit extreme.'

'Extreme! Good grief! If we all went around leaving things others to clear up for us....'

'Like Vanessa and Nicky, you mean?'

'You said it. I didn't.'

'No, but that's what you were thinking.'

Nigel tittered. 'How do you know what I was thinking?' he said, trying to steer the argument into safer waters.

'Oh, I just know you,' Jackie replied, nestling close to her fiancé, who lapsed into thoughtful silence because of the possessive way she said it.

The taxi turned into Jackie's road. As it neared her house, the taxi driver, who had been silent throughout the journey, suddenly became animated.

'Listen to that! That is some CD player. It's like a full scale rock concert.'

Alarmed, Jackie struggled to unbuckle her seat belt as the taxi stopped outside her front gate. A pulsating beat came from somewhere beyond the high privet hedge which concealed the house from the road.

'Oh no,' she groaned. 'It's coming from my house.'

The taxi driver laughed cruelly. 'Reminds me of the Isle of Wight, 1970. That was some concert.'

Thirty-Eight

After hurrying out of the house, Mike spotted Andrew about a hundred yards away, going along St. John's Road towards the centre of Tunbridge Wells. Instead of following him, Mike went into the Kelsey Arms, bought himself a pint of bitter, then sat on one of the benches outside. He dialled Maggie's number on his mobile. Her daughter answered and Mike heard her squabbling with her brother over who should deal with the phone call. The boy won and went to call his mother. When she came to the phone, Maggie answered 'Hello?' cautiously, as if she was expecting more bad news.

'It's Mike,' he announced. 'I know I said I'd ring on a weekday but I had to speak to you.'

'Why? What's wrong?'

'Nothing's wrong. I just wanted to hear your voice again.'

He heard her quick intake of breath and he felt insecure. Was she irritated by his phone call? Perhaps she didn't want to see him again.

'Mike,' she said, 'it's Sunday. Why aren't you at home?'

'I've got some work to do,' he lied. 'And as I'm between customers, I thought I'd give you a bell.'

A motorbike shot by on the main road, the decibels loudly deafening. He didn't hear what Maggie said.

'Sorry?'

'I said as long as you're sure everything's all right.'

'Why wouldn't it be? So when am I going to see you again? It's been nearly two weeks since we....'

'What about Thursday? About one o'clock.'

'That'll make it nearly three weeks. Can't you make it sooner? What about tomorrow?'

'No, I'm sorry. I can't.'

151

'Why not? Half term's over now.'

'No, Mike. I can't.' She sounded annoyed. 'It has to be Thursday. Like it or lump it.'

'Guess I'll have to lump it then,' he replied hurriedly. 'The time'll drag until Thursday. I miss you.'

'Yeah. Me too.'

'I love you.'

'Don't be stupid, Mike. See you.'

An abrupt click and she was gone. He stuck his mobile back in his pocket and took a sip of his beer, which was more lively than his mood, which had sunk to a flat feeling of impotence now that his conversation with Maggie had ended. It was an anti-climax and he quickly downed the rest of his pint, before going back inside the Kelsey to buy another.

***

A mighty wall of sound blasted Jackie and Nigel as they stood framed in the living room doorway, a look of stunned disbelief on their faces. Seeing them enter, the musicians exchanged looks, grinned, shrugged, and carried on playing. Vanessa and Nicky, who were sitting on speaker cabinets, drinking cans of beer, saw their mother's numbed expression as she attempted to absorb what she was seeing: the snake-like mass of wire and electronic equipment cluttering her living room.

Jackie turned and fled, followed by Nigel. Vanessa and Nicky scrambled across the clutter and caught them up outside the front door.

'How dare you!' Jackie screamed.

'It's only a rehearsal,' Vanessa shouted. 'They had nowhere else to rehearse.'

'We thought you weren't coming home until tomorrow,' said Nicky sheepishly, but no one heard her.

'Haven't you any consideration for the neighbours?' Nigel yelled.

Vanessa stared at him. 'What?'

He shouted louder. 'The neighbours!'

'Our immediate neighbours on the left are away. And on the right they said they'd go out for the afternoon.'

'And what about me?' shrieked Jackie. 'I can't stand this noise. And that mess.' She turned to Nigel. 'I'm taking you up on your offer. I'll move in with you right away.'

Nigel grinned and grabbed the handle of her suitcase. 'I'll put your things in my car.'

'But, Mum....' Nicky whined.

'I've had enough!' Jackie snapped. 'When Nigel and I get married, we'll sort something out for you two. But up until then I'm going to live at his place. And we'll eventually be putting this place on the market and combining both our properties into one big one.'

Vanessa looked miffed. 'But what about us?'

'That's your problem.'

'But you can't just leave us to our own devices.'

'You're both old enough to fend for yourselves.'

Nigel returned from having put Jackie's suitcase in the boot of his car. He had a smug, self-satisfied tilt to his mouth, which Vanessa wanted to slap.

'What are you grinning at?' she demanded.

'I don't think this is the time or place....' he began.

'Piss off!' she screamed.

'Charming!' he said, with an infuriating expression of self-righteousness. 'Come on, darling. Let's get to my place and unbend.'

As they walked to the car, Jackie corrected Nigel. 'I think you mean unwind, darling.'

'I expect I do,' Nigel smirked.

Vanessa and Nicky watched their mother depart with increasing dread. It had all gone horribly wrong. Now they would have to fend for themselves.

Thirty-Nine

Alone in his sister's house, Craig noticed a newly hung photograph of Gary on the wall by the breakfast bar. He scowled at it.

'Oily git!' he muttered; then grinned and added, 'But thanks for the chip shop, Gary.'

The kettle boiled and he made two cups of instant coffee. Minutes later, Maggie arrived.

'Kids go to school without any problems?' he asked.

She nodded thoughtfully. 'They're better now they've settled back into a routine.' She looked her brother up and down. 'Craig, I hope you don't mind me saying this – I hope you won't take it the wrong way....'

'What?'

'Well, we are seeing a solicitor. Couldn't you have worn something a bit smarter?'

He took his coffee mug and sat on a stool by the breakfast bar, glaring at her. 'I've only got casual gear,' he said, with a trace of annoyance, but his sister was aware that he was also shielding himself from any criticism or hurt.

'You wore a suit to the funeral.'

'Oh that! I got it from the Hospice Shop. It's still in a heap on the floor where I left it.'

'Well, you could at least....' She avoided looking at him. 'At least roll your shirt sleeves down.'

'Do my tattoos embarrass you?'

'It's not that.'

'What then?'

She glanced at her watch and changed the subject. 'Gary's estate's going to take months to sort out. But I don't see any reason why you shouldn't be running your own chip shop right now. It'll be your responsibility, and you'll own it eventually.'

Craig gave her a warm smile. 'It'll be the best chippie in the south east. Who's running the others? I mean, won't you find it difficult, what with having the kids to look after?'

Maggie stared into her coffee. 'I'm selling the others. And, if anything, I'm taking on a bigger commitment. A full time headache, probably.'

She giggled self-consciously, turned away and poured her remaining coffee into the sink.

'Well come on – don't keep me in suspense. What are you up to, Maggs?'

She rinsed her mug under the hot tap, placed it on the draining board, then swung round to face him again, suddenly keen to share her plans with him.

'I haven't told anyone yet, Craig – you're the first to know. I'm planning to open a wine bar – here in Tunbridge Wells. I've found the premises I want. I'll have to apply for a licence, of course, but I don't see any reason why I should get turned down. So what d'you think?'

'I think it's a brilliant idea.'

'Do you? You're not just saying that?'

'No, I think it's a great idea. But I don't think you ought to go it alone. Hey! I've just had an idea.'

Frowning, as if she could guess what was coming, Maggie crossed the room to collect a pink, cardboard file from a pile of clutter on the pine dresser.

'I mean,' continued Craig, 'once you've given me the chippie – officially I mean – I could sell it, buy a share in your wine bar and help you run it.'

'No, I don't think it'd work.'

'Why not?'

'I just don't.'

Craig stood up, staring closely at his sister. When he spoke, his voice was quieter, feeling he was about to be hurt. 'You haven't given me a reason, Maggs. I mean, we get on alright, don't we?'

She nodded slightly but avoided looking at him.

'So why not? Give me one good reason.'

She studied her brightly painted fingernails closely and said, 'It's like this, Craig – I want this wine bar to be smart. Special. To attract the right sort of customers.'

'Oh! And I'm not good enough, is that it?'

She forced herself to look him straight in the eye. 'We get on great guns – we always have done. But there was a time we disagreed violently. Remember why?'

He held his arms out angrily. 'They're only tattoos, Maggs. They won't contaminate your customers.'

'I know they won't. That's not the point..'

'The point is: you're still a snobby little cow.' Craig raised his voice, pointing at Gary's photograph. 'It never occurred to me before: what a perfect match you two were.'

Maggie's eyes flashed and Craig held his hands palms up towards her.

'OK. I'm sorry. I didn't mean it. I don't want to upset you. I might lose the chip shop.

'I wouldn't do that to you, Craig. I wouldn't go back on my word.'

'I know you wouldn't,' Craig mumbled miserably. 'I don't know why I said it. I was just upset because I can see my life mapped out for me. I know exactly what I'll be doing in ten years' time.'

'Most people do.'

'Yeah, great life, ain't it?'

Maggie tapped her watch. 'We're due at the solicitor's. We'd better go. Cheer up, sweetheart. A fish and chip shop's a safer bet. In a few years I might be coming to you, my tail between my legs, to borrow some money.'

'No, I've got a feeling you'll make a go of it. And I promise, whenever I come into your wine bar, I'll wear a long-sleeved shirt.'

***

Marjorie had just left for her habitual Monday morning jaunt to see Freda at Ramslye when the doorbell rang. Ted thought she must have forgotten something. But when he opened the front door, the shock he had was like a punch in the stomach.

'Donald! What are you doing here?'

Donald's voice shook. 'I'm sorry, Ted, I had to come round. I... I needed someone to talk to.'

Ted's eyes darted towards Mount Ephraim. Marjorie hadn't yet rounded the corner, he could just about make out her figure near the top of the road. If she happened to look back....

'Quick!' Ted grabbed Donald and pulled him inside. 'You must have walked right by Marjorie. She's only just left.'

Donald showed his friend the clipboard he was carrying. 'I didn't want to make things awkward for you, so I....'

He didn't get a chance to finish. Ted slammed the door shut. 'Let's go through to the kitchen. I'll make you a coffee.'

Donald followed him. 'I don't suppose you've got anything stronger?'

'Only cream sherry.'

Donald pulled a face. 'Coffee'll be fine.'

Ted switched the kettle on. When he turned to face Donald, he noticed there were tears in his friend's eyes.

'How's Bamber?'

'He's had the operation, poor kid. It's not looking good. His mother's with him. But it's not Bamber. It's just a lump of breathing flesh, wired up to all sorts of....' Donald broke off and slumped into a chair at the head of the kitchen table. His clipboard fell onto the floor.

'If there's anything I can do,' Ted began, then stopped, suddenly alert as he thought he heard a key in the front door. The latch clicked, followed by footsteps and the sound of the door closing.

'Oh God!' whispered Ted. 'It's her! It's Marjorie! She's come back. She must have forgotten something.'

Forty

Donald picked the clipboard up off the floor, whipped a pen out of his pocket and asked Ted how many times a month he purchased savoury snacks such as crisps or peanuts. Ted looked confused. Donald repeated the question as Marjorie entered.

'What's going on?' she demanded.

Ted was seized with panic, although his face registered nothing. 'It's... er....'

Donald came to the rescue. 'Consumer research. Your husband kindly agreed to do a short interview about savoury snacks. It's a random survey. Door-to-door.'

Marjorie rifled through an untidy bundle of free newspapers, unpaid bills and junk mail on the dresser, turning to glower at Donald.

'Waste of time, if you ask me.'

Donald smiled innocently. 'I know it seems like an intrusion but – who knows – you might win our star prize.'

'Prize?'

'Yes! Prize!' Donald said with exaggerated enthusiasm. 'We're giving every participant the chance to enter our grand draw. First prize a holiday for two in Florida.'

Marjorie looked astounded. Donald didn't dare look at Ted, in case he laughed.

'That's bloody typical, that is,' said Marjorie, and found what she was searching for. 'I go and book us a holiday in Florida, now you come and tell us we could win one.'

She waved a glossy travel brochure in the air like an exhibit in a murder trial. Donald suddenly seemed less sure of himself.

'You and your husband are going to Florida?'

Marjorie almost hugged the brochure. 'Week after next. I've always wanted to go.'

Donald looked at Ted, as if to say "you never told me". As usual, Ted's face was deadpan.

'Still, I don't s'pose we'd have won,' continued Marjorie. 'So it's just as well we booked. And we got a very good deal.'

As Marjorie went towards the door, Donald looked pointedly at Ted. 'I'm sure you'll both have a wonderful time.'

Marjorie stopped in the doorway. 'I nearly forgot the brochure to show Freda.' She stared at Donald. 'How long's this going to take?'

Donald shrugged. 'Oh, not long.'

'Only you said you'd pop down to the Halifax, Ted.'

Recovering his poise, Donald said brightly, 'It shouldn't take more than ten minutes. And I'll still enter you in the free prize draw. If you win, you can return to the land of milk and honey next year and relive some of those precious moments.'

Marjorie was studying him closely and he thought he might have gone too far. Perhaps she could see through his subterfuge.

'Would you mind if I asked you a few questions about savoury snacks?' he added hurriedly. 'It's always useful to have a partner's opinion.'

'Sorry, I'm in a rush.'

She turned and exited. Donald congratulated himself on that last little touch. It had done the trick. Got rid of the old cow.

'Now, I'd like you to tell me which brand of cheese and onion crisps you might have purchased in the last month?' he said loudly. Then the front door slammed and he burst into laughter.

Ted looked far from happy.

'I think I handled that brilliantly,' Donald boasted.

'Did you just happen to have the clipboard?' Ted asked.

'Bit of forward planning.'

'It was taking a bit of a risk.'

Donald smiled. 'But that's good in a relationship. An element of risk. Forbidden fruits have been denied me for so long.'

'You talk as if....' Ted stopped, finding it difficult to verbalise his confused thoughts.

'As if we're a couple?'

'What about Bamber?'

Donald pursed his lips, a fleeting guilty look passed across his face, and then he shrugged it off. 'Life must go on, dear boy.'

'But he's not....'

'Not dead yet? No. That's why I had to see you. When the inevitable happens, I'm going to need a close friend I can turn to. But now you're swanning off to Disneyworld with she of the sharp tongue.'

'It was Marjorie's idea.'

'So you're going off and leaving me just when I need you most.'

Ted looked down miserably. 'I like you, Donald. I enjoy going to the theatre with you, but....'

'But that's as far as you want it to go. Why do I always have to finish your sentences for you? You always leave them half finished.'

Ted looked up and grinned. 'I half start them, you mean.'

'I do believe that was a joke. You really are most attractive when you smile, Ted. Why don't you pop upstairs and put your uniform on for me? I like a man in uniform.'

Ted blushed. Donald laughed.

'The day you put your uniform on for me, I'll know it's the day our relationship has arrived.'

***

Savita stood in front of Malcolm's desk. He was clearly annoyed about something but was doing his utmost to restrain himself.

'Since when have you taken it upon yourself to alter my letters?' he said, patting the A4 sheet in front of him.

'I'm not with you,' Savita replied.

'You changed "at this moment in time" to "at present". Why?'

Savita shrugged. 'I thought it was less... well, better to use plain English and all that.'

Malcolm stared at her for a long time. She could tell he was thinking: What gives this little Asian girl a right to correct the big white chief's letters? But he didn't dare say it. Eventually he moved the letter to one side and spoke in a more reasonable tone.

'You and Nicky. I've seen you together. You seem to be very close. You were holding hands at the water cooler this morning.'

'Nicky was showing me a new ring she's just bought.'

'Pull the other one. You're both dykes, aren't you?'

Savita hesitated. This was going to be a test of her acting skills. 'Well, as a matter of fact....' she began.

Malcolm pounced. 'I thought as much.'

'No you're wrong,' Savita said, shaking her head. 'Nicky and I like the best of both worlds, if you know what I mean.'

She could see by the licentious glint that came into Malcolm's eye that his fantasies had gone into overdrive.

He gave a nervous, testing-the-water chuckle. 'You're not up for a threesome, are you?'

She tilted her head to one side, as if giving it serious consideration. 'We might be. But there's a huge "but" attached to it.'

Malcolm's eyes widened, like a child feasting them on mountains of ice-cream. 'Go on,' he urged.

'Nicky and I'll think about it. But only if you stop bullying us.'

Another nervous chuckle. 'I don't bully you. Just having a laugh, that's all. But I promise, if the three of us do have a scene together, things will be very different round here.'

Savita smiled and nodded. 'Okay. I'll go and have a word with Nicky, then I'll let you know when's a good time to come round to my flat.'

Leaving Malcolm palpitating and day dreaming, Savita returned to the main office. She went over to Nicky's desk and told her:

'Hook, line and sinker.'

Forty-One

The smell of grilled bacon wafted tantalisingly through the house. Betty sighed, looking at her watch. It was only 9.30. She reached for her goody-goody mid-morning snack, thinly-spread cream cheese between two slabs of Ryvita.

'Hungry?' Nigel said, making her start at she took her first bite.

Betty nodded guiltily, almost choking on the dry biscuits. Nigel grinned from the doorway. He had a habit of sneaking up on her like this and it always made her nervous.

'It's the smell of bacon that does it,' she mumbled through a mouthful of crumbs.

'Jackie's treating me to a cooked breakfast this morning. Later than usual, I'm afraid.'

Betty was irritated by the boastful way he said it, making it obvious that he and Jackie had been having fun and games in bed. She felt jealous. It was a long time since her Ron had felt amorous. Always too tired.

'Don't forget you've got a tender to get out this morning,' she reminded him, pleased to see his smile fade. 'Deadline's twelve o'clock.'

'I'll deliver it in person.'

'You've got to re-write the proposal first. All ten pages.'

Nigel tutted loudly.

'Breakfast is on the table, darling,' sang Jackie, sugar-sweetly from the kitchen.

'Coming!' Nigel called back. He smiled and winked at Betty. 'I'd better go and eat it. Keep her happy. I won't be long.'

Betty gave her Ryvita a resentful crunch and switched on the computer.

'Here we are, darling,' said Jackie as Nigel came into the kitchen. 'Don't let it get cold.'

Nigel sat at the table and stared approvingly at his full English breakfast, then frowned as he surveyed the rest of the table.

'Something wrong, darling?'

'There doesn't appear to be any brown sauce.'

'Oh, I forgot to buy any. There's tomato ketchup.'

'Tomato's not the same. I like brown sauce with my breakfast. I told you to make out a proper shopping list.'

'I thought I'd remember. When I got to the shop, it must have slipped my mind.'

Nigel squeezed a liberal blob of ketchup onto his plate. 'Oh, well – it'll have to do. But you must try and organise yourself, Jackie. Instead of just buying bits and pieces as and when we need it. If you can't remember things, write them down. It's always been my golden rule.'

Jackie slid into her seat opposite Nigel, and avoided looking at him. They ate in silence for a while. But the angry clatter of Jackie's cutlery indicated that something was wrong.

'Something the matter?' Nigel asked, sensing the change in his fiancée's mood.

'Brown sauce!' she hissed. 'Who cares a damn about brown sauce?'

Nigel chuckled, attempting to lighten the situation. 'Well, I do for one.'

'It's unfair of you to criticise like that. You know how worried I am about the girls.'

'What's that got to do with it?'

As she watched him greedily gobbling his food, something tightened inside her. 'It's got to do with the fact that perhaps I should go back home.' she snapped.

'Perhaps you should, if that's how you feel.'

His remark, she observed, didn't put him off his stride as far as eating was concerned. Somehow his enjoyment of the breakfast made her angrier. She was about to fire another shot across his bow when the doorbell rang.

'Oh no!' exclaimed Nigel. 'I'd forgotten, my hair's being trimmed this morning.' He scraped the knife around his plate hurriedly, and shovelled an enormous forkful of food into his mouth. He swallowed noisily and swilled it down with a gulp of tea.

'Can you let Mike in for me? While I give my hair a quick wash.'

Jackie frowned. 'Yes, but....'

'It's a simple enough request,' Nigel said as he left the room.

Sighing, Jackie followed Nigel into the hall. She dreaded meeting the hairdresser following all that business about his daughter's abortion. It was not the sort of confrontation she felt able to cope with, especially this morning, after Nigel's petty comments about the brown sauce.

***

Malcolm sat at his desk, staring at the screen saver on his PC monitor. His chosen image was of a subjective camera viewpoint weaving in and out of a maze. How fitting this image seemed now as he waited for the revenge he knew was winging its way towards him like a bird of prey.

God! What an idiot he'd been. To fall for a stunt like that. He went over and over the previous night's events. He couldn't get over the way he'd been set up. The way Savita answered the door to her flat, wearing that sexy negligee, and giving him the eye. Nicky was already lying in the double bed, duvet tucked up around her. He remembered thinking at the time, how peculiar this was, as if the girl was shy of showing any nakedness. It was only much later, when the disastrous event played back in his mind, that he realised Nicky was probably fully dressed.

How could he have fallen for such an obvious trap? He had let his stupid fantasies overshadow his reason. Savita had been so transparently acting out the part of a siren, luring him to his doom.

'We've already started without you, Malcolm,' she whispered sexily as she joined Nicky in bed. 'Why don't you get undressed and see what fun we can have?'

What an idiot! He couldn't believe he'd fallen for it. Undressing hurriedly, he saw the cruel amusement in Savita's eyes as she watched him. But he was too dumb to comprehend it at the time. As he walked, naked and proud towards the bed, that's when the young man dressed in black sprang through the doorway. Flash of the camera. Then he was gone. And Malcolm felt like bursting into tears. How could he have been such an arsehole?

To distract himself from more worrying thoughts of revenge and retribution, he opened up his emails, telling himself that maybe the two girls would just demand that he treat them a bit better in future. Neither of them had shown up for work this morning, so he had no idea what their demands would be.

He had about fifty emails. There were several with attachments, but the one that leapt out at him had as its subject "our insurance policy". He frowned. Even though they were an insurance company, there was something peculiar about the wording. He opened it up. It contained one sentence. It said:

"Unattractive, maybe. But an excellent likeness. Open it up, Malcolm."

Hands shaking, Malcolm clicked the mouse on the paper-clip icon. The colour photograph hit him like a ramrod in the guts. A full frontal of him, leering at the two girls in the background of the shot. And it was so obvious what his intentions were as he stood there. Naked. Naked and proud.

Forty-Two

When Jackie opened the door to Mike, she felt awkward; unable to look him in the eye.

'Nigel's got an important tender to get out this morning and his secretary's working on it,' she said in an affected manner. 'I wonder if you'd mind cutting his hair in the kitchen?'

'The kitchen's fine by me,' Mike replied, following her. Still unable to look at him, Jackie busied herself with clearing the dirty plates.

'Sorry about the mess.'

'Well, I don't expect you've had much time for housework.'

Jackie looked at him sharply.

'Haven't you just been on holiday?'

'Oh. Yes.'

Mike was enjoying her discomfort. He half smiled to himself, making certain she saw it, then pulled a chair from under the table for Nigel to sit on.

After an awkward silence, Jackie said in a subdued voice, 'I'm sorry if I caused you and your wife any problems when I rang up.'

Mike shrugged. 'Oh well... it's all water under the bridge now.'

'Your daughter... did she... has she....'

'Has she had an abortion, you mean? Yes, she has. And now it's all forgotten. Finished.'

Jackie put the plates carefully on the draining board, too embarrassed to disturb the awkward silence that hung in the air between them. Mike watched her, waiting to say what she had in mind. He saw the tension in her shoulders, and he saw her summoning the courage to speak as she turned to face him.

'Do you mind if Nigel and I pray for your daughter and her unborn child?'

'If that's what turns you on.'

'Why should it "turn me on"?'

'Well, own up, you wouldn't do it otherwise.'

He grinned at her. He felt he'd let her off lightly. And why not? He was in a good mood. He was seeing Maggie later on.

***

When Savita and Nicky strolled into his office at gone eleven, Malcolm noticed the malicious hint of a smile at the corners of Savita's mouth and the cruel glint in her eyes. Nicky seemed less sure of herself, almost as if she was still scared of him, although she now had the upper hand.

Savita was enjoying the drama of silence, while she watched Malcolm squirm. He coughed lightly before speaking, in a voice he barely recognised as his. More of a feeble croak.

'All right. What is it you want?'

'We're going for gold,' said Savita.

Malcolm frowned, genuinely puzzled. 'I'm not with you.'

'Exactly. You won't be with us for long. I want you to clear your desk. Sudden resignation.'

'You must be joking.'

'No. I'm serious. I want you gone by this afternoon.'

'But I can't do that.'

'My boyfriend followed you home two nights ago. He knows where you live. He can make sure your wife gets a copy of that photograph. You can choose. Marriage or job? What's it to be?'

'But – but this... this is ridiculous,' he stammered. 'It's blackmail.'

'We're not demanding any money.'

'It's still blackmail.'

'You're not in any position to argue or accuse us of any wrongdoing.'

As he stared up into Savita's vengeful face, Malcolm knew he would get no quarter from her. Maybe if he appealed to Nicky, she might be able to persuade her colleague. Once she saw how sorry he was.

'Nicky,' he began in a tremulous voice, 'I'm fifty-two years old. I've been in this firm now for nigh on twenty years. If I have to leave, I'll find it difficult to get another job. Especially if I walk out, resign for no reason at all. Please, Nicky. I'll let you have loads of time off work. I'll give you brilliant appraisals – so brilliant you'll have to have a pay rise. What do you say?'

Nicky pursed her lips. 'Well, I'm not sure.'

'I am,' snapped Savita. 'You're a worse than useless toad. A fat pathetic amoeba, and you're finished.'

Malcolm's eyes suddenly swam with tears. 'This isn't fair,' he blubbered. 'Please don't do this. Please. I beg you. I'll do anything.'

Nicky was embarrassed and looked away. So he looked pityingly into Savita's face, searching for some small deposit of mercy.

'Please, Savita. I know I behaved abominably, but... I've learnt my lesson. Everyone deserves a second chance.'

Then Nicky offered Malcolm his one last grasp of hope, the lifeline he was praying for. She turned to Savita and spoke softly, as if afraid to disturb all the emotion and turmoil that was happening before her.

'Savita, I think we ought to discuss this in private.'

Savita scowled at her. 'There's nothing more to discuss.'

'I think there is. Let's go out for a coffee and talk about it.'

Savita sighed and shook her head. 'Oh, Nicky. We mustn't weaken over this....' She threw a disparaging gesture in Malcolm's direction. 'This nasty tosser.

But... OK... if that's what you want. Let's have a nice long break and talk about it.'

They left Malcolm drying his eyes with a grubby handkerchief. 'Take as long as you want,' he called after them.

***

As soon as Mike had departed, Jackie rushed into the kitchen. Nigel was sweeping his hairs off the kitchen floor with a dustpan and brush.

'Darling, I'd like a word with you.'

'Not now. I've got an urgent tender to get out.'

'It won't take a minute. This is important. I don't want that man to cut your hair in future.'

'Mike? Why on earth not?'

'There's just something about him.'

'That's hardly a reason for dispensing of his services.'

'Please, darling, will you do it for me? There must be lots of other hairdressers.'

'But I still don't understand why.'

'Please. Will you do it just to please me? Because I love you.'

Nigel put the dustpan and brush on the work-top and put his arms around Jackie. 'I wouldn't want a haircut to come between us. And I'm sorry I complained about no brown sauce.'

She giggled contentedly and kissed him.

'I do wish though....' he began.

'What?'

'Remember what I told you about my sock stock rotation? You still haven't got that right yet.'

She pulled away from him and he could see she was struggling to contain her irritation.

'I'll buy you new socks. They do plain socks with different colours on the toes and heels. So there's no need to have one of your slaves darning in your sweatshop.'

'That's not the same, Jackie. I've tried those socks and they don't work. You can sometimes see a little bit of colour showing at the top of the heel. And that drives me insane.'

Jackie's eyes blazed. 'Drives you insane? You are insane!'

She swept out of the kitchen, and later on he heard the slam of the front door.

Forty-Three

As soon as they had sat down in Café Nero with their Cappuccinos, Savita shook her head, as if anticipating Nicky's objection to how she had handled the Malcolm situation.

'I'm not changing my mind about that man,' she said.

'But, Savita, we can't destroy his life.'

'Don't tell me you feel sorry for him.'

'Well... yes, I do.'

Savita blew on her coffee then took a tentative sip.

'The punishment,' Nicky went on, 'hardly fits the crime. So, okay, the man's a bully and a slimeball. But does that mean we have to totally destroy his life? It's probably true what he said: I doubt if he'll get another job at his age. Especially if he walks out for no apparent reason. And what's he going to tell his wife? My God! He'll be suicidal. He might even kill himself. Do we want that on our consciences?'

Savita stared thoughtfully at the froth on her coffee. After a while she looked directly into Nicky's eyes and said, 'I'll make a deal with you. I'll go along with his offer of good appraisals, and maybe a pay rise, and having an easy life at work....'

Nicky sighed. 'Thank God for that.'

'Providing,' Savita emphasised, 'that he doesn't find another whipping boy.'

'What d'you mean?'

'I mean, the leopard doesn't change his spots. Malcolm will leave us alone but he'll find someone else to pick on. So here's the deal. If we find out he's bullying someone else, we proceed with plan A. We destroy him. If he behaves himself, fair enough, we leave him alone – apart from having an easy time of it ourselves, of course.'

Nicky nodded thoughtfully as she considered this. 'So do we tell him? About what happens if he picks on somebody else, I mean?'

'Definitely not,' snapped Savita. 'What is the most common characteristic of bullies?'

Nicky shook her head and waited for the answer.

'They don't bully people in front of witnesses.'

'So,' said Nicky, 'how will we know if he's picking on someone else?'

'We both know,' Savita replied, 'from bitter experience, how miserable life becomes. If we see anyone looking depressed, we ask them what's wrong. Show some concern and compassion. They'll be glad to get it off their chest. And if it turns out to be Malcolm – well, that's it! He's finished. Is that a deal?'

Savita thrust a hand out towards Nicky.

'Deal!' said Nicky, and they shook hands on it.

***

'I love you,' said Mike.

Maggie ignored him and conjured up her diary on her iPhone. 'What are you doing on Friday the seventeenth?'

'Becoming an entry in your busy schedule,' Mike replied huffily.

'Don't get heavy, Mike.'

'Well, I thought it was supposed to be men who are supposed to treat sex casually.'

She tapped in the entry in her diary, deleted the image, and started to push him towards the front door. 'Time you were off.'

'Is that all you can say?'

'What d'you want me to say?'

'Didn't you hear me say "I love you"?'

She swung open the front door. 'Oh, grow up, Mike!'

He opened his mouth to speak but she cut in. 'Did you buy your wife those flowers?' He looked at her blankly. 'No, I didn't think you had.'

She slammed the door shut behind him.

'Women!' he shouted at her through the mottled glass. 'I'll never understand them.'

***

Dave, whose performances at Cromer ran for five days from Tuesday to Saturday, had driven Mary and the boys home to his house on Sunday, so that they could be back at school first thing Monday morning, having only missed one week following half term.

On Monday lunchtime, he was sitting in the kitchen with Mary, drinking tea and studying the form in the racing pages of his newspaper. 'Just popping out to see a man about a nag,' he suddenly announced, and rushed towards the back door, looking at his watch.

Mary looked up from the cook book she was reading. 'Dead cert, is it?'

Dave laughed. 'Something like that.'

As soon as he had gone, she became restless. He had left his newspaper behind and she noticed he had marked at least six horses in three races. She thought he would probably be out of the house for a good hour, at least. This was the opportunity she had been waiting for. Time to satisfy her curiosity.

She went out into the hall, pulled open the hall table and rummaged around until she found the key to the third bedroom. She hurried upstairs and pushed the key into the lock, nervously enjoying the film-like drama of the situation, which was a welcome relief from what had become a boring day.

The key turned easily and she pushed open the door. It was dark. Heavy curtains were drawn closed. She felt for the light switch and clicked it on. The room, lit by a naked light bulb, blazed with synthetic brightness.

Mary stared, frowning, unable to fully comprehend what she was seeing. Then she felt a movement behind her. She swung round just as his hand reached out to grab her.

'Dave!'

In his other hand he held the rolled-up newspaper that he had forgotten and come back for. How could she have been so stupid?

'You just couldn't keep your nose out of it, could you?'

He tightened his grip on her arm.

'Dave!' she cried. 'You're hurting me.'

Forty-Four

Seeing the fear on Mary's face, Dave let go of her arm. 'I'm sorry,' he said. 'I didn't mean to hurt you.'

Now that his anger had drained away, she saw the wounded look in his eyes and she felt sorry for him.

'It's my fault. I shouldn't have....' she began, and faltered.

'You were curious. Can't say as I blame you. In your shoes, I'd probably have done the same.'

He walked over to the window and drew the curtains. Daylight flooded into the room and Mary blinked, trying to take in what she was seeing.

'It's some sort of shrine,' she said slowly. 'To her.'

Dozens of framed photographs covered the walls; they were all of the same woman, mostly glamorous ten-by-eights. On a table, carefully arranged, lay toiletries and make-up, covered in a thin layer of dust. In front of the table, silk dressing gown neatly draped the back of a bentwood chair. A bundle of scrap books and photograph albums were stacked in a tidy pile beside the table. But the dominating feature of the room stood in a corner to the left of the door – a sequined dress, in shimmering silver and blue, adorned a dressmaker's dummy, crowned by a wig block with an auburn wig beneath a large floppy hat.

Mary stared at the faceless wig block and shivered, letting her breath out slowly. 'My God! This is so weird. It's like that film with – um – Anthony Hopkins. You know....'

Dave smiled thinly. 'I think you mean Anthony Perkins. In Psycho. Unless you mean Silence of the Lambs. But I hope I'm harmless, even if I am a bit round the twist.'

Mary felt the tight knot in her stomach relax. She smiled at him, then peered carefully at one of the framed photographs.

'She really beautiful, Dave. She must have been really special.'

'Oh, she was special all right!'

Mary continued to stare at the photograph, missing the irony of his tone.

'I couldn't hope to compete with her. Look at those breasts. So perfect. They've just got to be silicone implants.'

Dave laughed gratingly. 'Or hormone treatment.'

Mary stared at him, her eyes narrowing shrewdly as she began to suspect the truth.

'You'd never guess the truth, Mary. Not in a million years. Oh well – I guess it's confession time.'

He crossed to the pile of albums and selected a scrap book. He turned over a page as Mary peered over his shoulder. A newspaper cutting caught her eye.

'I knew it! She's a man! She's had a sex change!'

Mary read from the cutting. 'Yorkshire born civil servant Marilyn Whitby, previously known as John Whitby.'

Dave sank into the chair with a sigh. Mary bit her lip quickly as she tried to work it out.

'John Whitby. But that means he's your... brother?'

Dave picked up a mascara stick and fiddled with it. Apart from a buzzing in his ears, everything seemed deathly quiet. Unreal.

Mary waited for him to speak.

'I never really knew me dad. He left us when I were a nipper. Can't have been more than two – two and a half, maybe. When I was older, I asked me mam about him, but all she'd say was that he'd gone away to another country. And she'd no idea where. So that seemed to be that.

'Then, when I were about eleven – just about to start secondary school – Dad came home. Only I didn't know it were me dad. He'd changed, you see. Completely.'

Mary could feel her heart beating against her ribs. 'My God, Dave! This woman is your father.'

'And Mam never told me. Not till after he died. It took me a long time to get used to calling him "Dad" after that. I'd always known him as Aunty Marilyn, this mysterious, glamorous, long-lost relation who came to stay with us.'

'But... why didn't your mother tell you?'

'I don't know. How do you explain to a kid in his formative years that his old man's changed into a ravishing redheaded woman that most of your schoolmates fancy?'

Quietly, Mary replaced the scrap book on top of the pile. There was something she needed to ask Dave. She had already made up her mind that she would become his lover, but now there was something she had to know. She stood close behind him, both hands massaging his shoulders.

'Did you used to fancy your Aunty Marilyn?'

He nodded slightly. 'She used to sit me on her lap, cuddle me, and tuck me in at night. I used to get turned on. Though I never let it show. But as soon as the lights were out....'

'It's not your fault, Dave. You weren't to know.'

'There I'd be, hoping one night me Aunty Marilyn would climb into bed with me; enjoying every schoolboy's fantasy of being seduced by an attractive older woman. And all along it's me dad. No wonder I became a comedian. With an upbringing like that, what else could I be?'

Mary leant forward and gently kissed the side of his head. 'Try not to worry about it. You've got me to look after you now.'

Dave stood up and turned towards her, smiling. 'Come here, gorgeous. Let me kiss you.'

He pulled her towards him and she let him kiss her briefly. Then she pulled away, and said, 'Dave, just a minute. I want to hear the rest of it.'

'I'll tell you later. Right now, why don't we consummate our relationship?'

Mary glanced at one of the photographs. 'This is seriously weird. She still turns you on, doesn't she?'

'Does it bother you?'

Mary giggled and pressed herself closer to him. 'This is the best sort of therapy I can think of for now.'

Forty-Five

Nicky and Savita decided to take full advantage of the situation with Malcolm, so instead of hurrying back to the office they window-shopped in the Victoria Centre for a while, then had a buffet lunch at a new Chinese restaurant. When they returned to the office in the afternoon, other staff members stared at them, and it was obvious they had been the subject of office gossip.

Savita didn't care, without bothering to knock, she marched boldly into Malcolm's office, followed by Nicky. Malcolm was on the telephone.

'Er, listen, Roger, something important has just cropped up. As in crisis. Can I call you back in half-an-hour? OK. Speak to you later, mate.'

He hung up, then stared hard at Savita, his eyes glassy and remote, trying to conceal the hatred he felt for her. She let the silence stretch excruciatingly before she spoke.

'You're off the hook,' she said. 'Nicky felt sorry for you. Though I can't think why, you fat slug.'

Ignoring her insult, he looked towards Nicky, and mumbled, 'Thanks, Nicky. So what happens now? Where do we go from here?'

Nicky pursed her lips and thought about it. 'Well, we had a two hour lunch break.' She giggled. 'I expect we'll be having a lot of those.'

Malcolm shook his head, as if he couldn't quite believe what was happening. He cleared his throat noisily. 'I... er... I will of course be giving both of you excellent appraisals, with recommendations for a pay rise, but we have to be a bit subtle about your timekeeping. If the MD suspects something's going on, then its curtains for all of us. And about the photograph, I don't suppose there's any way you could....'

But Savita was already shaking her head. 'Don't be ridiculous,' she said. 'That was a digital photograph. And there's no way Damian's going to delete it. That's our passport to good behaviour, wanker. You don't mind if I occasionally call you wanker from now on? Just between the three of us, of course.'

There was a sharp rap on the door; it opened, and in walked Jeremy Clarison, the company MD. He raised his eyebrows quizzically and gave the two employees a half-smile and a nod.

'Malcolm,' he announced, 'I hope I'm not disturbing anything important.'

Malcolm swallowed noisily. His lips felt dry and his throat was parched. 'No, not all, Jeremy. Just going through some preliminary details of Savita and Nicky's quarterly appraisals which we are reviewing next week.'

The MD eased himself into a chair and crossed his legs. 'In that case, don't mind me. Pretend I'm not here. I'll be a fly on the wall, like the camera in a reality TV show. Please carry on.'

Malcolm's tongue felt furred-up, large and cumbersome when he tried to speak. 'Um – well – thank you for the hard work, girls. Carry on as you are doing. I mean, keep m-motivating the team as you have been doing, and your appraisals will be....' Malcolm's brain seized up. He made two forward slices with his hands instead. Then recovering slightly, he said, 'Excellent work so far. Excellent. Thank you for coming in to discuss it.'

Savita and Nicky exchanged an amused expression before exiting. As soon as they had gone, Malcolm offered the MD a feeble smile, as if this would suffice as an explanation for his odd behaviour. After an uncomfortable pause, the MD frowned and studied his fingernails carefully before speaking.

'What was all that about, Malcolm? I mean, if you are doing quarterly appraisals next week, why a sort of preview? Bit of a waste of time, if you ask me.'

Beads of sweat had broken out on Malcolm's forehead, and his face was mottled. 'I – um – just wanted a quick word with them. Good workers. Good workers.'

The MD stared at Malcolm in deep concentration. 'Are you feeling all right, Malcolm? You really look most peculiar.'

Just for an instant, it occurred to Malcolm to confide in Jeremy. Bloke to bloke, he might understand. I mean, he thought, what bloke hasn't been tempted like that? A threesome. Bit of lesbian coupling. Male fantasy, and all that. But Jeremy Clarison was old school. A bit old fashioned. About to have an enormous twenty-fifth wedding celebration. No, bit too risky. He might find himself clearing his desk in double-quick time.

'As a ma-matter of fact,' Malcolm stammered, 'I don't feel well. Might be a virus that's doing the rounds. I feel hot and cold all the time.'

'I think you'd better take the rest of the day off,' Clarison said. 'What a nuisance. I interrupted my annual leave to come and ask you....' He sighed deeply and shook his head.

'What?' Malcolm said.

'I fancied a round of golf at the Neville, and I'd got no one to partner me.'

***

Mary snuggled close to Dave, her hand gently stroking the hairs on his chest.

'How was it for you?' she giggled softly.

'Fair dos. It were awright that!'

She giggled again, then became serious. 'That's something I noticed about you – your accent. It became really broad when you were talking about your childhood.'

'It's impossible to escape from the past.'

'Is that what you're trying to do?'

'Not escape, exactly – no. I've just not been able to confront the past – up until today. But I'm glad I was able to tell you. To share it with you.'

She pecked his cheek. 'So am I.'

From downstairs there came the sound of the letter box swinging open, followed by the plop of something heavy dropping onto the mat. Dave looked at the bedside clock.

'Bit late for a second post.'

Mary got out of bed and threw on her dressing gown. 'I'll go, and I'll make us a cup of tea.'

While she went downstairs, Dave leapt naked out of bed and peered through the net curtains at the window. He was just in time to see his argumentative neighbour's son crossing the street back to his parent's house.

Mary screamed: 'Ugh! This is disgusting! Someone's posted something....'

Dave grabbed his dressing gown and dashed downstairs.

'It's all right,' said Mary, shaking. 'I thought at first it was dog's muck. But it's a pile of tea leaves and tea bags.'

She was surprised to notice that Dave looked pleased.

'I saw him,' he said. 'It was my neighbour's son. That's him what's been making all those phone calls, I'll bet. And now we've got him. Bang to rights!'

Forty-Six

'Can I come in?' Claire knocked lightly on Andrew's door and entered. She caught him hurriedly hiding an A4 sheet under a magazine on his desk.

'I was just....' he started, a trace of guilt in his tone.

Claire sat on the edge of the bed, waiting for him to continue. He sat at his desk, half turned away from her, absently doodling on the magazine.

'Just what?' she ventured after a brief silence.

He shrugged. 'Oh – nothing much. Just making a few notes.'

'What about?'

'Nothing that would interest you.'

'How d'you know it wouldn't?'

'I just know.'

'Who's this Mr Bannerman who wanted you to phone him?'

'Oh – I've already spoken to him.'

'So who is he?'

'Just a bloke who's doing some work for me.'

'What sort of work?'

'He's an investigator, if you must know.'

'An investigator! You mean like in private investigator?'

Embarrassed, Andrew turned toward the computer screen and moved the mouse.

'Andrew, has this got anything to do with that writer Chloe was telling us about?'

'I wish I hadn't told her now. I should have kept my mouth shut.'

'What's going on? What are you up to?'

Andrew tensed briefly, then turned round to face his mother, suddenly feeling the need to share his feelings with her.

'I hired this bloke from an ad in the Yellow Pages, to see what he could uncover about the writer.'

'Oh Andrew! What the hell d'you think you're up to?'

Andrew turned back to the computer screen. 'I knew you wouldn't understand.'

'How much is this costing?'

'What's that got to do with anything?'

'Because I don't want to see you throwing your money down the drain. The money Nanny left you.'

'Exactly. It's my money. She left it to me.'

'I'm sure she didn't intend you to chuck it away on some – some hair-brained nonsense.'

'I wish I hadn't told you now.'

'Andrew, why do you get so obsessed about everything?'

'What d'you mean?'

'It was the same with the computer. Then the fruit machines. You never do anything in half measures; you become thoroughly wrapped up in them, to the exclusion of everything else. Why can't you just behave normally?'

'You saying I'm abnormal?'

'Of course not – it's just that – why d'you get so involved with something that doesn't concern you?'

'It does concern me. It concerns all of us. You know what the book was about, don't you?'

Claire tried to stop herself from sighing, knowing it would irritate her son, and let her breath out slowly.

'I know it's about the arms industry.'

'Yeah... well... it's pretty sickening. I've been researching it myself – on-line. Never mind this new deal for Africa and all that rubbish about wiping out debts. D'you realise how many billions of pounds this country is still making selling arms to countries like Malawi and....

Concerned, Claire automatically pressed her hand onto Andrew's. He snatched it away, as if he'd been scalded.

'Look, we all know how terrible that sort of thing is....' she began weakly.

Andrew slammed his hand down on the desk. 'But we don't know. We only think we know.'

Claire tried to remain calm, speaking softly, almost in a whisper. 'And what have you asked this Bannerman bloke to do?'

'Try to find out who was printing the writer's book. They might still have a copy.'

'So you're paying this bloke good money to do something you could easily do yourself.'

'How d'you mean?'

'Well, you don't work during the week. Presumably this firm of investigators will just contact all the local printers, which is something you could have done yourself. Dad would have helped you.'

Andrew looked surprised, then frowned and shook his head.

'You could have tried asking him,' Claire persevered. 'Maybe it's the sort of thing he would have liked to get involved in.'

A moody, sullen expression clouded Andrew's face. 'I doubt it.'

Claire suddenly ran out of patience. 'So now what? What happens if you manage to find this a printer who's got a copy of the book? What then?

'That's my business.'

'Oh, suit yourself. Chuck all that money away.'

Claire stormed angrily out of the bedroom and clumped downstairs to the kitchen. As soon as she had gone, Andrew tugged the A4 sheet from beneath the magazine and studied the notes he'd written about arms dealing. He frowned deeply. If only he could spell. And if only he could find the right words to express himself.

***

Thrusting the bag of old tea leaves and tea bags under the uniformed constable's nose, Dave said, 'What you gonna do about it then?'

The constable wrote laboriously in his notebook. 'Teabags were posted through your front door.'

'And tea leaves,' said Dave, indignantly.

Mary sat in the armchair opposite the policeman and felt sorry for him. He could have been quite good looking if it wasn't for the fact that he was plagued by spots and his ears stuck out like jug handles.

The constable, struck by inspiration, stopped writing and looked up. 'Which would seem to indicate that the perpetrator of this act uses fresh tea as well as tea bags.'

Mary caught Dave's eye and put a hand over her mouth. The policeman saw her and blushed.

'Never mind that,' said Dave. 'I told you who it was. My neighbour's son.'

'But you didn't actually see him posting the tea, sir. Only walking away from the house. What other reasons have you got for thinking it might have been him?'

'I had words with his father.'

'Oh?' The policeman regarded Dave suspiciously. 'What about?'

'Well, I....' Dave began floundering.

Mary came to his rescue. 'It was an argument about car parking. Dave bought an old banger and left it outside his house. It was in the papers.'

'Oh, so that was you, was it?' The policeman's tone was censorious.

'I was proving a point,' Dave said defensively. 'It's not there anymore. I've had the car removed.'

The policeman flipped his notebook shut and stood up. 'I think the best thing I can do is wander over to the neighbour's house and have a word.'

'Is that all? What about the phone calls? The bloke ought to be prosecuted.'

'It might be difficult to prove, sir. Right – I'd best be on my way.' He nodded to Mary.

Dave followed him to the front door. 'I'll see you out.'

'Just be grateful, sir, it was nothing worse than tea bags.'

Mary smiled to herself as she pictured Dave's reaction to this parting remark. The front door slammed and a second later Dave was back in the living room, spluttering with indignation.

'Did you hear that? Bloomin' heck! I know they say you're getting old when coppers start to look young, but he still had teenage acne!' He noticed Mary smiling at him. 'What are you grinning at?'

'I think you're sweet.'

He came over and puts his arms around her.

'Just a minute, Dave: apart from the kids coming home from school any minute now, don't you want to see what happens in the house opposite?'

'Quick!' he yelled. 'We can get a better view from the bedroom.'

They ran upstairs, giggling and snorting like naughty children.

Forty-Seven

No direction, no meaning to life, nagged and worried Claire as she sat at the kitchen table, surrounded by piles of advertising material that needed collating. She stared into space, feeling empty and depressed.

She heard the front door opening and, not wanting to be caught in an indulgently introspective mood, continued working. Mike entered and made a beeline for the kettle.

'What's all this?' he demanded, as if she had no right to use the kitchen table.

'Alan's got these "Pub Grub in Summer" leaflets to get out.'

'Bloody weather,' Mike complained. 'I can't stand this heat.'

'You complain when it's cold, you complain when it's raining; in fact, all you ever do these days is complain.'

'I wouldn't mind if it was sunny, but it's oppressive heat.'

'If it wasn't for the weather, I wonder what we'd find to talk about.'

'It's the country's favourite topic.'

'I was talking about us.'

'Yes,' said Mike, as he stood over the kettle, waiting for it to boil. 'Ditto.'

Claire stared at him, wondering if he was joking or serious. His humour often verged on the sarcastic, and he was downright rude occasionally. But she had felt the sting of truth in his statement. Their communication seemed to have broken down a long time ago.

'Mike,' she began tentatively, 'why don't we take a short break? Go away somewhere for four or five days. France, maybe. It wouldn't cost much.'

He shook his head. 'I can't. I've got too many clients who want their hair cutting right now. Especially on a Saturday.'

'But everyone's entitled to a holiday. Put them on hold for a week.'

'I can't do that.'

Claire felt some anger welling inside her. 'It's like you don't want to spend time with me.'

Avoiding her eyes, Mike fetched milk from the fridge.

'Don't be daft.'

'What with Chloe and Andrew, we've been under a lot of pressure lately. We need some time together – on our own – to recharge the batteries.'

She got up from the table, walked over to him, and touched his hand gently. As if stung, he withdrew it, almost knocking over his mug.

'What's wrong?'

'Nothing. I just can't stand being touched like that.'

'Like what?'

'Softly. It's repulsive.'

Hurt and angry, she glared at him. Their eyes met, and in that brief moment she knew.

'Who is she, Mike?'

'Who? What are you talking about?'

But the innocent, puzzled look didn't fool her. And no matter how hard he would try to deny it – and perhaps go on denying it – she knew.

***

'Hello! I'm home,' Jackie called out, dreading what she might find. She heard the blaring theme tune to the Pointless quiz coming from the living room and breathed a sigh of relief. Everything appeared to be normal.

Vanessa, wearing the designer scruffy denims Jackie hated so much, came out of the kitchen, clutching a pot of yoghurt.

'Oh. Hi, Mum!'

Jackie wondered if her daughter was surprised or disappointed that she had come home.

'Where's Nicky?' she asked.

Vanessa inclined her head towards the living room. 'Watching Pointless.' She nodded at her mother's suitcase near the front door. 'You're back then.'

Jackie hesitated. 'Well... I felt guilty about leaving you both for so long.'

Vanessa smiled with amusement. 'Understandable. It wasn't a party, though. It was a rehearsal.'

Jackie tittered apologetically. 'It was still pretty loud.'

Brushing past Vanessa, she entered the kitchen. 'I suppose there's piles of washing-up to do... Oh! It's not as bad as I expected.'

'You sound disappointed.'

'Well, I suppose I miss a little bit of mess after being at Nigel's. He's such a fusspot. He likes to keep everything "ship-shape".'

Vanessa's lip curled scornfully. 'Don't I know it. So does this mean you've come home because you miss us both, or because you've had another row with him?'

'I... I don't know what he expects. Everything I do is wrong.' Her face crumpled and she burst into tears. 'Oh, Vanessa! I'm so unhappy. I just wanted to come home.'

She launched herself at her daughter and sobbed on her shoulder. Toffee flavoured yoghurt spilled out of the pot in Vanessa's hand onto the carpet tiles.

Hearing her mother crying, Nicky popped her head round the door, though with some reluctance.

'Oh, Mummy... er... sorry you're upset. I'll just find out what happens to the final two contestants in the head-to-head, then I'll be right back.'

Forty-Eight

Heaving and puffing, Ted struggled through the door pulling the heavy suitcase, and he was also carrying Marjorie's heavy overnight case. Marjorie carried a bag of Duty Frees and an enormous Mickey Mouse soft toy.

'Mind the paintwork,' she said, as she hurried to the hallstand mirror to admire her sun-tanned reflection.

Ted slammed the door shut with his foot. 'We should have got a taxi,' he grumbled, letting Marjorie's bag drop.

'We're not made of money. It's not as if we're far from the station.'

Ted straightened his back and groaned pointedly. 'It's all right for you. You didn't have to struggle up the hill with them.'

'You're out of condition, that's your trouble.'

Marjorie took one last look at herself, then walked down the hall towards the kitchen. 'I'm exhausted after that journey. Could do with a cup of tea.'

Ted followed her into the kitchen. She put the bag of Duty Free gin, cream sherry and perfume on the table, then propped Mickey Mouse sitting up against them. She flopped into a chair.

'Put the kettle on, Ted. I've had it.'

Instinctively, Ted did as he was asked, but couldn't resist commenting, 'Yes, you must be tired. You've had to lug that rodent all the way from America.'

'There's no need to be sarcastic.' She touched Mickey's nose affectionately. 'I've always had a soft spot for Mickey Mouse – ever since I was so high.'

Ted slammed a mug down forcefully. 'Cost a fortune it did.'

'Everyone's entitled to come back from their hols with a souvenir of some sort.'

'It was embarrassing. Sitting on the plane cuddling it. It's not as if....' He broke off, afraid to say what he thought.

'Not as if we've got any children. Is that what you were going to say? And whose fault is that?'

Ted felt the side of the kettle, wishing it would hurry up and boil.

'You could have had tests, you know,' Marjorie continued accusingly. 'But you were too embarrassed.'

'If I remember rightly, it was you who didn't want me to have the tests done. You refused to talk about it. I was quite willing to....'

Marjorie snapped, 'Then why didn't you? Why d'you always have to do everything I say?'

Confused, Ted looked down at his feet, feeling he was in a no-win situation.

Irritated, Marjorie stormed to the larder in a renewed burst of energy and fetched the biscuit tin.

'Not that it matters now,' she said. 'I'm forty-five and you'll be fifty-two soon. Doesn't time fly when you're having fun?'

Ted stared at her. The way she chomped on a chocolate Hobnob made him want to throttle her. As if she could sense what he was thinking, her eyes fixed him in her sights.

'What's wrong?' she demanded.

His voice uncomfortably husky, he asked, 'Do you regret not having had children?'

'You know I do.'

'No, I don't know that. We've never talked about it. Not since – not since years ago, anyway.'

'Does it matter?' Her hand disappeared into the biscuit tin and she speared another Hobnob.

Ted sighed deeply. 'No, I don't suppose it does.'

Marjorie crunched into the biscuit and spoke through a mouthful of crumbs. 'I think I'll take my tea upstairs. Have a nice soak in the bath.'

'There'll be no hot water yet.'

Marjorie tutted. 'Run upstairs and put the immersion on, would you?' She saw the pained expression on his face. 'Or must I do everything myself?'

***

As he began cutting Nigel's hair, Mike said, 'You know, it's strange, but I thought I'd lost a customer for a minute.'

Nigel could feel himself colouring. After a telling pause, he asked, 'How d'you mean?'

'Well, after that business about your girlfriend phoning my wife up, I thought it would lead to... I don't know... I got the impression your girlfriend wouldn't like to see me around.'

Nigel cleared his throat nosily. 'Actually, I'm still master of my own house.'

'Where is she?' Mike asked pointedly.

Another pause. 'She's gone back to her place for a few days. We had a disagreement.'

'Not about me, I hope.'

'Don't flatter yourself, Mike.' Realising it came out sounding rude, Nigel chuckled and added, 'It's just that it's hard to understand women.'

'Tell me about it,' said Mike, his mind winging its way into Maggie's bed.

Although there was no one who could overhear them, Nigel's voice dropped to almost a whisper. 'If I tell you....' he began.

'What?'

'You know how I met Jackie, through the dating service? Well, this other woman got in touch with me only yesterday. She looks very attractive. And she sounds as though she's really up for it, if you catch my drift.'

Intrigued, Mike pretended ignorance. 'I'm not with you. When you say "up for it"....'

Nigel sniggered like a dirty schoolboy. 'I spoke to her on the phone. Sounds like she just wants a good stuffing.'

Mike choked back a laugh. 'Really. How come?'

'Some of the things she was saying. Suggestive, rude things. Yes, I think she's really up for it. What would you do, if you were me?'

However boring Nigel was, a little bit of intrigue would liven up Mike's occasional visits to cut his hair. So he said, 'There's only one rule in life, where philandering is concerned. Don't get caught. Just treat it as a final fling before you get married.'

Nigel nodded his head vigorously, so that Mike had to shift the scissors back.

'Thank you, Mike. I think I might do that. I mean, what harm can come of it?'

'None at all,' said Mike, hoping and praying that Jackie would find out.

Forty-Nine

While Marjorie was soaking in the bath, Ted dialled Donald's number and waited, tense and alert. As soon as Donald answered, he spoke quickly and quietly.

'It's me – Ted. I'll have to be quick. Marjorie's in the bath.'

Donald chuckled. 'I had a feeling you were going to ring tonight. How was the holiday? Rekindled any old amorous feelings towards wifie?'

'I'll tell you about it later.'

Donald exaggerated the eagerness in his voice. 'Really!'

'I mean about the holiday.'

Flatly, Donald replied, 'Yes, that's what I thought you meant. So can we meet later?'

'No, I can't. Not tonight. I was phoning to see how Bamber is.'

'I haven't escaped the assault of Heavy Metal on my eardrums.'

'What?'

'Bamber's fine. It wasn't malignant. He's recuperating at his mother's in Lewes.'

The news was slow to hit Ted. He opened his mouth to speak but couldn't find the right words.

'Hello? You still there, Ted?'

Ted panicked. 'I've got to go. Marjorie's coming. I'll ring you tomorrow.'

He hung up. It was a lie. Marjorie was still soaking in the bath. Why had he hung up so suddenly? Was it because he was disappointed? Had he been expecting news of Bamber's death, and was now disappointed because he was going to have to share Donald's friendship again?

***

As Dave drove down Yew Tree Road his depression lifted a bit. He was flat broke, but at least he now had someone to share his problems. His credit cards were already stretched to breaking point, but what the hell! Soon he would find some solace in Mary's embraces. He glanced at his watch. It was just gone half-twelve. They would have a few hours in bed together before the kids were due home from school.

As luck would have it, he found a parking space near his house, and noticed his neighbour opposite had taken to putting a cone outside his house when they were out. Trying to stop the High Brooms to London commuters from parking. Dave found this annoying. After all, the man had no right. It was all very well stopping the commuters from parking, but Dave had every right to park his car wherever he chose.

As he opened the front door, he heard the pounding beat of music coming from the kitchen. He didn't want to make Mary jump, so he called out:

'Hello! It's me. I'm home.'

The radio was switched off. Mary looked startled as he entered.

'Dave! What are you doing home? I thought you'd be performing tonight.'

'The management have gone bust. It's all gone belly up.'

Mary opened her mouth wide before speaking, pantomiming alarm. 'Oh, what! I hope they paid you off.'

'A big fat nothing. Sod all. The management went into receivership before anyone got a penny. What a washout.'

***

'It's for you,' said Vanessa, handing her mother the phone. 'Lover boy.'

199

Jackie tutted and scowled at Vanessa as she took it. She heard Nigel's braying laugh at the other end of the phone.

'I heard that,' he said.

'I'm sorry....' Jackie began.

'So am I,' he purred. 'I know I'm not the easiest person to live with but I intend to mend my ways.' He dropped his voice to an affectionate whisper. 'Sugar-pie?'

'Y-e-s?' Jackie answered cautiously.

'Wedding bells will still ring out in the Autumn, won't they?'

'I still love you, Nigel. But I think it would be better if I lived here with the girls until then.'

She pressed the telephone closer to her ear. Nothing. A wall of petulant silence. 'Hello? Nigel? You still there?'

'It's about the open air concert I said I'd take you to next week. It's a bit tricky. I've got to go away on business. A C.T.I. course.'

'A what?'

Computer Telephone Integration. Must keep abreast of the latest technological developments, you know.'

Jackie sighed understandingly. 'Oh well, not to worry. You mustn't let a concert stand in the way of work. It's your livelihood, after all.'

She was so understanding, Nigel began to feel guilty. They said their goodbyes, blowing kisses down the line, then gently clicked down their telephones.

Nigel sat at his office desk, thoughtfully chewing his lip. On the desktop lay his Bible. He picked it up and tears swam into his eyes.

'Forgive me,' he whispered. 'I won't ever lie like that again. I promise. But it's not as though we're married yet. And I could do with a little....'

He searched hard to find the right words, not wishing to offend the Almighty, or whoever might be listening. Eventually he found the least offensive euphemism.

'A little break,' he said. 'After all, I've worked hard this year.'

Then he opened the bottom drawer, tucked the Bible out of mind, and telephoned his lonely heart contact.

Fifty

A ndrew lay on his bed, eating his lunch – a bowl of Coco-Pops. His father barged into the room and jumped straight to the point.

'I hear you've been spending your money hiring a private eye.'

Andrew flushed. 'So what?'

'When are you going to start growing up?'

Andrew looked up at his father's towering figure and shrugged irritatingly. 'It's my money.'

Mike felt like smacking the cereal bowl out of his hands. He controlled himself and said, 'It won't last long, the way you're carrying on. Then what're you gonna do?'

'I'll cross that bridge when I come to it.'

'What's that supposed to mean?'

'I haven't a clue. But you're always saying it.'

Shaking his head, Mike sat heavily on the flimsy plastic chair by his son's desk. 'So how much have you spent so far?'

'Not much.'

'Can you be more specific?'

'Between four and five hundred.'

'And what has this gumshoe come up with?'

Andrew stopped spooning cereal into his mouth and frowned. 'You what?'

'Gumshoe,' Mike explained sarcastically, 'is an American word for a private dick.'

'There's no need to make it sound so....' Andrew felt ridiculed and lapsed into a sulky silence.

'Corny is the word you're looking for,' continued Mike. 'As in cloak and dagger. And what exactly has this investigator found out so far?'

Andrew avoided his father's eyes. 'The trail went cold. The printers didn't have a single copy of the book. Someone had been along to collect them. Every single one.'

'So that's that then.'

Andrew pursed his lips. 'I suppose so.'

'And you paid over four hundred quid just to find a firm of printers?'

Andrew nodded unhappily and picked at a hang-nail.

'So now what?' Mike demanded.

'The investigation agency said the only possibility was to try and trace whoever took the books away.'

Mike laughed humourlessly. 'I bet they did. It's a nice little earner for them.'

'Actually, they recommended that I drop the investigation. Don't waste your money, they said.'

Andrew's head sunk miserably onto his chest. He looked so vulnerable, Mike went over and eased himself onto the bed, facing him.

'Listen, Andy, I know how important this has been to you....'

'No, you don't. You've hardly talked about it.'

'Why don't we pop out for a beer tonight? You can tell me all about it then.'

Andrew seemed embarrassed. 'You wouldn't be interested. And I know what'll happen in the pub. You'll start mouthing off about what I'm doing – all the research about the arms industry and that – and you'll get into an argument.'

'We needn't sit near the bar.' Mike stared at his son, waiting for him to capitulate. 'Well?'

'I'll think about it.'

Mike lost patience. Sighing, he glanced at his watch and stood up. 'I've got to get back to work. I'll see you later.'

Andrew didn't reply. As soon as he heard his father leaving the house, he got up off the bed and took a sheaf of A4 papers out of the bottom drawer of his desk. He took a last look at the untidy hand-written notes. Not being academically inclined, he had found the research demanding. He consigned the notes into the waste-bin, slumped into his chair and switched on the computer.

***

'Ted!' Marjorie yelled. 'What d'you think you're doing?'

Ted was about to open the front door. 'I told you. I'm off to work.'

Marjorie, almost speechless with shock, stammered, 'But you... you... you're wearing your uniform.'

Ted smiled. 'That's because I work on the railway.'

'Yes, but I thought we agreed that....'

'I never agreed to anything,' Ted interrupted. 'It was your idea.'

'What about the neighbours?'

'Oh, bollocks to the neighbours!'

Ted marched out of the house, relishing the stunned expression on his wife's face. He was equally delighted to bump into his next door neighbour, the wife of an advertising executive.

'Good afternoon,' he said brightly.

She didn't answer. She wore the same stunned expression as Marjorie.

***

'Nearly done,' Mike said snipping the last few hairs at the nape of Graham Harlow's neck. 'It's a bit too hot for work. Humid.'

'Oh, I love this weather. Can't get enough of it. It makes me feel really positive.'

'Any success with the book yet?' Mike asked with genuine interest.

Graham Harlow, in his early sixties, was an ex teacher who had taken early retirement to work as a writer. He had had one novel published, which hadn't made him very much money, and had written mainly technical booklets and magazine articles. But the huge success always seemed to be teetering, just out of reach.

'I finished my new novel, which is set in America. And now I've got an American literary agent, and she's sent it to a Hollywood producer – a contact of hers.'

'Oh, nice one, Graham. Fingers crossed, eh? And how's your love life?'

'Fantastic. Two years we've been together now.'

Mike took the mantle from around Graham's shoulders and shook the hairs onto the carpet. 'No plans to move in together?'

'We both like our own space. We intend to keep it that way. Pauline's a keen golfer, and I'm not really interested. Four times she's played this week. So I only get to see her once this week, at the golf club dinner and dance.'

'That's more than enough time to spend with a partner,' said Mike.

Graham laughed dutifully, then became serious. 'Oh I'd like to spend a lot more time with Pauline. But she's always so busy.'

He paid for the haircut and showed Mike to the front door of the flat. Then he went and got the vacuum cleaner out of the cupboard, intending to clear the hairs from the carpet. Instead, he was distracted by the open window, and went and looked out into the communal garden. Life felt so good. His relationship made him feel positive about his chances of making a success of his second novel. Little did he realise that his life was about to fall apart.

Fifty-One

Following Ted's outburst, Marjorie stood in the hall, paralysed by shock. She felt nauseous and thought she might faint, so she steadied herself against the hallstand. Gradually the feeling passed, giving way to a sudden craving to eat something sweet and sickly.

She rushed into the kitchen, opened the fridge, grabbed the remains of a Black Forest gateau, then sat at the table and shovelled it into her mouth as if she hadn't eaten for weeks.

'That's better,' she sighed when she had finished. She looked towards the larder, wondering if she could still fancy a chocolate biscuit, and the picture calendar that hung from a rusty hook on the wall nearby caught her eye. She stared at the beach scene with a blazing sun, and frowned. Then she got up, fetched the calendar from the wall, and turned back the pages slowly until she reached March, a picture of lambs gambolling in a field. Her lips felt dry. The cake had made her thirsty. She fancied a cup of tea now. But that would have to wait. She went out into the hall, picked up the phone and dialled the number she knew off by heart. It rang a long time before the receptionist answered.

'It's Mrs. Blackburn. Marjorie Blackburn,' she said when she got through. 'I'm a patient of Doctor Jordan. Would he be able to see me today?'

***

At midnight on Saturday, the golf club dinner and dance began to wind down for a half-twelve finish. Graham and Pauline got up for a final smoochy slow number. He held her tight while she sang along to James Blunt's "Your Beautiful", softly in his ear.

Their taxi arrived bang on half-twelve and they both fell into the back. When they got back to her house, she invited him in for a brandy night cap, then they lay back on the sofa, both a little tipsy after so much wine.

'I checked in my old diary,' Graham said. 'On Wednesday it will be the second anniversary of our first date. We ought to do something.'

She avoided looking at him. 'I'm playing golf on Wednesday.'

'In the evening. I'd like to take you out for a meal to celebrate.'

'There's a meal being laid on after golf. I will have eaten.'

'OK then,' he persisted. 'Maybe we could go out somewhere for a drink afterwards.'

There was the briefest of silences, before her rush of words. 'I can't go on like this anymore. I really can't. I can't carry on this way. It's got to end. I can't make love to you anymore.'

It was so unexpected, at first he couldn't take it in. But he could see by the tension in her body that this was for real. It was showdown time and floods of uncontrollable tears ran down his cheeks.

'But we can't split up,' he sobbed.

'I just don't think we can be lovers anymore. I'm not in love with you, and I feel it's wrong when we make love.'

'But why now, so suddenly?'

'I'm sorry,' she sighed. 'I didn't want to hurt you. I really didn't. I did try to tell you some time ago. I said I wasn't in love with you. I like you, but I don't love you.'

'Yes, I remember. That was last September, when we got back from that barbecue. And at the time I said I didn't want to replace your Colin's love. I know how much you loved him up until his death. But I remember telling you that I wasn't trying to replace him, or airbrush him out of your history, and I was quite happy to settle for affection and respect. And our relationship seemed to be

OK after that. For a good nine months for Christ's sake. So what's suddenly happened to change all that?'

'Nothing,' she said, her mouth setting tightly.

He gulped back the brandy and demanded another. She brought the bottle and he poured himself an enormous measure. As he stared down at the drink, more tears blurred his vision, and his voice shook with emotion.

'There's someone else,' he said. 'You've met someone else.'

'I haven't. It's just that I don't want to carry on making love to someone I'm not in love with.'

Anger crept into his voice. 'In these scenarios, there's always someone else. The reason you've given me is... well, it's pathetic. There must be another bloke.'

He gulped back another mouthful of brandy, his head now reeling from the drink and the bad news.

Her voice dropped to almost a whisper. 'Don't take this the wrong way. There is someone I've known for thirty years. Before I met Colin. And I always fancied this person. I still do. I had a do here last Saturday, and he stayed the night. But he slept in the spare room. And I promise you nothing happened. And perhaps nothing will. It's complicated. He's having an affair with a woman who's married.'

'Oh, this gets better and better,' Graham shouted, then took a swift gulp of brandy. 'And you had a do last Saturday. Barbecue, was it? And I expect you invited all your friends round. Most of those we saw tonight. So why wasn't I invited?'

'I feel guilty – so guilty – about that. But it wasn't possible to invite you as well.'

'You mean, as well as this other bloke.'

Almost imperceptibly, she nodded her head.

'Can you remember the Friday before your do, by any chance? You came round to my place for dinner. And we made love afterwards.'

'I'm sorry,' she whispered. 'I really didn't want to hurt you. I like you. But I just can't go on with it anymore.'

He knocked back more brandy. By now he was slurring and feeling numb from the depression that had hit him. They talked for another hour but found nothing new to say. Eventually, having drunk three-quarters of the brandy, he fell asleep on the sofa, dead to the world.

He woke up at eleven in the morning, and rather than feeling weirdly disoriented from the hangover, and the fact that this was the first time he had slept in her spare room, he knew immediately where he was and what had happened. His trousers and jacket lay in a crumpled heap on the floor, but he was still wearing his dress shirt. Then he happened to look out the window into the back garden, and the anger rose in his throat like bile. He let out the worst obscenities he could think of, cursing over and over, disgusted by what he had seen.

Pauline came running in from the garden, saying, 'What's wrong?'

'What's wrong,' he yelled indignantly. 'I fell in love with you and my world is falling apart. And what do you do? You stand out in the garden practising your golf swing. That's priceless. A real George-fucking-Bush moment.'

Then the anger left him feeling weak, and he sobbed again. 'I'm sorry. It made me angry. It's just that I fell in love with you.'

She sat on the edge of the bed and took his hand. 'I didn't want to hurt you, I really didn't. I'd still like to be your friend. But if your not in love with someone....'

'You can't force them to love you,' he finished for her.

And now he knew the horrible truth. It was over. There was no going back now, no second chance or "Let's try again" as in a crumbling marriage. When he got home he flaked out on his bed and sobbed again, and spent most of the afternoon going over and over what was said. Eventually, he dragged himself to his feet and telephoned Pauline, leaving a message on her answerphone.

'I'd sooner be your close friend than lose you altogether,' he said 'Maybe we could have a picnic at the seaside. No strings attached. Ring me.'

Fifty-Two

Ted almost had second thoughts as he walked along Warwick Park, looking for Donald's house. But the heart pounding fear and tingling nervousness he felt seemed so dangerously attractive. Besides, he had already telephoned Donald, who was expecting him. There was no turning back now.

Glancing nervously around, he rang the doorbell. His friend must have been waiting impatiently for his arrival, because the door was thrown open almost immediately. He gave Ted a welcoming grin.

'At last, dear boy! I thought this day would never come. Well, don't just stand there. Come in.'

As Ted stepped inside, Donald stifled a giggle.

'What are you laughing at?

Donald laughed aloud. 'You silly boy. You're wearing your uniform. I appreciate the gesture, Ted. But I was only joking.'

***

Graham spent the whole of Monday brooding, needing answers to questions he had not asked Pauline, either because he was too drunk or too distraught. He made up his mind he would go and see her in the early evening. He knew she went line dancing every Monday night and he could catch her just before she left. He decided not to telephone in advance, in case she put him off coming.

Because it was warm and sunny, her front door was wide open and she saw him arriving and came out to meet him. She gave him a weak smile, wondering what he wanted.

'I've come round to talk about yesterday,' he said. 'Everything was a haze and a nightmare. Now I've had time to think, there are

211

things I need to get clear in my mind. I don't think I can move on unless I have answers.'

She invited him into the kitchen and he sat on one of the breakfast bar stools while she made him coffee.

'Saturday night,' he began. 'Sunday morning, the alcohol had really hit me. But I can vaguely remember when I asked you about the early days in our relationship, that you may have said something like you supposed it was lust on your part. So when did you fall out of lust with me?'

She looked flustered as she fidgeted with the coffee mug. 'Well, not really lust. I liked you. I still do. But I don't feel I want to spend the rest of my life with you. It had to stop sometime. It couldn't have gone on any longer. Not from my point of view.'

'But after we'd started our affair, you seemed to want to be with me for quite some time. Six months after we started going out together, you made the train journey to see me in Scarborough for a long weekend, that time I had my play put on in the studio theatre there. And that first Christmas you spent it with me. But not last Christmas. So when, in between those times, did it go wrong?'

She shook her head with frustration. 'I don't know. All I know is I'm not in love with you. It's just... I don't need or want sex. I can live without it. It's bottom of the list on my priorities.'

He thought about this for some time before he spoke, and watched her pour water on to the coffee.

'When I was married,' he said, 'for about three or four years before we split up, on the odd occasions my wife and I had sex, we used to have to use a lubricant. It was the only way we could manage it. But you always felt like I aroused you.'

Pauline laughed. 'I always used to put a lubricant on, every time I came round to you, or before you came round here.'

He looked surprised. 'But why did you always do that in advance?'

'Because I knew you always wanted sex. And I'm sixty years old. Women of our age tend to dry up. But I don't want to do that anymore.'

She handed him a coffee. As he took it, she noticed his hands were shaking.

'But I've fallen in love with you,' he said feebly. 'And you know that time after the barbecue, when you told me you weren't in love with me. I made certain I never said I love you again.'

'I know you did. I realised that.'

'I didn't want to force you into a corner. And I stuck to my side of the bargain. When you agreed to sleep with me for the first time, you said you'd only agree if we kept our own space. Perhaps I should have played things differently.'

'No, I think I always will want my own space.'

He pounced on this. 'Think! You mean you might not want that with this new chap.'

She sighed. 'Look there's nothing going on. I only told you about him because you went on about it, convinced that was the reason for this. But nothing may come of it.'

'And is this bloke a golfer? Was he at the dinner and dance the other night?'

'No, Jack comes from Hastings. And I play near there once a year. I'm playing golf down there on Thursday.'

His hand trembled as he raised the mug and blew on his coffee. 'I've got the shakes.'

She smile sympathetically. 'I'm sorry. I didn't want to hurt you for the world. I'd still like to be your friend. We can be friends, can't we?'

He smiled sadly. 'You got my phone message?'

'Yes.'

After that, it was small talk, while she showed him the latest water colour she had painted in her art class. As he left, she gave him a smile and a small wave from the porch.

'When it's sunny, let's do that picnic,' he said. 'Ring me.'

She nodded and shut the door. As he walked away from her bungalow, he had doubts about their remaining friends. If there entered a new man in her life, he couldn't see her wanting to spend any time with an ex-lover.

As he walked back to his flat, thoughts about what had been said tormented and tortured him. And there were still things he had wanted to ask but had forgotten.

He would have liked to know why she hadn't told him this a week ago. Why she had waited until after the do at the golf club. Then the cynical thought struck him Perhaps she wanted someone to partner her for the evening, and not sit at the table next to an empty chair. Perhaps it was a case of out with the old, in with the new. All done and dusted. Neatly. Like a theatre show ending on a Saturday night. He was history.

When he arrived back at his flat, he decided to call Kathy. She was a feisty attractive woman, and he had fallen in love with her. But she was married. They occasionally had dinner together and enjoyed each other's company; and she always made him laugh with outrageous, sometimes inappropriate, comments.

When she came on the line, he told her how depressed he was about his split with Pauline, without going into too much detail.

Then Kathy said: "You ought to stop going with us shrivelled old menopausal women; we need to find you some young totty.'

He giggled. 'Forty-seven, Kathy. To me you're a babe. If only you'd dump that husband of yours. You know I love you.'

She laughed. 'And I love you, Graham. But you know why, don't you? It's because you're still a teenager.'

Fifty-Three

Dave put two plates of thinly spread cheese on toast on the table, and on hearing Mary sigh, he said, 'Sorry it's nothing more exciting, but times is hard.'

Mary smiled at him. 'This is fine. I'm not that hungry.'

Dave bit into the toast without looking at her. 'That's all right then.'

'Is something wrong?'

'Like I said: times is hard, and now I seem to have three more mouths to feed.'

Mary shifted uncomfortably in her seat. 'I'm going to start looking for a part time job soon. Then I can help with some of the bills.'

He looked directly at her. 'It would be appreciated.'

She hadn't expected this. Everything had been rosy in the garden up until now. Any thoughts of contributing to her children's upkeep had been pushed to the back of her mind. Especially as she thought Dave was earning good money doing his summer season – until it collapsed. Now she felt herself being put under pressure again. And, when all was said and done, Dave's house was paid for. He had no mortgage to worry about.

'The children break up for the holidays in a few weeks' time. I'll have to try to find something I can do working from home.'

Dave pouted. 'Well, I get on very well with them. I can always be the stay-at-home step-dad.'

Mary thought it was time she changed the subject. 'There's something that's been bothering me,' she began, frowning deliberately. 'Well, not bothering me as such... but....'

'Go on,' Dave prompted.

'I just wondered about the time your father died. You were doing quite well on television back then. How come I don't remember reading about your father in the papers?'

Dave gave her a wry smile. 'It made the papers, but not many column inches. Dad had a heart attack on the seventh of December, 1980. By the time the press got on to it, a young nutter called Mark Chapman stole the headlines.'

'That name rings a bell.'

'He shot John Lennon. Yeah, Chapman did us Whitby's a favour. It's an ill wind as they say.'

Mary was silent for a while, and idea forming in her mind. 'Dave,' she said, 'if you want to get back in the limelight again – and they say there's no such thing as bad publicity...'

Dave looked wary. 'I couldn't do that.'

'But why not?'

'I just couldn't.'

'Oh well, it was just a thought,' said Mary, sounding miffed.

***

As Ted made himself a late breakfast, Marjorie sniped at him. She still hadn't recovered from the shock of his recent behaviour.

'It's me who's got to clean this house from top to bottom.'

Ted ignored her, and concentrated on the kitchen wall clock as he timed his boiled egg.

'So the sooner you get out from under my feet,' Marjorie went on, 'the sooner I can start cleaning the kitchen.'

Ted felt like asking her why she couldn't start on one of the other rooms first. Instead, he muttered, 'I'll be out of your way in just a minute.

She tutted noisily. 'Look at the time.'

Her voice grated on Ted. His jaw tightened. 'I can't help that. I want my breakfast.'

With growing anger he stared at the boiling water and imagined himself hurling it at her, and her anguished cries as she clawed at her burning face, like a scene from a horror film.

'Oh!' Marjorie exclaimed in a voice dripping with sarcasm. 'Ted's on the late shift, so we've all got to suffer and run round after him.'

'No one's running round after me. I'm getting my own breakfast.'

'Too bloody right, you are!'

Ted sighed heavily. 'I suppose your in such a bad mood because of the uniform. Well, you don't have to worry, because today I've put it in the sports bag as usual.'

He stared at her defiantly. The reason for changing at work as he had done in the past was because he intended visiting Donald before starting the late shift.

His eyes were drawn back to the clock. Six minutes had gone by. 'Damn!' he yelled vehemently. 'While you were yapping on, I forgot to time my egg.'

Marjorie was dumbfounded. He had never spoken to her like this before. Except for that time when she discovered he'd been seeing that man. He'd sworn blind he hadn't seen him since, but you could never tell with Ted. He was such a dark horse.

'Have you been seeing that man again?'

'What man?'

Ted had his back to her. She couldn't see the sly smile on his face.

'Don't pretend you've forgotten. His friend – that fat queer bloke who came round here.'

'Oh him!' Ted said, dismissively. He brought his breakfast over to the table and sat opposite Marjorie. 'That bloke was a trouble maker.'

'But you haven't answered my question. Have you been seeing his friend?'

'Of course not.' Ted guillotined the top of his egg and stared at the yoke. 'I can't eat this.'

He got up from the table and threw it in the bin.

'What are you doing?' Marjorie demanded.

'What's it look like?'

'Waste of good food. I don't know what's come over you. You're behaving like a child.'

Ted dropped the plate into the washing-up bowl and headed for the door.

'Where d'you think you're off to?'

'To work.'

'I thought you were on the late shift.'

'Staff sickness,' he lied. 'Chance of some overtime.'

He slammed the front door harder than usual, then walked briskly across the common towards Warwick Park and Donald.

Fifty-Four

Vanessa sat at the kitchen table, eating toast and jam while reading about Coldplay in a magazine. Her mother bounded excitedly through the door, making her jump. A dollop of jam dripped onto Chris Martin and Gwyneth Paltrow's picture.

'Ta-ra!' fan-fared Jackie, showing off her dress. 'What do you think?'

Vanessa nodded. 'You're still going through with it then.'

'The first week in September. Before you're back at college. And Nicky's on annual leave – so neither of you will have an excuse for not attending.'

'So we pop along to the Registry Office, have a few drinks after....'

'A meal,' Jackie corrected. 'Nigel's taking us all to the Hotel du Vin.'

Vanessa made a point of looking unimpressed. 'Oh, great. I can just imagine what that's going to be like.'

Jackie let out a low moan. 'Oh, why is it that nothing we do is right? It's not as if either of you are young children. And I know it's traditional for children to hate their stepfathers, but just what is it you've got against Nigel?'

'I don't want to see you get hurt, that's all.'

Jackie frowned. 'I can't see why....' she began, but the sentence died in mid-air.

'I'm sorry,' said Vanessa. 'But I've got to say this. I don't trust him.'

Jackie sighed deeply, and blinked away her tears. 'But he's never given me – or you, for that matter – any reason not to trust him. I think you're being most unfair.'

'What about this seminar he's supposed to be at? Almost a week gone by, and he hasn't phoned once.'

'He's probably busy. A lot on his mind. And sometimes it's difficult to get to a phone.'

Vanessa mimed a telephone. 'Oh hello-o! We don't have mobiles.'

Jackie felt the tears about to burst. 'He did send me a big bunch of flowers.'

Vanessa wanted to end the conversation, and said, 'Oh yes, I'd forgotten about the flowers. I'm sorry, I was wrong about him. Completely wrong.'

Jackie glared at her daughter then stormed out of the room.

'Now what have I said?' Vanessa called after her.

***

Graham had been drunk for over a week now. Everyone in his local pub knew about the split, and they had been sympathetic to begin with, but now the sympathy was becoming a chore. And when the e-mail came from his American agent, saying they were going out of business, it was the last straw. To have to start all over again seemed a Herculean task and didn't bear thinking about. So he opened another bottle of wine and thought about ending it all. He spent all day thinking about it, going over all the different methods he might employ.

He even imagined his funeral, wondering if suicide precluded a good attendance. Or did one have to die a more respectable death from natural causes? He pictured his first wife and his ex-wife attending, and actually chatting about him familiarly. He wondered if Pauline would attend, then decided she might not. She might think he had killed himself deliberately to get back at her. The dreaded guilt trip. It would probably make her angry. And if she had an important golf match on the day of the funeral, bitterly he suspected that golf might win out.

After he had opened the second bottle of wine, he had sunk to an all time low, and thought about asphyxiation from car exhaust fumes. A painless way to drift away. By the time the second bottle had hit home, he had worked out that he would need a hose pipe and gaffer tape and decided to drive to Homebase. He knew he wasn't fit to drive. But so what? If he was done for drinking and driving, did it matter?

All the same, he drove carefully down to Homebase. It was all very well to kill oneself, but he didn't want another death on his conscience. As he went down Major York's Road, the heavens opened up, and rain cascaded down his windscreen.

Rivers of tears, he thought bitterly, as he switched his wipers and headlights on.

Homebase was empty. He staggered around drunkenly; everything seemed a blur. God knows how he I managed to drive down here. Eventually, he managed to find an assistant, and asked, 'I need some gaffer tape and a hosepipe. Urgently.'

The spotty-faced youth regarded him with a look that was both quizzical and fractious. 'That aisle over there for the garden hose,' he mumbled. 'And over there for gaffer tape.'

As the youth shuffled off, Graham watched him go, and called after him, 'Your simian features do you a disservice. You're actually very efficient.'

When he got back to the car park with his purchases, he discovered his headlights were still on, and remembered the bleeping warning signal had packed up for some reason.

Oh well, he thought. Not much point in getting it repaired now. I'm free. Free of the burden of living.

Then he drove home extremely carefully, and only clipped two wing mirrors from cars parked at the bottom end of Major York's Road.

Two bottles later, he was out of it. He came to, as he suspected he would, in the early hours of the morning. He went out to the flats' car park at the rear of the building. There was a half moon and just enough light to see what he was doing, although he was staggering, swaying and bumping into things, and everything he did took an enormous amount of time and effort. But eventually he managed to tape the hose to the exhaust pipe and threaded it through the window by the driver's seat. Then he went indoors and got the fifth bottle of wine, uncorked it, and returned to the car. He sat in the driving seat and covered the gap in the window with masses of tape. Then he took an enormous swig of wine, almost a quarter of a bottle in one gulp. After all, what did it matter? It could hardly be bad for his health. Not as bad as carbon monoxide.

Bye-byes time, he told himself, and turned the key in the ignition. Click! He turned it again. Click! Nothing. The car wouldn't start. He had left the headlights on and the battery was flat.

Fifty-Five

Her lips drawn tight, Maggie slammed the cordless phone down onto the breakfast bar table.

'Who was that?' asked Craig. 'Sounded a bit heavy.'

Maggie shrugged. 'Oh, just a friend.' Seeing her brother smiling, she added, 'Yeah, well, I suppose Mike was more than just a friend.'

Craig nodded slowly. 'How long have you known him?'

'A long time. It's Gary's hairdresser. And no I wasn't having an affair with him while Gary was alive.'

Craig gave his sister an innocent smile. 'I didn't say anything.'

'But you were thinking it. Would you like another beer?'

Craig shook his head. 'I ought to get back.'

'Yeah,' agreed Maggie, 'that's enough skiving off for one night.'

'Well, I am the boss now. I can do what I like.'

Maggie threw her brother a warning look. 'For crying out loud, Craig! Don't do a Gary on us – otherwise you'll be out of business.'

Craig laughed. 'It was a joke. Awright?'

***

Tony Rice sat at the bar and stared at Mike. 'If you want my advice, smack the bitch. Keep her in line.'

Mike swivelled slowly on his bar stool and glared at Rice. 'Sorry?'

Rice grinned. 'I couldn't help overhearing your conversation on the mobile. She was giving you a hard time.'

'Oh yeah? What's that to you, pal?'

'Just making conversation.'

Mike swallowed the last of his draught Stella and called the barman over. 'Yes please, Mark – when you're ready.'

He turned towards Rice and said, 'So you call that making conversation, do you? I call it poking your nose in where it's not wanted.'

Rice's grip tightened around his glass. His eyes were deadly as he stared at Mike. 'What's your problem then?'

'You tell me. You seem to know all about it.'

Rice smiled coldly. 'It ain't my fault your skirt's given you the heave-hoh. If you don't wanna make conversation, sit somewhere else. Usually, when people sit at the bar, it's 'cos they wanna socialize.'

Mike smirked. 'You want to be sociable, do you? Come here for a conversation, have you? So what shall we talk about? Politics? Religion? Literature? That's a good one. Let's talk about literature. Or do you still move your lips when you read?'

The barman brought Mike's fresh pint. Oblivious of the dangerous look on Rice's face, Mike indicated a pile of loose change on the bar.

'There you go, Mark – help yourself.'

As the barman took the coins, Mike downed almost half of his fifth pint. He wiped the drops off his upper lip and turned to face Rice again.

'So what do you do for a living then?' Rice hesitated long enough for Mike to pounce. 'Let me guess. You look like a manual worker who's never done an honest day's graft in his life. I'd say you were a recidivist. And if you don't know what it means, you can always look it up.'

Rice's lip curled slightly. 'Congratulations. You guessed right. So what do you do?'

Mike raised two fingers in front of Rice's face. Before the ex-convict had time to react, Mike made a snipping motion and explained, 'I'm a hairdresser.'

Rice gave Mike another cold smile which set off sobering alarm bells in his fuddled brain.

'Sorry,' he began, slurring his words. 'I didn't mean to be rude. Woman trouble. You know what it's like.'

Rice shrugged confidently. 'OK. No problem.'

'I've had too much to drink.'

'Forget it.'

But there was something in Rice's manner which disturbed Mike. He glanced at his watch and downed the rest of his beer.

***

Craig turned at the kitchen door and said, 'This bloke you've been seeing – was he on the rebound?'

Maggie pursed her lips thoughtfully. 'Maybe. But I don't think it was on the rebound of Gary's death. I think our marriage broke down years ago. I just didn't want to admit it.'

'So now you've given this hairdresser bloke the elbow.'

'I didn't want to.'

'Is he married then?'

Maggie nodded. 'Yeah. And as far as I'm concerned, I don't want to be responsible for breaking up his marriage.'

'So what was the problem?'

'He was getting serious. He's already had two yellow cards. But tonight he was... well, you heard most of the phone call. He was behaving like a lovesick schoolboy.'

Craig laughed. 'Most married men want an uncomplicated affair. This guy must be no ordinary idiot.'

Maggie's eyes became distant, moist. 'I like Mike. He's fun to be with. I'm going to miss him.'

They heard a scuffling, snuffling noise from the hall. Daryl appeared in the doorway, rubbing sleep and tears from his eyes.

'Mum!' he cried. 'I had a dream about Dad. Will he come back for the holidays?'

Craig stepped aside for his nephew, who rushed into his mother's arms and sobbed.

***

Mike had parked the car in a side street, well away from the pub. As he fumbled with his keys in the lock, he heard a rush of sound from behind and started to turn. He had been aware of someone following him along the street but had thought nothing of it.

The fist that smashed into the side of his face was like a battering ram. His body jarred with pain as he crashed to the ground. A foot came down heavily on the side of his neck and he was choking, fighting for breath. He was dimly aware of a recently familiar voice saying, 'I usually get paid for this. But for you I'll make an exception.' His right hand was wrenched upwards and then came bone-splitting pain as each finger was systematically broken. The pain was unbearable. He passed out.

Fifty-Six

A drunken scream pierced the air of Accident and Emergency. 'Excuse me,' said the young nurse. 'I'll leave you to it.'

After she had gone, Mike looked up at Claire and Andrew and mumbled an apology.

Claire frowned. 'You've been beaten up, darling. Why should you be sorry?'

'I meant....' He stopped. He couldn't think of anything to say. He looked down at his plastered hand and winced.

Andrew felt awkward. He cleared his throat softly before speaking. 'You all right, Dad?'

'I'll survive.'

'What did you tell the police?' Claire asked.

'That I'd been beaten up, of course. What else could I say?'

'You could have told them the truth. Nobody stole anything from you. You weren't mugged. Someone had it in for you, didn't they?'

Mike suddenly realised that Claire, who already suspected him of having an affair, now thought he'd been beaten up by a jealous husband.

'All right,' he began, sighing deeply to highlight his confession. 'I had one too many beers.'

Andrew turned to his mother and said, 'I told you. He picked an argument with someone in the pub.'

Claire's eyes narrowed as she stared at Mike. 'Is that what happened?'

Mike nodded sheepishly. 'This time I picked on the wrong bloke.'

'But he's broken your fingers. Cold bloodedly. Don't you think you should have told the police?'

227

'The bloke was a professional villain. Been in prison. I don't want my other hand broken.'

Claire tutted impatiently. 'What the hell are you going to do for a living?'

Mike shrugged and stared miserably at his hand. 'Guess I'll have to take a short break.' He looked up and laughed weakly. 'If you'll pardon the pun.'

'Oh, very funny, Mike. We're all laughing. What an enjoyable summer it's going to be. Not only will you be unemployed and lose half your customers now, that'll be any chance of a holiday out the window.'

***

With just over a month to go before the wedding, and with what seemed like a million and one things to attend to, Jackie felt unsettled and nervous. Eventually she decided she would summon up the energy to bake a superb coffee and walnut cake for Sunday. Nigel would be home by then, and she had invited friends over for a barbecue, mainly to introduce them to Nigel.

Vanessa and Nicky, who had been upstairs in Nicky's room, watching television, suddenly appeared in the kitchen, exchanging furtive glances at each other. Right away, Jackie knew something was wrong.

'What's the matter?' she asked.

Silence. She saw their pitying looks and repeated her question with more urgency.

Vanessa coughed and turned towards her younger sister. 'I thought you were going to tell her.'

'I can't.'

'You're so spineless. Why does it always have to be me?'

Jackie slammed a packet of chopped walnuts onto the work surface. 'I suppose this is something to do with Nigel. I know you're both determined to sabotage our marriage. Well, come on – out with it. Then I can get on with my baking.'

Vanessa shrugged, giving her mother a well-you've-asked-for-it look, and said, 'You know he said he was going up north for that seminar?'

Jackie's lips twitched angrily. 'Oh, not that again. Why do you refuse to believe him? What's wrong with you two?'

For once, Vanessa looked genuinely sympathetic. 'I'm sorry, Mummy. I really am. We've just seen him on television. On the news. He was in a hotel in Brighton. And early this morning, the guests were evacuated. There was a bomb went off. No one was hurt. It was a controlled explosion.'

Jackie felt a nervous tic in the corner of her eye. 'Are you sure it was Nigel.'

Vanessa nodded gravely. 'Yes, they interviewed him and this woman as they came out of the hotel. He had his arm about her. I'm sorry, Mummy. I really am.'

***

Mike eased himself into the chair facing the television, pointed the remote awkwardly with his left hand, and switched on the news. Claire passed behind his chair, stopping to gently kiss the bruised side of his face.

'Shall I pop out to get a DVD and some cold beer?' she offered.

'I'm on the wagon.'

Claire laughed. 'For how long?'

'I'm a changed man.'

Claire looked towards the flowers in the crystal vase. 'I can see that. You've never bought me a dozen red roses. Well, not since we've been married, you haven't. Why this gesture now, of all times?'

Lowering his voice, Mike said, 'Because of all the trouble I've caused you.' He indicated his plastered hand. 'And because I still love you.'

'I love you too, darling. Break a few bones more often, will you? Now I'm going to have a glass of wine. D'you want one?'

Mike shook his head. 'I wouldn't mind another coffee.'

As Claire went towards the door, Mike gave a loud whoop as he stared at the television screen. 'It's him!' he yelled excitedly. 'Nigel whatsit.'

Claire stopped in the doorway and peered at the television. 'Someone you know?'

'One of my clients. The chap whose fiancée phoned you up and started preaching.'

Claire scowled at the screen. 'Oh, him!'

After she had left the room, Mike giggled softly. He had been the one to encourage Nigel to go ahead and have an assignation. And now the idiot was being broadcast nationwide, with his arm round another woman. Mike hoped and prayed that his fiancée had watched this evening's news. It would serve the hypocrite right.

Fifty-Seven

On Saturday Nigel clambered out of bed, put his dressing gown on, and delayed telephoning Jackie. There was something niggling at the back of his mind. Like himself, he knew she rarely watched television, and liked to listen to the news on the radio. But what if she happened to switch the television on for a change? It didn't bare thinking about.

He made himself a bowl of porridge and a cup of tea, then showered and dressed. By then he was feeling more confident. If Jackie had seen the television news, she would surely have attempted to ring his mobile, and there were no messages on his voice mail or any texts.

At ten o'clock he took the plunge and rang her. Her voice was calm and sweet when she answered.

'Hello, Nigel. How did it go?'

'Oh, it was hard work but stimulating.'

'Where was it you went for this seminar? I know it was up north, but....'

'Sheffield,' he lied.

'So when did you drive back from Sheffield?'

'Last night.'

'Was the M1 busy?'

'I always cut across from the new M6 toll and down the M40.'

'So you were definitely in Sheffield yesterday.'

A shiver ran down his spine. Why was she pushing him on this point?

'Hello, Nigel. Are you still there?'

'Sorry. Yes. I was distracted. I think I heard the post coming through the letter box.'

'I expect you're tired after that long drive last night.'

'Not really,' he purred, in what he felt was a voice of assurance. 'I feel fresh enough to come over and cuddle my bunnykins.'

'So you were definitely in Sheffield all day yesterday.'

He thought they had moved on from Sheffield. Now alarm bells were clanging inside his head.

'Well?' she demanded, her voice hard and cold.

'Yes, I told you. The seminar was in Sheffield.'

'So you haven't been to Brighton recently.'

A harsh neon message screamed inside his skull. She knows! He had already worked out a story in advance, just in case she saw the television news item. But she had deliberately set him a trap, letting him think she was blissfully unaware of the Brighton bomb incident and his television appearance.

He felt a nauseous tremor in his stomach, then took a deep breath and launched into his explanation. 'I'm sure I told you last week: the conference was in Brighton. The seminars were in Sheffield, but the week culminated in a Brighton conference. The venue was too small in Sheffield.'

'But you said you got back from Sheffield last night.'

'No, no. Thursday night I drove to Brighton.'

'That's not what you said.'

He began stammering. 'W-well, you... you see, I'm still in a state of shock. It was terrible. T-terrible. There was a bomb at the Brighton hotel... and I still haven't got over it.'

'You poor thing.'

Jackie's voice oozed sympathy. But it was overdone. Behind it lay shark infested waters.

'Yes, it was terrible.'

'It was on the television,' she snapped. 'And you came out of that hotel with your arms around another woman.'

'She was distraught. Frightened. I found her in the reception area in a state of shock. I had to do something to comfort her and get her outside. After all, any moment that bomb could have gone off.'

'How brave of you, Nigel. So now you won't mind if I telephone the hotel in Brighton and find out just what conferences were booked in for yesterday.'

'What? Why would you want to do that?'

'Because – frankly – I don't believe you.'

'Don't be silly, darling... I've told you....'

But the line had gone dead. He tried ringing back, but got the engaged tone. How could he have been so stupid? And why, why, why had he agreed to that brief interview with the television reporter? It was his ego. A big, fat, stupid ego. And now his relationship was in tatters because of it.

**

Hot oil sizzled and spat as Ted tipped potatoes into a roasting tray. Marjorie sat at the table, trying to fold paper napkins in the fancy way she had seen in their Florida hotel.

'I hope you've done enough potatoes,' she said. 'You know what an appetite Alec's got.'

Ted tittered. 'Not to mention Freda.'

'Now, now.'

Marjorie got up from the table, went to her handbag which was lying on the dresser, and took out an envelope. Ted put the roasting tray back in the oven. When he turned round, Marjorie thrust the envelope at him.

'What's this? It's not my birthday for another fortnight.'

'I wanted you to have this now. I couldn't wait any longer. It's an early present.'

Puzzled, Ted tore open the envelop and pulled out a Congratulations card, a picture of a champagne bottle fizzing with silver and gold. He opened the card. Inside, Marjorie had written:

"To Ted, love to a father to be."

Ted looked into Marjorie's eyes, uncomprehendingly at first. She smiled.

'I'm over three months pregnant. I thought I'd save it as a birthday surprise, but... well, you might try and look happy about it.'

Fifty-Eight

Mike sat at the kitchen table reading the Sunday Times without taking it in. His mind was filled with images of Maggie and him making love in some remote spot on Ashdown Forest. Andrew stood by the fridge, drinking beer from the can. Claire pushed him to one side.

'Oh, darling!' she complained. 'Why don't you help instead of getting in the way?'

'What d'you want me to do?'

'Lay the table.'

'OK,' he said with a sigh, and began taking cutlery out of the drawer.

Claire opened the fridge, took out a carton of whipping cream, then glanced at the wall clock. 'It's nearly half one. They should have been back by now.'

Andrew shook his head and smiled incredulously. 'Who'd have thought my sister would get a dose of religion. Her boyfriend must be a smooth talker.'

'That's not the only reason Chloe's....' Claire stopped herself in time. She didn't want to mention her daughter's abortion. Or even think about it.

'Mike,' she said hastily, 'I'm going upstairs to put my face on. Can you put the vegetables on for me?'

Mike stared at his uninjured hand and flexed his fingers. 'I think I can just about manage it. But shouldn't we wait for Chloe and Mark? Just in case his car's broken down. It looks a bit clapped out, if you ask me.'

'No one's asking you.'

They heard a key in the latch. 'Here they are now,' said Andrew.

Chloe, wearing a beatific smile, came into the kitchen, holding her boyfriend's hand. He had blonde hair, was slight, fractionally

235

shorter than Chloe, and had conventional good looks, and reminded Claire of a young Robert Redford.

'Hello, Mark. You two look very pleased with yourselves. Was it a good service?'

Mark beamed at her. 'It's happened! Chloe was touched. The spirit came upon her.'

Mike looked as if he wanted to throw up, and Andrew stared open-mouthed at Mark.

Chloe giggled feverishly. 'It was amazing. I fell down. It was as if... as if I was drunk with happiness. And everyone was singing and chanting.' She looked at Andrew. 'You ought to try it sometime.'

Embarrassed, Andrew looked down. 'Yeah. Cool.'

Chloe giggled again. 'I'm starving now. When's dinner ready?'

Claire, barely unable to disguise the irritation she felt, left the room, saying, 'I wish you'd help your father. His hand's giving him problems.'

***

Only three hours to go and Jackie's friends would be turning up for the barbecue, keen to meet her fiancé. What on earth could she tell them? That Nigel had been seen leaving a hotel with another woman, and that it was all over between them? Somehow the social disgrace seemed worse than her fiancé's deception. Fighting back tears of frustration, she picked up the telephone and dialled Nigel's number. His voice was soft and subdued when he came on the line.

'It's me,' she said. 'I want you to come over here at least an hour before the barbecue and tell me to my face what you told me on the phone yesterday, so that I can see if you're telling me the truth.'

'I promise you I am,' he said. 'I was confused and shocked after the bomb incident, and....'

She interrupted him. 'Tell me to my face. That way I'll know if you're lying.'

'OK. I'll come over soon. Then you'll see I'm telling the truth.'

After she had hung up, Jackie saw Vanessa framed in the living room doorway.

'I don't believe I just heard that. You're actually going to give that creep another chance.'

Something snapped in Jackie. 'Mind your own damn business,' she screamed.

Vanessa pulled a face. 'Oh, sorry I spoke,' she said, and shot back into the living room.

***

When Graham arrived in the White Hart everyone could tell by the state he was in that he'd been drinking. His eyes were bloodshot, his face had a deep barroom flush that was in danger of turning purple, and there were dewdrops of sweat on his top lip and forehead. And when he handed money over for a glass of wine, his hands were shaking.

'You've sunk a few already, haven't you, Graham?' challenged one of the regulars.

'Last night I did,' he replied. 'I haven't been drinking this morning, if that's what you mean.'

'Pull the other one.'

Graham ignored it, tried to tug a pound coin out of his pocket and dropped it on the floor. Stooping to pick it up, he almost fell over. Regular customers watched with fascination, and muttered to each other about the state he was in, and the reasons for him being that way.

'Yes please, Marion,' he said. 'I'll have a strip for the meat raffle.'

The landlady handed him a strip of five raffle tickets, and he stared bleary-eyed at the numbers, while he raised his glass carefully and downed half the wine in one gulp.

The bell rang for the start of the raffle and the first number drawn was Graham's. At first he didn't comprehend that it was his, until one of the regulars standing next to him told him he'd won. He chose the pork joint.

Usually, whenever anyone won one of the five meat prizes, it was followed by friendly banter. But this time the regulars were silent and embarrassed. Then after all the meat had been won and disposed of, Ken, the landlord, shouted:

'We're losing money on the raffle, but we'll still throw in a bottle of wine.'

Someone down the far end of the bar won it. Graham staggered over and offered to exchange the pork joint for the wine. The customer couldn't believe his luck. He didn't like wine much anyway.

After he'd had another couple of glasses of wine, Graham became incoherent as he tried to discuss politics with someone. He tried to organise his thoughts so that what he said made some sense, but he kept starting a sentence and forgetting where it was leading. It was time to leave. He picked up the bottle of wine, gave a cursory wave to everyone and staggered up the path towards the road. By now he was sweating profusely, and the bottle slid from his hands and smashed on the concrete path. He stared at the rivulets of red wine running down the path, cursed loudly, then weaved drunkenly towards the road. He got as far as one of the benches under the trees. It was as far as he could manage to walk. He slumped onto the bench and fell into a deep sleep.

Fifty-Nine

Dave stared across Grosvenor Recreation Ground, watching Mary's children clambering over the metal frames, the older boy showing off and telling the younger one what to do. Mary sat next to him on the bench, thoughtful and distant. After a long silence, Dave cleared his throat noisily and spoke.

'They'll not be having much of a holiday this year.'

'Same as last year,' said Mary.

'You've not talked much about their father. Correction. You've never talked about their father. Don't they miss him?'

'Ronnie was a 22 carat bastard. Possessive and obsessively jealous. He put me in hospital once.'

'Wife battering?' Dave asked.

Mary nodded. 'Once was enough. I had an exclusion order put on him. I think the authorities knew he could be dangerous. Especially as he'd spent some time in a young offenders institute for GBH.'

'So what became of him?'

'He buggered off to the USA, thank God. It was a long time ago. Thomas was only two, and even Simon barely remembers him.'

Mary heard one of them shouting, 'Look at me, Mum,' and she waved and smiled. 'Thank you for coping with their behaviour,' she said, giving Dave's arm a squeeze. 'They seem to like their Uncle Dave.'

Dave turned and reassured her with a gentle smile. 'Well, I know what it's like growing up without a father.'

Mary opened her mouth to speak, but Dave cut in: 'I never knew me Aunty Marilyn was me dad until after his death, did I?'

'No, of course not.'

'No wonder I was mixed up.' He put his arm around her shoulders, pulling her close. 'But thanks to you, I feel it's something that happened to someone else, in another life. For the first time in my life I feel one hundred per cent normal.'

She laughed. 'A slight exaggeration I feel.'

'Listen, I've been thinking....'

'I thought I could smell burning.'

'No, seriously: Simon and Thomas would be better off if they each had their own room. So I've decided to clear out the spare room..'

She squeezed his hand on her shoulder. 'Oh, Dave!'

'It was a monument. A shrine. Very unhealthy. I'd sooner it was a jumble of toys. So, as soon as they go back to school, I'll clear the room out.'

'What are you going to do with all the stuff?'

'Stick it in the loft.'

'Oh.' Mary sounded disappointed. 'You're not getting rid of it then?'

'Why should I trash it? That's my history. can't change it.'

'Well, if that's how you feel, what's wrong with selling your story to the papers?'

'No.'

'It'd make us a lot of money.'

'Us?'

He removed his arm and looked round at her. Annoyed and hurt by his suspicious stare, she began to raise her voice. 'Yes, us! We're a couple now. But you still manage to make me feel like a lodger; a tenant who's behind with the rent. I hope you won't chuck us out if we can't pay our way.'

Dave frowned. 'I didn't think....' he began.

She interrupted him impatiently. 'I know I haven't made much effort to bring in money, but I do have two boys to look after. All

I'm asking is that you treat me as your partner. Not the lodger you happen to be screwing.'

'I'm sorry,' he mumbled, 'if I gave you that impression. I love you. It's just the work situation's been bugging me. I've had a worrying time. What with that summer season going up the swanee.'

She softened, moved closer to him and kissed his cheek.

'I'm sorry, too. I hope you didn't mind my saying the way I felt.'

He shook his head. 'I'm glad you did. It's best to get these things out in the open.'

She gave him a cheeky grin. 'Tomorrow night, why don't we all sit down as a family and have a Chinese takeaway and bottle of wine?'

'Where's the money coming from?'

'My Family Allowance is due tomorrow.'

***

When Nigel came round, Vanessa found it difficult not to stare at him with loathing, so she disappeared into the garden. Nicky was sitting in the living room watching television, so Jackie took Nigel up to her bedroom for their confrontation. She stood directly in front of him and looked into his eyes.

'Now tell me the truth, Nigel, what were you doing in that Brighton hotel, having told me you were in Sheffield?'

'I'm sure I told you about Brighton....'

'Sheffield, you said.'

'No, I mean a long time ago, when I first found out I was going on this course. I'm sure I told you it culminated in the Brighton conference. You must remember, surely.'

He knew how scatterbrained she could be, and would think she had forgotten him telling her, or hadn't listened to what he was saying.

She shook her head and frowned. 'I really can't remember. But I did phone up the hotel. There were no conferences that sounded like anything to do with telephones or computers.'

Nigel had also telephoned the hotel and found out what seminars or conferences were taking place that day.

'That final day at Brighton was about Diversity Awareness.'

Her frown deepened. 'Diversity Awareness! What's that got to do with telephones?'

Straining to look sincere, he said, 'We sell to all races, religions and ethnic groups. We have to be trained in diversity. It's mandatory, I'm afraid. Then when that bomb was going to go off....'

'Were you frightened?'

'Petrified. And Jackie, I have to say this: can you honestly believe I'd openly allow myself to be interviewed on television if I was doing something as underhand as... how can you even think it?'

She smiled at him, wanting to believe him, pushing her suspicions to the back of her mind.

'As long as you tell me you promise that's the truth.'

He returned her smile. 'I promise.'

Then he caught her glancing towards the dressing table, on which lay her bible. And he wondered if it was going through her mind to make him swear on it.

Just in case she was, he thought he'd get it in first, as if it was his idea.

'Would you like me to swear on the Bible?' he asked.

'No, you've given me your word, Nigel. I trust you.'

'All the same, I'd still like to swear on it, just to make absolutely certain you believe me.'

His double-bluff worked. She shook her head emphatically, glad that their lives could now be restored to normal, and be just a little bit ordinary. Then she kissed him full on the lips, and the Brighton hotel incident was behind them.

Sixty

Early on Monday morning, ignoring the closed sign on the door, Maggie swept into Craig's fish and chip shop. Her brother was standing at the fish fryer, diligently polishing the chrome.

'You're putting elbow grease into that,' she said. 'It wasn't like that when Gary was alive.'

Craig grinned at her. 'Well, now I'm the owner....'

Maggie bit her lip thoughtfully. 'Which is what I want to talk to you about. I've been thinking about what you said about selling this place and becoming a partner in the wine bar. I'm game if you are.'

Craig frowned. 'Well, you've taken me unawares, like. I don't know what to say.'

'I don't want you to make a snap decision. We won't be opening until the late autumn. Think about it.'

'As a matter of fact, Maggs, I can give you my answer right now. I think I'll stick to the chippie, thanks.'

Maggie looked put-out. 'Oh!'

'I think you're right. I just don't think I'd fit in.'

Maggie sniffed disdainfully. 'Some people have no ambition.'

'Yeah, well, if it's a question of needing more money, I'd be happy to flog this place for you.'

Maggie coloured. 'What makes you think I'm short of money, Craig?'

'Nothing. I just thought....'

Maggie turned and walked towards the door. 'And I thought you'd be pleased. Oh well, forget it.'

'Don't be like that, Maggs.'

'Like what?'

He began polishing the chrome again. 'It doesn't matter.'

Maggie slammed the door as she left. Craig watched her crossing the road, thinking how well suited she and Gary had been.

***

When Philip, the new administrative assistant in the claims department, returned from the toilet, both Nicky and Savita could see he was really upset about something, and his eyes were red, as if he'd been crying. And he'd been in the toilet a good fifteen minutes. Prior to that, he'd been summoned to Malcolm's office, and Savita suspected that this visit had something to do with his sudden depression. As he passed her desk, Savita asked him what was wrong.

He looked like a startled creature caught in the glare of headlights. 'Nothing,' he muttered, and hurried across the office to his own desk.

Savita watched him. He was an effeminate young man in his mid-twenties. When he was standing, he drew himself up to his full height, with his chest thrust out, as if he was trying to appear masculine. But it was a parody of masculinity, and this over-compensation made him appear even more effeminate, and it was not helped by the sibilance of his speech. But everyone in the office seemed to like him. He seemed a very genuine person, interested in others, harmless and gentle. Savita made up her mind that she would get to the bottom of what was going on.

***

As they sat drinking coffee outside one of the cafés in the Pantiles, Donald suspected Ted had something to get off his chest. It was the way his friend's eyes moved around, unable to settle on any one object.

'Something wrong, Ted?' Donald asked after a hefty silence.

Ted glanced at his watch. 'I haven't got long. I've got to get to work.'

'But you said you wanted to see me. Said you had something to discuss.'

'I don't know how to tell you this....' Ted began, then focused his attention on the bottom of his coffee cup and lapsed into silence.

Donald sighed. 'Are you trying to tell me it's all over? Ended as soon as it's begun?' He laughed humourlessly. 'I sound like a character from a Noel Coward play.'

'That's not what I'm saying. No.'

Donald frowned, waiting for him to continue. Ted took a deep breath and spoke hurriedly.

'I'm going to be a father.'

'Donald's mouth fell open. 'I don't believe it.'

Ted smiled. 'Now you sound like Victor Meldrew.'

For once Donald seemed at a loss for words. 'But when... I mean how...' He laughed foolishly. 'Well, of course I know how. What I mean is, I didn't think you and she who wears the trousers did it any more.'

'Well. Once in a blue moon. I never thought she'd become pregnant. Not at her age.'

'How old is she?'

'Forty seven.'

Donald chuckled. 'Well, well, well. So you're going to become a geriatric father. If it's a boy, you can teach him to play football. It'll help you through your retirement.'

Almost involuntarily, Ted reached out and put a hand on Donald's arm. 'I know how you feel.'

Donald shook his head and smiled grimly. 'I doubt it.'

'It's the last thing I wanted. To become a father.'

'Well, dear boy, that's where you and I differ. I'd love to have children. Well, don't look so – why should that surprise you? I had an extremely happy upbringing in a large family. But my sexuality being what it is....' Donald gestured helplessly. 'I hope we can still go to the theatre occasionally.'

There was a pause before Ted's eyes met Donald's. 'Of course we can. Why can't we just carry on as we are?'

'Well, there is the small problem of Bamber's return. But I'm sure we can manage something.'

Ted nodded. 'I'd better go. Or I'll be late.'

Ted rose and squeezed Donald's arm gently before walking away. Donald watched as his friend hurried along the Pantiles. He laughed to himself and muttered:

'If someone had told me I'd have fallen for someone in a British Rail uniform....'

Sixty-One

Sitting nervously in front of the bank manager, Maggie felt intimidated and patronised. He thumbed through the sheaf of papers on his desk, raising his eyebrows as if surprised that the little girl who sat before him was as capable as her late husband. Maggie, who had deliberately worn her short skirt and black stockings, crossed her legs. The bank manager, distracted by the rustle, glanced furtively at a stretch of her thigh. He cleared his throat.

'Shame you can't sell the Maidstone shop.'

'I only need a bridging loan until it's sold.'

'But it only has a seven year lease.' The manager shook his head with disbelief. 'Suppose no one wants to buy it? And you have seriously underestimated the shop fitting costs at the wine bar.'

'Are you seriously saying you're going to pull the plugs on the wine bar before it's even opened?'

'It's not a question of "pulling the plugs", as you put it. You need another loan. You're asking me to risk the bank's money in a venture.'

Maggie uncrossed her legs and leaned forward in her chair. 'Are you telling me no? After my husband's banked with you for all these years?'

The bank manager gave her a lascivious smile. 'There are certain conditions.' He paused, staring at her breasts. 'I know of this hotel – lovely quaint little place in darkest Sussex – and my wife's off to Scotland to stay with her mother next weekend....'

Maggie couldn't believe she was hearing this. But then, any bank manager who had wined and dined with Gary....

'Naturally,' continued the manager, 'I should deny this conversation took place. But you have rather painted yourself into a corner. So how about it?'

***

Savita and Nicky managed to persuade Philip to come to lunch with them. Although they didn't usually have pub lunches, they thought the occasion warranted a few glasses of wine, and they decided on Wetherspoon's at The Opera House.

While they waited for their meal, Savita asked Philip bluntly if he was having trouble with Malcolm. The young man looked frightened, and gazed around the bar, as if there could be spies lurking, waiting to report back to his boss.

'It's OK,' Savita assured him, 'we've all been bullied by Malcolm. But he's stopped picking on me and Nicky now.'

Philip looked at each of them and raised an enquiring eyebrow.

'Yes, I know that's hard to believe,' Savita continued, 'but the reason he's stopped picking on us is a bit complicated.'

'Very complicated,' Nicky added, feeling she had to make a contribution.

'So what's Malcolm been doing to you?' Savita asked.

Philip lowered his voice. 'I'm – I'm gay, you see. And he must have picked up on it. I can't think how he knew or found out.'

Savita threw Nicky a surreptitious look which he noticed. He went bright red.

'Is it that obvious?'

'Well, I....' began Savita, feeling awkward. 'I hadn't really thought about it.'

Philip shrugged. 'It doesn't matter. What matters is, he's making my life unbearable. He sends me emails asking me to go into his office for the stupidest things. This morning I went in, and he told me the clock on his wall was two minutes slow and got me to put it right. And while I was doing it, he was coming out with all the most awful euphemisms for my sexual orientation. He's the worst homophobe I've ever met.'

'You don't think....' Nicky began.

'What?' prompted Savita.

'Well, it's just a thought: you don't think he's like Kevin Spacey's neighbour in that film American Beauty, do you?'

'I see where you're coming from,' said Philip, 'but I think it's a bit glib to say that just because he's a homophobe, he must have those tendencies himself.'

'Does it matter?' snapped Savita with rather more vehemence than she intended. 'What matters is that we must stop him bullying you, Philip.'

'Yes but,' He frowned. 'How are you going to do that?'

Savita looked at Nicky. 'Shall I tell him?'

'I don't see why not.'

Savita explained to Philip about the photographs they had of Malcolm in a compromising situation. After she had finished, he said:

'That's all very well, but if you threaten to expose him again, and he stops bullying me, he'll probably find someone else to pick on.'

'Exactly,' agreed Savita. 'Which is why I am going to send his wife a copy of the picture, and the MD will get it by email. By this time tomorrow Malcolm will be looking for another job, and his wife will be starting divorce proceedings.'

Nicky and Philip stared at Savita, both cowed by the enormity of her intentions.

'What?' said Savita. 'What's wrong?'

Nicky pursed her lips. 'I don't know,' she said, 'if we should go that far.'

'So what's the point in threatening him, if he knows we have no intention of carrying out the threat?'

'But it could seriously backfire,' said Philip.

'How?'

'I don't know. But if you take away his job and ruin his marriage, you'll leave him in ruins.'

'Tough,' snapped Savita. 'He should have thought of that before he started picking on people again.'

'Yes but if you leave a person with nothing left to lose, who knows what they're capable of doing.'

Savita clenched her lips tightly before speaking. 'I don't care. All I know is, I'm sick of the evil bastard, and I want him out of our firm for good. Goodbye, Malcolm. I'd like to say it's been nice knowing you, but it hasn't.'

That was when their food arrived.

Sixty-Two

Craig slammed his beer glass onto the grubby, pub table. 'He said what?'

Maggie gave her brother an ironic smile. 'He made it obvious the bank will pull the rug from under me unless I went to bed with him.'

'The filthy little git. He needs sorting out.'

'What are you gonna do? Go round there with the boys?'

'As it happens, I do know someone who could....'

'Leave it out, Craig. That's not the answer.'

'No, well....' Craig shrugged like a hard man and picked up his pint glass. 'So what did you say to this little merchant banker?'

'I told him I'd think about it.'

Beer dribbled from the corner of Craig's mouth as he stopped in mid-sip. 'You what!' Then he noticed the teasing look on his sister's face. 'I thought you were serious for a minute.'

'Oh, thanks.'

'So now what?' said Craig, wiping his mouth with the back of his hand.

Maggie pursed her lips. 'I don't know. Change my bank for a start. Trouble is....'

Craig interrupted her. 'The trouble is you're strapped for cash, and you need to sell my chippie.'

'It's not mine to sell, sweetheart. It belongs to you now.'

Craig shook his head. 'It was never really mine. It belonged to Gary. Own up. And I know what he'd have thought of me having it. So I guess I'll have to learn about running a wine bar now.'

Maggie smiled and toasted him with her wine glass.

***

As Malcolm passed through the open-plan office, he sensed an atmosphere. Nicky and Philip had their heads buried in paperwork, trying not to catch his eye, but Savita was staring at him with a vicious smile, watching him like a predator waiting to pounce. He hurried into his office and closed the door. His breathing was shallow and he felt a nauseous quake in his stomach. He could tell something was seriously wrong. The threatening atmosphere was solid and palpable, like a hand gripping his throat.

He sat at his desk and shifted his computer mouse. His maze screen saver vanished and he was about to open up his emails when his mobile rang. The display told him it was Jeremy Clarison, the managing director, ringing. Apprehensively, he clicked the OK button, and answered with a bogusly cheerful voice.

'Jeremy! What can I do for you?'

The MD got straight to the point. 'I don't want to come into the office today, Malcolm. But we need to talk business for a few minutes, then I've got a train to catch to Charing Cross. I'll wait for you in the street outside, just round the corner from reception, outside that pizza place. We'll go for a coffee. It won't take long.'

'Oh, right,' Malcolm began. 'Can you give me some sort of clue what it's about? Forewarned and forearmed and all that.'

Silence from the Jeremy's end of the phone. The MD had already hung up and Malcolm realised he was talking to himself. Frowning, he grabbed his jacket from the back of his chair and left the office, wondering if there was any reason to be alarmed. Jeremy had sounded perfectly normal, so maybe there was nothing to worry about. He convinced himself that it was his own imagination that was running amok.

But as he crossed the open-plan office again, his legs weakened, and he felt his energy being sapped by the hatred of his staff. Braving it out, he stared straight ahead, avoiding a glance in Savita's direction, although he could feel her eyes piercing the transparent thinness of his demeanour.

As soon as he was outside the building, Malcolm dashed around the corner, expecting to find Jeremy waiting for him, but the MD was nowhere to be seen. Malcolm waited as instructed outside the pizza takeaway, wondering where the MD had got to. Perhaps he'd gone into the newsagent's opposite to get a paper to read on the train.

He watched customers entering the newsagent's, and saw them leaving again. There was no sign of Jeremy. Frowning deeply, and becoming more worried by the minute, Malcolm placed a call on his mobile to the MD's mobile, but all he got was his voice mail. He left a brief message, saying he was outside the pizza takeaway as instructed. Then he waited, glancing nervously at his watch every few minutes. After waiting for fifteen minutes, he decided that perhaps the MD had to rush to catch his train, so he returned to the office. At reception, Frank, the security man, stood in his way.

'Sorry, sir,' he said. 'I'm afraid you can't go in there.'

'What! Why not?'

'Instructions from Mr Clarison. I'm very sorry, sir, but Mr Clarison says that you are no longer an employee of the company, as of today.'

Malcolm felt like crying. It was the worst case scenario, and it was actually happening to him. The thing he had always feared. The anxiety dream that had haunted him at nights. The dreaded desk clearance. Being booted out unceremoniously.

In a small thin voice, almost pleading with the security man, he said, 'Frank, I've left some things in my office. If I could just....'

He moved forward slightly, and the security man raised the flat of his hand, but resisted touching him.

'That's far enough, sir. Any personal effects, we'll put in a bin bag and you can collect them later. But for now, I'd vacate the building if I were you.'

He stared uncomprehendingly at the security man, searching for a glimmer of sympathy in his face; but the security man wore a deliberate mask of inscrutability.

Feeling as if he was a zombie, walking without purpose, Malcolm turned and left the building.

He drove home in a daze. What on earth could he tell Sheila, his wife? That he had lost his job, and it couldn't have happened at a worse time. Their daughter was soon to be married, a wedding with all the bells and whistles, and now he wouldn't be able to contribute anything towards the cost.

He felt tears of shame pricking his eyes. Perhaps Sheila would be sympathetic and understanding. Somehow he doubted it. In recent years they had been having problems, always sniping at one another. Always angry and pent up.

'Sheila!' he called out as he walked through the front door. 'Where are you?'

She was waiting in the kitchen. He could see she had been crying. And there on the kitchen table, the photograph stared at him accusingly. She came towards him. He had never seen an expression of such hatred before. The slap caught him by surprise, stinging and biting, bringing tears of pain into his eyes.

'You disgusting animal,' she hissed. 'I want you out of this house, and out of my life. You disgust me, you filthy stinking animal.'

And like a wounded animal, he lowered his head and whimpered. 'Please, Sheila,' he pleaded.

'I want you out of here,' she snapped. 'And I never want to see you again.'

Sixty-Three

While Mike helped Chloe's boyfriend to load up the car for their holiday at a Christian festival campsite in the midlands, Claire had a last minute word with her daughter in the kitchen.

'I haven't had a chance to speak to you since you've come home,' she said hurriedly, glancing towards the door in case Mark came in. 'I wanted to ask a few things.'

'What about?'

'Well, you seem to be serious about Mark....'

'I told you: in a few years' time we'll be getting married.'

'Yes but....' Claire frowned as if she was struggling to work something out. 'He's very religious.'

'I know. So am I.'

'And does he know? About the abortion?'

Chloe chewed her lip nervously and nodded slightly.

'And how does he feel about it?'

'At first he was devastated. But Mark's very strong; it would take a great deal to shake his belief.'

'I'm glad you told him.'

'You didn't think I'd....' Chloe was shocked her mother thought she might contemplate marrying Mark deceitfully. Did her mother think so little of her?

'Of course not,' Claire said hastily. 'I'm just glad he's so understanding.'

'It took a long time. A lot of soul searching and a lot of prayer. You see, Mark believes God knows everyone; even before they're born.'

Claire felt embarrassed and irritated, wanting to say what she really thought of that concept. 'So now what?' she said, unable to conceal her annoyance.

'What d'you mean?'

'What about your career? I mean, you had your heart set on something in the media. Television journalism.'

Chloe shrugged, pursing her lips. 'It doesn't seem quite so important now. I suppose I really want to spread the word. There's always Christian cable television.'

'Oh, Chloe! I'm sure once you're over this religious phase,...'

'It's not a phase, Mum.'

'I know, but people – once something bad happens to them – they often turn to religion. The affluent and healthy really don't need it.'

Chloe looked annoyed, and was about to answer her mother when Mike entered, and told them the car was all packed up. Andrew was summonsed from his bedroom, and they all went out to watch the young couple depart. As they waved them off, Mike noticed Claire wiping away a tear.

'What's wrong?'

She shrugged. 'I don't know. Just a bit disappointed with the way it's worked out, I suppose.'

Mike turned to Andrew and asked him, 'What was Chloe talking to you about in your bedroom? Not trying to convert you, was she?'

'No, she was giving me advice. She's right. I might study; take a few exams. See if I can get into college and do computer studies.'

Mike beamed. 'That's great, Andy!'

'Wonderful, sweetheart,' added Claire, and stroked his hair, noticing that for the first time he didn't seem to resent it. Perhaps, she thought, he's coming out of his Kevin phase.

***

At just gone nine-thirty that night, having spent some time with her boyfriend at his flat, Savita left to catch the bus back to her place in Rusthall. She dashed along to the station when she saw her bus go by. She cursed, knowing that at this time of night there wouldn't be another one for about half an hour. At first she thought she might get a taxi, but it was a warm night and thought the exercise would do her good. It was only about a mile and a half from the station, and she knew she could be home by around ten fifteen, which was when the next bus was due.

As she began walking up Major York's Road, with the dark common to her right, she suddenly began to feel nervous. She knew it was irrational, having walked along the road many times before, often later than this. Occasional cars drove by, and the road was well lit, but she couldn't help feeling anxious. It was instinctive. A feeling that she was being followed or watched.

A car cruised slowly by, and she saw the shadow of the driver's face staring out at her. She slowed down, wondering if she should turn round and run back towards the Pantiles, go into the nearest pub and call for a taxi. But the car continued slowly up Major York's Road. Perhaps the driver had just been curious, wondering what a young woman was doing walking alone by the common late in the evening.

She decided to ignore her fears and put on a spurt. Then she saw the car turn right into Fir Tree Road, which was a dead end. It led towards the cricket ground and car park, an odd place for someone to be going at this time of night.

As she got closer to Fir Tree Road, the car reappeared, turned into Major York's Road, coming in her direction. The driver parked in one of the vacant parking spaces and the headlights faded. Then the driver got out of the car and crossed the road and began walking along the path towards her. She froze. He was probably less than twenty yards away. She hesitated, turning to see if there were any cars coming along the road. There was nothing. The road was deserted. And when she turned back she saw that the figure heading perilously close to her was Malcolm.

'You bitch!' he shouted. 'I'm going to destroy you, like you destroyed me... fucking little bitch.'

She turned and ran. But it was too late, and Malcolm's full force hit her in the back and she crashed to the ground, hitting her head on the hard surface. She tried to open her mouth to scream for help, but the fall and Malcolm's weight had winded her.

She felt him grab her hair and one of her wrists and pull her towards the bushes on the common.

'No!' she pleaded. 'Please, Malcolm. No!'

She struggled and tried at least cling to the path, where perhaps a passing car might see her. But Malcolm overpowered her and soon she was in the pitch black of the trees. She felt him tearing and tugging at her trousers. She opened her mouth to scream and his fist smacked her hard across the mouth, then his other hand tightened around her throat.

'I'm sorry,' she cried. 'Malcolm, I'm sorry.'

But she knew it was useless. It was too late for that.

Sixty-Four

On Friday evening, as soon as she got home from work, Nicky ran upstairs to shower and change. For once, she was glad to be alone in the house. Her mother was over at Nigel's place, and Vanessa had gone away to stay with friends in Canterbury. So Nicky felt relieved about not having to explain to anyone about her date, the first she'd had in ages.

She had met Jason at a party more than three weeks ago, and he had asked for her phone number. But when almost three weeks had gone by, she had wrongly assumed that he wasn't interested and was unlikely to hear from him again. Then last night, out of the blue, he had called, apologising for not having been in touch due to pressure of work, and asked her out to dinner. She found it difficult to control her excitement, and throughout her day at work she couldn't stop thinking about him. Her life had been so dull recently. Other than all that business with Malcolm, and that was the sort of excitement she could well do without.

After her shower, unable to make up her mind what to wear, she tried on three different sets of clothes, and finally decided to wear the first thing she thought of, a peppermint low cut top and white denims. She was admiring herself in the mirror when the doorbell rang. She glanced at her watch and frowned. Jason wasn't due for another hour. Panicking, she hurriedly brushed her hair and sprayed perfume on her neck. Then, as the doorbell ran again insistently, she rushed downstairs.

She was surprised to find two of them standing in the porch, holding up their identification, as if this was a scene from some television crime drama. The older of the two, although he couldn't have been more than thirty-something, enquired, 'Nicola Ingbarton?'

Puzzled, she nodded dumbly, wondering if this was something to do with her date.

'I'm Detective Sergeant Ryland, and this is Detective Constable Swade. I wonder if we could have a word with you?'

'Yes, of course,' she said, in a small frightened voice. She took them into the living room and they both sat next to each other on the two-seater sofa. The older one sat leaning slightly forward, while the younger of the two leaned back and produced a notebook and pen from his suit pocket. She sat in an armchair immediately opposite them. The detective sergeant cleared his throat before speaking.

'Do you work for Instant First Insurance?'

Nicky nodded. 'Yes, I've been there about eighteen months. What's this all about?'

'And how well do you know your work colleague Savita Kapoor?'

Nicky hesitated, sensing there was something very wrong. 'I... er... I know her quite well. We're friends at work. We often have lunch together. Why? What's wrong?'

The sergeant exchanged a brief look with his colleague before answering. 'I'm sorry to have to tell you this, but Miss Kapoor was found dead on Tunbridge Wells common this morning.'

Nicky felt something awful stirring inside her, like a hand clutching at her heart. 'But when... I mean how....' she began, uncertain of how she could express herself.

Realising she was at a loss, the detective decided he could be open with her. After all, she was hardly a suspect, just someone who could help with their enquiries.

'We think she was murdered. It looks like she was strangled.'

Nicky could contain herself no longer, and she choked back the tears, apologising to them for her reaction.

'It's OK,' the detective told her, as he watched the tears streaming down her cheeks. 'I'm just sorry to be the bearer of such news. But we need to move quickly on this one. Do you know her boyfriend by any chance?'

Nicky nodded. 'Does he know?'

'Yes. Apparently he works for a travel company, and he had left for the middle east, probably some time after she was murdered.'

Horrified, Nicky wiped away the tears with the back of her hand, and said, 'You don't think he had anything to do with it?'

'We've managed to get in touch with him and he's on his way back. How well did you know Miss Kapoor. Her background and history, I mean?'

Nicky shrugged. 'Well, I think she and her parents were born in this country....'

'But her boyfriend wasn't Asian, was he?'

Nicky shook her head.

'So was she on good terms with her family over her relationship with him?'

Suddenly, Nicky realised what the detective was driving at, and said, 'I don't think her family would have objected to the relationship, if that's what you mean.'

'Were they Muslim?'

'No, I think they were Catholic.'

'Well, was there anyone else, in your opinion, that might have wanted her dead?'

Nicky hesitated, and in her mind she could see Malcolm's face looming like a hideous beast of prey.

'Miss Ingbarton?' prompted the detective.

Then she told them about Malcolm. And when she got to the bit about them setting up their boss to make him think they were going to have a threesome, she could feel herself colouring, and she couldn't look at either of the detectives. She felt their eyes boring into her and the atmosphere was electric. After a brief pause while they digested this information, and she could hear the DC scribbling on his notepad, the sergeant said:

'What happened? Did she carry out her threat and expose her boss?'

Tearfully, Nicky explained, 'I didn't want her to. Neither did Philip. And Philip thought it was dangerous, destroying his career and his marriage. He thought Malcolm would have nothing left to lose.'

The detective sergeant rose hurriedly, as did his colleague, snapping shut his notebook.

'Look, thanks for your help. We'd like you to be of further assistance, but for now....' He took out his mobile as he moved towards the door. 'We need to get over to your ex boss's house.'

***

Two squad cars and the detective inspector in charge of the case screeched to a halt outside Malcolm's house in Southborough. After an urgent, insistent ringing of the doorbell, his wife opened the door. When she saw the police, her eyes widened in disbelief.

'Mrs. Ellison. Is your husband home?'

'He left, and he hasn't come back. I told him to go. Filthy animal. What's happened to him? Nothing too trivial I hope.'

'Any idea where he might have gone?'

She shook her head, and as she did, she noticed something a little way down the street. 'That's his car. He's parked it a little way down the street. Probably hoping I wouldn't notice. He's probably spent the night in his bolthole.'

'His bolthole?'

'Yes, he built his outhouse from masses of old pallets. Often, if we had an argument, he'd spend the night there.'

'Mind if we take a look?'

'Of course not.'

They traipsed through the house, out through the kitchen, and into the long, narrow back garden. At the end of the lawn were some apple trees, and behind these stood a large timber building with several windows. As they neared the shed, they could see the outline of a human form, a dark shadow through the glass.

As the detective threw open the door, he said, 'You'd better not come in Mrs. Ellison. Quickly. Someone find a knife and cut him down.'

But they could all see that it was useless trying to revive him. The boss from hell was dead.

Sixty-Five

Forensic evidence revealed that Savita Kapoor was raped and strangled on Tunbridge Wells Common, and the DNA tests proved that the perpetrator was Malcolm Ellison, as if anyone could have had any doubt about his guilt.

The daily papers and the Sundays carried front page stories of the murder, and for days Tunbridge Wells swarmed with reporters and paparazzi trying to milk as much as they could from the story. Sheila Ellison, much to her children's disgust, sold her exclusive story to one of the tabloids, exaggerating her husband's animal lusts and habits between the sheets, thus justifying the hefty sum the tabloid was paying her.

Savita's funeral service was held at a Catholic church in Wembley. Nicky took the day off work to attend, but was worried about meeting Savita's parents and relatives, since all the newspapers ran the picture and story of the way Malcolm had been set up when he anticipated a threesome. At the last minute, she changed her mind about going, and went instead to St. Augustine's Catholic Church in Crescent Road, where she knelt and said a prayer for her friend and colleague, and lit a candle for her. Feeling slightly guilty for her cowardice, she walked aimlessly through Calverley Park, then sat on a bench and toyed with her mobile. She sent Jason a text message, telling him she missed him. He had his own business, as a central heating engineer, and she thought he was probably at work and wouldn't respond quickly. But he responded in less than three minutes. His text message said:

> Like 2 cheer u up babe
> cum 2 my place 2nite &
> b my lover. all u have 2
> say is yes. luv Jason xx

She deliberated for less than a minute, then sent him a text in the affirmative. The die was cast. She was committed. She put the recent events behind her, brushed them away like so many niggling doubts and troubling thoughts. Now life was moving on.

***

As Tunbridge Wells shopping centre teems with shoppers going in and out of the Victoria Centre, anyone watching the monitors of the CCTV security cameras will see nothing more than another uneventful, typical Saturday afternoon, pretty much like the previous one, and the one before that; people going about their business and spending money. However, keen observers of body language might notice Nigel and Jackie, standing outside Argos, having a quarrel over something as trivial as the empty yoghurt pot Jackie had abandoned on the coffee table in Nigel's house because she didn't want to miss the start of an episode of Silent Witness. Nigel was peeved to discover that Jackie, who had implied that she watched little television, was in fact quite addicted to many programmes, and the strain of the impending marriage is beginning to take its toll.

Do CCTV cameras single out Dave Whitby, who stands outside Superdrug? He looks like a man loitering with intent. But the reason for his shifty demeanour is the recent argument he's had with Mary over his intention to do a six week summer season in Blackpool. Now she is part of his life, she has objected to him leaving her to cope on her own. 'Tough!' he said. 'It's what I do for a living.' And this had erupted into a major scene, followed by sulks, and a refusal to follow her and her sons into Superdrug. He shuffles about, like a man with something to hide, hands deep in pockets, head sunk low, unaware that we can all be seen by the myriad cameras in our shopping centres, and without the Big Brother element of sound, our demeanours are open to any interpretation.

But no CCTV observer would have been suspicious of Nicky and her new boyfriend, as they stop outside HMV in the Victoria Centre. They look like many a young couple in love as they exchange lingering kisses. Now that their relationship has been consummated, not only are they blissfully unaware of the Big Brother presence of shopping mall security cameras, they don't even notice the people around them as they hold each other close, lost inside their own sensual world.

Because there are so many shoppers milling about in the centre, no camera can actually single out Vanessa. Unless it is with an imaginary telephoto lens of a feature film camera zooming in on her as she heads towards HMV where she is bound to bump into the young lovers. She stops and the camera goes in tight on her face. This female Cain, who has no boyfriend at the moment, is consumed with jealousy as she watches her younger sister kissing the rather good looking Jason.

Avoiding them, she dashes into Marks and Spencer's, hurries through the store and out the other side, then goes round to Criminal Records, where she can probably by the latest Coldplay album a few pounds cheaper anyway.

On her way through the precinct, she doesn't notice the middle-aged couple gazing into the window of Mothercare. Anyone focusing a camera on Ted and Marjorie couldn't fail to notice his hangdog look, sharply contrasted with her assertive body language as she discusses her plans, and it is obvious as he nods absently that his mind is elsewhere. Perhaps it is in an antique shop in the Pantiles, where Donald is giving a potential customer his best price on a china teapot.

Any camera able to pan across from Mothercare over to Starbucks, would pass Maggie and Craig, sitting on stools in the window, heavily discussing their plans to sell Craig's fish and chip shop. Like Ted, he nods while Maggie does most of the talking. He is reluctant to join his sister in this venture, but feels he has no choice.

If the same camera were to track on a dolly, rounding the corner from the precinct into Monson Road, it would pick up on Claire and Mike, standing outside a travel agent's. Naturally, he is unaware that his ex-lover is less than a hundred yards away, drinking a medium cappuccino. But now he is reconciled with his wife, and they have just exited the travel agent, having booked a fortnight in Crete. He holds his plastered right hand up in front of her and grins, asking her to be gentle with him. She kisses him briefly and lightly on the lips, and he reflects on his dissatisfaction with life in general, and is now also reconciled with the realisation that he has returned to the ordinariness of his life, which is perhaps as it should be. His plastered hand is a reminder that he now wants his life to be uneventful.

But the man responsible for his recent pain is not far away, standing in the queue by the checkout at Tesco Metro. Having wrapped the few groceries he is buying, he hands the checkout girl a ten pound note. As soon as she opens the till, he leans over and snatches the notes, then – abandoning the groceries – he legs it out of the supermarket and across the road. Squeal of tyres and the blast of a car horn. He runs round the back of Meadow Road. Nobody pursues him. He walks up to the fifth floor of the car park, picks up his Renault, and drives back to Tonbridge. And it's that simple. No CCTV cameras have got a clear image of Tony Rice as he dashed head down towards the car park. He has got away with it. Less than a hundred and fifty quid, but at least he has his beer money for the rest of the weekend.

Back on his own manor, strutting towards his local, he knows he won't be pursued for such a petty crime, and he has become just one of the many ordinary people going about their business on a Saturday afternoon.

Also Available

From Andrews UK

More Careless Talk

by David Barry

The sequel to Careless Talk, in which Dave Whitby's new relationship turns sour as Mary's ex-husband begins terrorising and stalking her, and Mike's hair cutting is compromised by his drinking and his marriage goes belly-up. All his customers relationships go from bad to worse, but henpecked Ted, the railway guard finds a new life that has always been denied to him.

Also Available

From Andrews UK

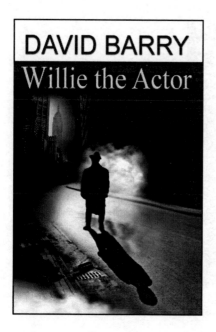

Willie the Actor

by David Barry

Glancing quickly over the bar, he saw the bartender lying face down in a pool of blood, senselessly gunned down simply because he was in the wrong place at the wrong time... New York City in the prohibition era, and Bill Sutton's wife thinks he earns an honest crust as a rent collector. Instead, he leads an extraordinary double-life as 'Willie the Actor', a notorious bank robber. Based on a true story, the novel's protagonist is a gentle gunman who never once fires a shot. However it was believed he was jinxed and almost everyone he works with comes to a violent end.